TO KILL A DEVIL

TO KILL A DEVIL

A MASON COLLINS CRIME THRILLER 4

JOHN A. CONNELL

NAILHEAD PUBLISHING

COPYRIGHT

TO KILL A DEVIL

A Nailhead Publishing book

Current version published in 2020 by NAILHEAD PUBLISHING

ISBN 978-1-950409-15-0 (hardback)

ISBN 978-1-950409-08-2 (paperback)

ISBN 978-1-950409-07-5 (ebook)

"And now...farewell to kindness, humanity and gratitude. I have substituted myself for Providence in rewarding the good; may the God of vengeance now yield me His place to punish the wicked."

— Alexandre Dumas, *The Count of Monte Cristo*

1

A rustling outside the window startled Laura from her sleep. It had been almost a year since she'd moved into the house in Garmisch-Partenkirchen, and she had become used to its distinctive noises. This sounded different. She held her breath and listened. But all she could hear besides the beating of her heart was the autumn wind whipping through the valley and lashing the bushes underneath the windows.

She let out her breath, and her body sank back once again into the bedding. It was just the wind.

She admonished herself for being so nervous. Yes, she'd been a war correspondent, sometimes spending long nights in dangerous places, but the war was over. She pulled back the covers, swung her legs over the edge, and sat up. Her husband slept soundly next to her. The clock on her nightstand indicated it was 3:10 a.m. Lately, her thoughts, her worries, were waking her every night, and it was becoming a bad habit.

She wedged her feet into her slippers and stood. A single shiver coursed through her as she pulled on her robe. Richard stirred for a moment before resuming his steady breathing.

With each exhale, his lips fluttered like a tiny motorboat puttering across a sea of dreams. It gave her a chuckle; her previous lover, Mason, often made the same sound as he slept. Funny that she had fallen in love with two successive men with the same idiosyncrasy.

The floorboards creaked as she walked, but she wasn't concerned about the noise; Richard could sleep through a bombing raid. Mason, on the other hand, slept with one eye open, and the slightest sound would wake him up, thinking an enemy was sneaking in to slit his throat.

Laura exited the bedroom and closed the door as quietly as she could. She might as well get some work done. The deadline loomed for her article on a series of deaths in the area. On the surface, the deaths appeared to be from accidents or natural causes, but they occurred under suspicious circumstances, and all of them could be connected to her with only one or two degrees of separation. That gave her a sense of urgency to finish the piece, as if doing so might appease her sense of looming danger.

She went down the hallway to the front room that was both living and dining room and sat at the dining room table, which also served as her working space. She turned on the desk lamp beside her typewriter. The pool of light quickly faded to darkness outside the lamp's glow. On the edge, between light and shadow, she regarded the chair opposite her. It was, of course, empty, but in the ghostly light, she conjured up an image of the last time she'd seen Mason. He had sat in that chair and presented her with a massive amount of evidence to bring down a powerful crime ring of U.S. Army brass and a murderous cohort of soldiers, displaced persons, and ex-Nazis, giving her the biggest story of her journalism career. Then he'd left Garmisch, left Germany. As a consequence, he'd also left her. And though she was already living with Richard at the time, it had been hard that day to watch him walk away.

Mason had seemingly slipped off the edge of the earth, but in time, rumors came back to her that the crime ring had not been completely eliminated. Someone very powerful had been left standing, and that person was sending out assassins to hunt Mason down. Could these latest murders in this sleepy area of occupied Germany be related? Was this person extending his tentacles to mete out revenge?

Laura stared at the empty chair for a moment, still envisioning Mason sitting opposite her. She ached to see him again, and she hoped he was okay—wherever he was. She forced the image from her mind. After all, the man she now loved, who shared her bed, slept in the other room.

She pulled the typewriter closer, paused to gather her thoughts, and began typing. The sound of the keys striking paper was comforting, though it seemed loud in the quiet house. But just under the clack of the keys, she thought she heard another sound. A rustling, like fabric, outside near the bushes.

She rested her fingers on the keyboard and turned her head toward the side window. The curtains were closed. A gust of wind made the last of the autumn leaves flutter, the branches clack. Then the sounds subsided as the wind calmed.

An idea came to her for tackling a difficult passage, and she returned to her task, typing with rapid fingers. Lost in her thoughts, time passed without her noticing, until, finally, she finished the paragraph and lifted the edge of the paper to review the results.

A barely perceptible odor reached her nostrils. Cold

weather always congested her sinuses, and though it was faint, she could detect a distinctly pungent aroma. She lifted her head slightly and sniffed the air to determine the source. She rose from her chair. Cleaning fluid? She stepped into the kitchen, where all the cleaning items were stored. The odor was lighter in there than in the dining room. She reentered the living room and turned to face the hallway. The odor seemed to come from there.

The hair raised on the back of her neck. Her stomach clenched.

With hesitant steps, she moved across the living room to the hallway. The doors to the guest bedroom and bathroom came first, then their bedroom was at the end—maybe twenty-five feet from where she stood. She took two strides toward the bedroom, when a whoosh and a boom blew the bedroom door off its hinges. A searing wave of air knocked her backward. She fell to the floor as a ball of fire swirled into the hallway. A blanket of flame raged across the ceiling, igniting everything in its path.

Laura scrambled to her feet. Shielding her eyes from the heat, she cried out, "Richard!"

She screamed his name again and took a half step toward the inferno that had once been their bedroom. Fire consumed the hallway. She used her arms to shield herself against the intense heat. Black smoke roiled, obscuring the top half of the hallway. The house had become a furnace. The air burned her lungs, and she choked from the smoke.

She dropped to her hands and knees and crawled for the front door. Just then the windows exploded in the living room. Glass bottles shattered and flames roared. The whole house was now in flames.

Her lungs begged for oxygen, but only smoke came in. Her vision narrowed as she crawled for the door. Nothing but the roaring fire and black smoke. She felt faint. Her muscles threatened to seize. And in the inferno, she had no idea if she was still crawling for the front door.

She hacked and coughed. Her mind was shutting down. She kept crawling, praying she would find the door before it was too late.

And she prayed that whoever did this wasn't waiting for her in the dark night.

2

Catalonia, Spain
October 1946

The train crawled along, traversing a valley between dusty brown hills. It was somewhere south of Barcelona, but at the rate it was moving, it could be another couple of hours before it reached its destination. Though technically a train, it was pulled by a tractor truck. Seven years had passed since the end of Spain's civil war, but the country was still reeling from the devastation and loss of life. And the war had left the country so poor that train locomotives were even in short supply. Mason could walk almost as fast, but he'd been walking for days in Spain's hot October sun, and it felt good to get off his feet.

The train rolled through small villages, often stopping to let off passengers dressed in threadbare clothes with their chickens or lambs, or their arms burdened with bundles and children. It would take on more passengers, then lurch forward on its slow journey to the next town.

An old man had heard Mason mangle what little Spanish he'd picked up on the journey, and he sat next to Mason to practice his English. That was three hours ago, and the man had not stopped talking since introducing himself as Miguel Costa. His deeply creased face was a roadmap of a turbulent life, and now an impoverished one, though he hadn't lost the clear-eyed gaze of a man who drew wisdom from that hardship. To Mason's mind, Señor Costa resembled illustrations of Don Quixote, from the gray Vandyke beard to his thin, elongated face. Except that Costa's right arm was missing below the elbow, with the empty coat sleeve pinned to his pocket.

Costa's one-sided conversation had drifted from his experiences in the civil war to his life as an English professor at the university of literature and history before Franco's purge of intellectuals. Exhausted from the arduous trip, Mason tried to get some sleep, but Costa would tap his arm to get his attention and continue recounting his life story.

During a pause in the man's tale, Mason settled back again and put his fedora over his eyes, but Costa tapped him again.

"Why are you on the poor train?" Costa asked, abruptly shifting the conversation to Mason. "You are an American. You can afford better."

Mason lifted his hat to look at the man, who didn't pick up on his impatient glare. Miguel smiled and nodded in an attempt to prompt a response.

"I used most of my cash bribing your damn Guardia Civil," Mason said. "They didn't care whether I had proper identification or not as long as I paid them enough."

"No identification. No passport. No money. What is an American doing in Franco's Spain anyway?"

"I took a wrong turn."

"Yes, apparently you did. Americans aren't welcome—poor ones, anyway—because your government will not recognize Franco's Spain." He shook his head in despair. "This used to be a great country. Now look at us." Costa held up his intact arm to present the passengers as evidence of his claim. His right stump moved as well, causing the sleeve to bounce. He became aware of the movement and lowered his left arm. He leaned in and lowered his voice, "I lost my arm fighting for the Republicans."

Costa then started waxing on about the battle that caused the loss of his arm, but Mason was distracted by the two Guardia Civil policemen who entered the car. They immediately zeroed in on someone three seats ahead of him, a pretty young woman Mason had noticed when she got on the train at the last stop. The two policemen looked inebriated, and lascivious smiles spread across their faces. One of them leaned in, and the girl jumped. The other thought that was funny, egging on the perpetrator.

Mason couldn't see where the first policeman put his hands, but it didn't take much imagination to figure it out. The girl cried and begged in words Mason couldn't understand. None of the other passengers dared speak. Meanwhile, Costa continued to recount details of his life, occasionally tapping Mason with what was left of his right arm.

Mason looked at him and listened to a few words, then looked back at the policemen. A heat rose from his chest, which caused the veins in his neck to pulse against his shirt collar. He tried to get his anger under control, but it wasn't working. His whole mission was to keep a low profile and get out of Spain as quickly as possible. Getting into and through France would be another issue, but slipping out of a country straining under a dictator's rule and corrupt police was his priority at the moment.

The harassment continued, making Mason ball his fists and sit up straight. Costa tapped his arm again, and this time Mason whipped his head around.

Costa seemed unfazed by Mason's murderous glare. He wagged his finger at Mason. "I know what you're thinking, Señor Collins. Don't interfere. The Guardia Civil can be very dangerous. Drunk on power."

Mason said nothing and looked back at the policemen.

"I fear for the girl," Costa said. "This is not the first time I have witnessed such things."

The policemen were pulling the girl's arms, trying to make her stand. The young woman fought back. She cried and begged but didn't call for help. She probably knew no one would come to her aid; no one would dare defy the policemen's authority. They finally got her to her feet and started to push her toward the rear of the train.

Mason's face burned with rage. He tried to control it; he was so close to getting across the border without incident. Reaching the outskirts of Barcelona meant it was no more than three days on foot to the border. He couldn't screw this up now. Miguel kept tapping his arm and telling him not to do something he'd regret.

Just as the policemen pushed the girl past his seat, Mason stood to block them. He waved for the girl to go, and she rushed away in tears.

The lead policeman stood no taller than Mason's chin,

while the other was about Mason's height. They growled commands in Spanish. Mason shook his head. The lead policeman whipped out his nightstick and raised it to strike.

Mason grabbed the man's weapon arm and twisted it, wrenching the nightstick out of his hand. He then thrust his right elbow into the policeman's chin. The move was so fast that the policeman was unprepared. His teeth clacked, and his head jerked back, stunned.

The next instant, Mason yanked the stunned policeman's pistol out of its holster. The second policeman had gone for his gun, but Mason already had his leveled at the cop before he could get it completely out. With wide eyes, the second policeman let his pistol drop back into its holster and raised his hands in the air.

The lead policeman had recovered his senses and threw a punch at Mason's jaw. Mason blocked the punch and kneed the man in the groin. The policeman cried out and doubled over. Mason finished him off with a knee to the forehead.

Mason motioned for the second policeman to hand over his gun. The man complied, and Mason threw it out the window. He motioned for the policeman to go back the way he came. The man did as he was told with as much speed as he could muster. Mason then tossed the gun he'd taken from the lead policeman out the same window.

No one said a word or made a motion as Mason grabbed his bundle from the overhead rack, made an about-face, and dashed for the rear of the car. He blew through the door and stepped out on the platform.

The train was creeping along a stone viaduct that navigated a series of hills and ravines. To his right, a steep slope ran upward and was little more than hard earth covered in loose dirt and rocks. The only thing keeping the dirt or rocks from tumbling onto the tracks was a rickety wall of wooden planks. To his left, a wall of hewn stone marked the edge of the viaduct. Beyond the wall, the slope fell away into a deep ravine. He had four feet between the wall and the moving train, but it was his only option. He calculated the angle of his jump, then leapt off the platform.

Fortunately, the leisurely speed of the train allowed him to use the wall as a break, and he rolled along the wall until he could stop his forward momentum. He ran for the back of the train. The rock wall forced him to run alongside the cars. Above the sound of clacking train wheels, he heard shouting behind him, then the crack of a rifle. A bullet whizzed past his torso.

The wall fell away up ahead. Only thirty feet to go, then he could scramble down into the ravine and make his escape. The report of a rifle sent another bullet zipping past. Fifteen feet to go.

The long strides to freedom …

Four Guardia Civil jumped off the caboose, cutting him off. They aimed their pistols and pulled back the hammers.

Mason stopped, dropped his bundle, and put his hands in the air.

3

Rotting in a dark, dank cell or being beaten by prison-guard thugs was nothing new to Mason. He'd experienced that once before, at the hands of the Nazis during the war. But rather than toughening him up, those previous experiences had done the opposite, leaving him raw, marinating him, tenderizing his mind as much as his body.

Mason sat on the floor of an eight-by-eight-foot cell of cement stained by decades of blood, urine, and the breath of condemned men. The door of thick wood planks and steel banding allowed no light in and did little to suppress the screams, or pleas for mercy, or demands for confessions. And while a one-foot-square window mercifully let in some daylight and a hint of fresh air, it also let in the sounds of firing squads that echoed in the prison's inner courtyard.

His body tensed when heavy bootsteps approached the door, then relaxed when the sounds faded. The Guardia Civil had beaten him senseless on the day of his capture. Then the prison guards had their turn the next day. And they had come back at irregular intervals throughout his stay to beat him further. He kept track of the time by the church bells that clanged somewhere in the distance. On Sundays they rang five times during the day, meaning he'd been the guest of the Montjuïc Castle prison for three weeks and four days. Long enough to make him wonder if he was ever going to get out of there alive.

Up until a few weeks ago, his overriding mission was to track down the man responsible for sending assassins after him and his friends and colleagues. But now, after two years as a U.S. Army intelligence officer during the war, seven tumultuous months as an army investigator in occupied Germany, then six months as a penniless wanderer, depleted of energy and broken in mind and body, he had an irresistible urge to fade from the world, find a cabin in a forest on the top of a mountain; it didn't matter where.

And the one thing he needed to do before disappearing was to see Laura again. She never left his thoughts. The last time he'd seen her, she was with another guy and living in Garmisch-Partenkirchen on the southern border of Germany. He had no idea if she was still with the British journalist or even if she was still in Germany, but the hope of seeing her again—and possibly wooing her—was what had given him the strength to labor his way through Spain.

The sound of clomping boots stopped at the cell door. A key slid in the lock. Mason's body tensed once again, and he pressed his back against the wall. There was nowhere to go, and he was unable to run anyway, as his latest torture involved beating the soles of his feet, then being forced to stand for interminable hours. The door's latch screeched as it turned. The door swung open, blinding him with light. Silhouettes of the guards stepped in, dragging the body of Mason's cellmate,

Carlos. The guards stopped in the middle of the room and dropped the man. His head made a sickly, hollow sound when it struck the cement floor. Mason remained still and avoided meeting the guards' eyes. Any provocation, really anything at all, could prompt them to turn their savagery on him.

The guards exited the room and locked the door. Mason waited for their footsteps to fade, then he struggled to his knees and crawled on all fours to his cellmate. Carlos lay face-down. In the dim light, Mason couldn't see whether he was breathing. He turned Carlos onto his back as gently as he could. Fresh blood oozed from a wound where his head had hit the cement. The blood covered his forehead and began to run down his bruised and swollen face. Most of his teeth were missing, and dark bands of red and purple wrapped his neck where they'd garroted him countless times.

Carlos had been there weeks, maybe months, before Mason —no one lasted longer than that. The poor man's body was shattered. He'd been a university professor in Barcelona and was accused of urging his students to subvert the Franco regime. Mason was sure that whatever they wanted to get out of him, Carlos would have confessed long ago just to stop the relentless torture.

Mason put his ear to Carlos's chest and heard an erratic heartbeat. That touch of tenderness roused Carlos. He began muttering in Spanish. His voice was no more than a whisper. Mason tore off a corner of his tattered shirt and dabbed at the blood pooling in Carlos's right eye. Carlos stared at nothing, his gaze fixed on the ceiling. It seemed the guards had finally broken his mind as well as his body. Mason could pick out only a few words, though he could tell Carlos was reciting a prayer, speaking softly as if his lips were next to God's ears.

The screech and bang of the cell door opening startled Mason, but he remained still. His heart pounded. They had come for him to mete out more punishment.

The guard yelled at him in Spanish, but Mason refused to move.

"Are you Mason Collins?" another man's voice said, this one in English with an American accent.

"Yes," Mason said while continuing to watch Carlos pray.

"We're with the U.S. State Department. We're here to get you out of here and send you home."

Mason wondered if it was a trick or some kind of fantasy playing out in his mind. He turned his head to look toward the door. Three men stood just inside the cell. One uniformed guard accompanied two men in suits and fedoras. The two civilians held their hands to their mouths and noses, shielding themselves against the stench.

The guard yelled an order at Mason, and Mason said, "Somebody's going to have to help me get up."

Neither man moved. The guard called to someone in the hallway. Another guard pushed past the two civilians, and the two guards yanked Mason to his feet. The bottoms of his feet, his knees, and his legs exploded in pain. His stomach heaved and his knees buckled.

The guards dragged him out of the cell and down the corridor, just like every other time he'd been taken away for a torture session. His mind questioned whether the two civilians had been a figment of his imagination after all. But then he noticed he was being dragged in the opposite direction. The elation of pending freedom brought strength back to his legs. He found his footing and walked. He jerked his arms free from the guards, and though the soles of his feet begged him to stop, he continued toward the exit of his own accord.

He was exhausted by the time he exited the main gate of the prison. He stopped and lifted his head toward the sun. The two American officials came up on either side of him. They had yet to say much of anything. What he knew of diplomats, they would usually never shut up.

"How did you guys find out I was here?" Mason asked.

The taller man with a paunch and jowls said, "Diplomatic channels. They agreed to let you go, but we have to get you out of Spain fast before they change their minds."

"Not by boat, I hope," Mason said. "I hate boats." He looked at the other man, the one on his left. This man was younger, sinewy with a beak of a nose and a weak chin. The man flashed him something more like a grimace than a smile.

"I didn't catch your names," Mason said.

The jowly one said, "I'm Lou, and that's Mitch."

"And you're with the State Department?"

"That's what I said." Lou motioned toward the dirt parking lot. "Come on, let's get out of here. This place gives me the creeps."

As they walked toward a black Mercedes, Mitch said to Lou, "He's going to stink up the car."

"I picked up some kind of bug in there," Mason said. "Can't control my bowels. Something for you guys to look forward to."

Mitch curled his lip and hissed a curse. Mason remarked that his two companions hadn't spoken of taking him to a hospital, let alone seeing that he got a bath and clean clothes.

When they got to the car, Mitch held up a pair of handcuffs. "We gotta cuff you to the back seat. The Spanish insisted we do this until we cross into France."

"What about diplomatic immunity?" Mason asked.

"This is Franco's Spain," Lou said. "And we've got about four checkpoints to get through."

Mitch rattled the handcuffs at Mason and asked, "You want to get out of here or not?"

"You could hog-tie me, then lash me to the hood if it meant seeing the last of this place," Mason said and got into the back seat.

Mitch bent over to attach one of the handcuffs to Mason's wrist. When he did so, Mason noticed the .38 S&W in a shoulder holster underneath the man's suitcoat. Mitch forced Mason to lean forward so he could attach the other end of the handcuffs to a metal front-seat support. Mason had to slump forward, but just planting his butt on the plush seat was heavenly. Both men got into the car and immediately rolled down their windows.

Lou started up the car and exited the parking lot. The prison sat on a hill overlooking the southern edge of the city, obliging Lou to take a long, winding road down to the bottom of the hill. He turned right on a four-lane highway, heading toward the city, and in the span of a few minutes, they were in a dense urban area of Barcelona.

"What's next after we reach France?" Mason asked.

Neither of them answered.

"I'd sure like to get a hot bath and something to eat."

Nothing again.

Maybe Mason had been so desperate to get out of that prison that he ignored the signs. Maybe the torture, lack of food, the isolation had dulled his senses. Whatever the reason, it was clear to him now that these guys weren't there to rescue him, and by ignoring the signs, he'd willingly walked out of one sure death and into another. Only this way would be quicker. Valerius's assassins had caught up to him. Ever since Mason had busted up a crime ring in occupied Germany, a man Mason knew by only his nom de guerre of Valerius had sent assassins after him. He'd managed to elude several teams in Germany, France, and Morocco, but the crime boss had a very long reach, which, apparently, even penetrated into Franco's Spain.

Mason was sure that once they passed Barcelona and were out in some deserted area, they planned to put several bullets into his chest and a couple in the head. They'd avoid the face. They'd need his face intact to take photos of his body to take back to the boss as proof they'd made the kill.

Mason pushed down this rising alarm. He needed to think. There was no way he was going to let them kill him and leave his bullet-riddled corpse out in the barren landscape of Spain.

Or at least he'd die trying.

4

The Spanish police signaled for Lou to pull over at a checkpoint on the northern outskirts of Barcelona. A policeman bent over to look inside. Lou showed him a piece of paper. Enough daylight hit the paper to let Mason see that it was a signed letter, presumably from some high-ranking official suitably bribed by Valerius's agents. He figured it also implicitly stated that the bearer of said document would pass on an appropriate amount of additional funds to whomever was in charge of each checkpoint up to and including the border crossing into France.

After the policeman glanced at the letter, he motioned for Lou to follow him to a small guardhouse. Without the benefit of a breeze created by the forward motion of the car, Mason's stench caused Mitch to recoil.

"Goddamn," Mitch said and covered his mouth and nose.

"I have to take a crap," Mason said.

"At a checkpoint? No dice."

"I told you I got the GIs in prison."

"I'm sure your asshole got plenty of exercise in there. Use it now and hold it."

Lou got back into the car. The police lifted the barrier, and Lou took off, leaving the city behind. He whined to Mitch about how much money the checkpoint cop had extracted for safe passage—at least until the next checkpoint and the next cop.

Instead of taking the coastal route toward Girona, Lou steered them north-northwest into the more sparsely populated area among the jagged foothills of the Pyrenees mountains. They needed a desolate place to kill him, and Mason needed the same to pull off his escape. He wouldn't want to get away from Lou and Mitch just to end up in the Guardia Civil's hands again. He would bide his time.

A little over an hour north of Barcelona, and after passing several bigger towns, they were out in the rugged countryside.

"I told you, I've got the GIs, and I have to take a crap."

Neither of his would-be killers responded.

"You're not going to like what I'm about to do in the back seat of this fine Mercedes."

Mitch jerked his head around to glare at Mason. "You do that, and I'll put a bullet in your belly. Let you scream as your stomach acid eats your guts. You'll beg me to kill you."

"Now how is that supposed to save your car from a lifetime of stink?" Mason said, then doubled over as if in terrible pain. He gripped his abdomen and went for his belt to drop his trousers. "This ain't gonna be pretty, boys. Prepare yourselves."

Lou growled and looked for a place to pull over. Mitch's attention went to helping Lou, and he pointed with his right hand. "There."

That was what Mason was waiting for. He lurched forward and thrust his left hand inside Mitch's suitcoat. He had just enough time to grab onto the .38's handgrip.

"Son of a bitch," Mitch yelled as he went for Mason's hand.

Mason pulled the trigger. The pistol fired. Mitch cried out and grabbed his side. At the same instant, Mason jerked the gun out of Mitch's shoulder holster.

Lou steered wildly as he reached for his .38. He succeeded in extracting the pistol and was bringing it up to bear on Mason, but Mason fired first. Three in the chest.

Lou's head fell against the steering wheel. His foot slipped off the accelerator, but the car's momentum was enough to roll the car into a shallow ditch on the side of the road. The front bumper struck the embankment.

Mason braced himself against the impact, but Mitch, occupied with stemming the flow of blood from his bullet wound, was thrust forward. His head slammed against the windshield. He groaned and writhed as Mason reached into Mitch's coat pocket. He found the handcuff key. Mitch grabbed at his hand, but the motion caused him to cry out in pain, and he slapped his hands back on the wound.

Mason unlocked the handcuff around his wrist and jumped out of the car. He looked down the road in both directions. Luckily, it was empty from horizon to horizon.

He opened the front passenger door and pulled Mitch out of the car. Mitch screamed in pain and swung wildly with his fists. His right hip and thigh were covered in blood. The bullet must have torn through his right hip and exited somewhere near his groin.

Mason lifted him by his armpits and dragged him up the

short embankment, then down into a shallow ravine. He jammed the revolver's barrel into Mitch's abdomen and leaned into the man's face.

"Tell me who hired you, or I'll shoot *you* in thc gut."

Mitch clamped his mouth shut as he desperately took in air through his nostrils. Mason pulled back the hammer.

"Gyorgy Farkas!" Mitch yelled. "Farkas hired us."

"Where can I find him?"

Mitch hesitated.

Mason pushed the barrel deeper into the man's abdomen. "You know what a gut shot will do. Tell me where Farkas is."

"Lake Como, in Italy. He's got a big villa on the lake."

"Which one?"

"The only one with an army of guards around it."

"Is Farkas also known as Valerius?"

Fear spread across Mitch's face. He seemed to recover a moment later and snarled at the absurdity of the question. "Farkas is a small fish compared to that guy."

"But Farkas works for Valerius?"

Despite his pain, Mitch looked puzzled. "Are you crazy? You're one stupid son of a bitch if you think you can go after Valerius."

Mason ignored the question and asked, "Where can I find him?"

"I don't know. I swear."

Mason believed him. None of the assassins would know. Probably no one beyond Valerius's tight circle of associates would either. He put the pistol's hammer back into its resting position, engaged the safety, and put it in his belt behind his back. He started to lift Mitch by the armpits, but Mitch fought against his grasp.

"What the fuck are you doing?"

"I'll get you to the street. Somebody's bound to pass by."

"Let me bleed out. I ain't good for nothing now. We let you escape. If I live, Valerius will find me and torture me, just like he wanted us to torture you before we killed you."

"Suit yourself," Mason said.

As Mason turned to walk away, Mitch said, "You won't get within a mile of him. Valerius has assassins going after anyone associated with whatever you did to piss him off."

Mason stopped in his tracks. He whipped around, dropped to his knees, and wrapped his hands around Mitch's throat. "Who? Who did he send assassins after?"

"How the fuck should I know? Everyone."

Laura! Valerius was going after Laura.

Mason bounded over the embankment and ran for the car.

MASON KEPT HIS HEAD DOWN AS HE TOOK LONG STRIDES across the post office lobby outside the city of Narbonne, France. Like most of the post offices in the larger towns, it also had a telegraph office and a bank of telephone booths. He slipped into one of the booths and dug around for the loose change in his pockets. The money he'd taken off the two assassins was all in Spanish pesetas and U.S. dollars, so he had to persuade a café owner to exchange some of the pesetas for French francs. With his dirty face and the ill-fitting clothes he'd stolen from a clothesline in Spain, the owner probably thought Mason was a desperate fugitive, so he was more than happy to comply with Mason's frenzied demands.

He lifted the receiver and waited. The operator came on the

line. She said something, which Mason assumed was her asking for the phone number. Mason knew just enough French to recite the numbers to be connected to a telephone in Germany. She then asked, he assumed, for a certain amount of money to make the call. Mason kept dropping coins into the slot until he heard a series of clicks.

Finally, a phone in Garmisch-Partenkirchen rang, and a U.S. Army private at the 508th Military Police Battalion answered.

"I need to speak to John Tandy," Mason said, referring to a fellow criminal investigator he'd worked with at the army's Criminal Investigation Division, or CID.

"May I ask what this is about, sir?" the private asked.

"Tell him it's an old friend."

There was a pause, then the private said, "Mr. Tandy was killed in the line of duty."

The news hit Mason in the stomach. His would-be assassin Mitch was telling him the truth. Valerius had sent out assassins to kill anyone associated with the investigation that took down the crime ring.

"Sir, are you still there?" the private asked.

"Arnold Wilson, then," Mason said, praying that Wilson was still among the living.

"I've got to know what this is pertaining to, sir."

"Look, Private, I used to be an investigator there, and Wilson and I worked cases together. I've got some info for him."

The private told him to hold on a minute. Mason glanced at the clock. He had to know, and even this brief pause was killing him. Plus, it was only a matter of time before the French police caught up to him. He'd managed to talk his way past the border police, but an alert policeman might spot the car he'd stolen in a small town just inside the border between Spain and France.

After a couple of clicks in the telephone line, someone picked up another telephone receiver. "Wilson."

Mason had to refrain from yelling into the phone. "Wilson, it's me, Mason Collins."

"What the … you're still alive?"

"Arnie, I don't have much time. Is Laura McKinnon okay?"

"You mean that reporter who broke the news about the crime ring?"

"The same. Is she hurt? Alive?"

"My guess would be yeah. But she went missing after their house burned down."

An electrical shock surged through Mason's chest. "Their house burned down … What do you mean missing?"

"We only found her husband's corpse—"

Husband? Mason thought.

Wilson continued. "Looked like the husband was in bed when there was some kind of gas explosion. He was burned to a crisp, but we were able to use dental records to identify him as Richard Talbot. Some Brit reporter."

Mason's head spun from the news.

"By all accounts, Mrs. Talbot, uh Miss McKinnon, was home, or at least in town. But we didn't find a trace of her. And she never got in touch with us. She never came to identify the body or make funeral arrangements. Finally, we had to get in touch with Talbot's parents in England—"

"You've got to find her," Mason said, interrupting. "She's in danger."

"Mason, she could be anywhere."

"After busting up that crime ring, I've been hounded by assassins. I heard that the same guy who put the hit out on me is going after anyone associated with taking down the organization."

There was silence on the other end.

"Arnie?"

"Well, you know that OSS guy you busted? Schaeffer?"

Mason had a sinking feeling he knew what was coming. "Yeah?"

"They found him hanging in his cell. Best the prison guards could figure, there was no way he could have done that on his own."

"Christ, they're going after everybody."

"And Killion, the MP sergeant who helped you stop the train theft? He was murdered. Execution style. We thought it was one of the local gang leaders he'd arrested—"

"That means you'd better watch your back. And find Laura."

"Mason, either she's on the run, or … they've got her."

Mason slammed the phone down. The post office customers and employees were looking at him. He yanked open the door, hurried out, and headed toward the Citroen he'd stolen. He froze. Two policemen were checking out the car. Mason did an about-face and walked quickly in the opposite direction. He wanted to punch something or yell out in frustration and anger.

Wilson's words echoed in his head: *either she's on the run, or they've got her.*

A fellow investigator, John Tandy, had been murdered because of Valerius. In Tangier, a good friend was killed by an assassin's bullet meant for him, and those same men had put another in the hospital. And now Laura was missing. They wouldn't stop until they found him. Now it was clear he'd have to find Valerius before he could do any more harm. Before Mason could ever get his life back.

Mason's first stop was Gyorgy Farkas. No money, no car, trailed by assassins, and now the police, with close to six hundred miles ahead of him.

So much for going home.

5

Mason tore off a piece of the rabbit he'd cooked over a campfire. The meat burned his fingers, but he was too ravenous to care. He took a bite and sighed with satisfaction. The fire warmed his body against the cold wind blowing up the snow-covered slope. The surrounding trees blocked the worst of the easterly winds that caused the branches high above him to clack together.

The only other noise was the grunts of the man hog-tied five feet to his right. The man was naked. Rope bound his hands and feet together at his back. A second rope went straight up from the central knot and looped around a sturdy tree branch, with the rest of the rope coiled near the rock Mason used as a seat. His captive had stopped screaming threats or yelling for help only a few minutes earlier.

Mason savored the silence along with his food. He wore a long blond beard that was flecked with gray. His blond hair was matted with tight curls. He never realized that when his hair grew out it was that kinky. Or that his beard would have gray hairs. He figured the premature gray was a result of his life following a particularly bumpy road.

October, and the snows had already come to the Italian Alps. Two months had passed since he'd been sprung from the Spanish prison by the two now-dead assassins. The trek from the Spanish border to Lake Como, and now the South Tyrolean mountains, had involved stealing money, cars, and clothes. He'd worked a couple of weeks in Provence, in the south of France, during the grape harvest, then in an automotive plant in Turin, before coming upon his first target, a Hungarian named Gyorgy Farkas, in a villa on Lake Como.

Mason finished off a thigh and threw the bone in the fire. "Your friend Farkas gave you up—"

"He's not my friend."

"Business associate, then. The point is, I got him to talk. It didn't take long. Why don't you save us both the trouble and tell me where I can find Valerius?"

The man's name was Max Schliemann, another Valerius lieutenant and at least two rungs higher up the ladder than Farkas. His three bodyguards lay dead in Schliemann's chalet five hundred yards down the slope. Mason had locked the man's child-bride in the basement with warm clothes and enough food and water for the couple of days it would take for Schliemann's associates to check into his absence.

Mason licked his fingers, having finished off the rabbit. "You're going to tell me one way or another. Your gunmen murdered my friends and tried to burn my sweetheart alive. You can imagine that doesn't sit very well with me."

"Those weren't my gunmen."

"You work directly for Valerius. In my book, that makes you just as responsible."

The man growled in frustration and rage.

"I want Valerius's real name and where I can find him."

"Your friends' deaths are on you. If you'd had the balls to die without a fight, none of that collateral damage would have happened."

Mason shot to his feet and pulled down on the rope. His rage gave him the strength to hoist Schliemann into the air.

Schliemann cried out in pain. The pressure on his lungs made him struggle to breathe, and his cries came out as barks. When Schliemann hovered six feet off the ground, Mason tied off the rope to the trunk of a fallen tree. He took up the tag line attached to the rope supporting Schliemann and pulled. The tag line pulled Schliemann over the fire.

The man was too high above the fire to be burned—maybe slow-cooked if held over the flames long enough—but he'd certainly feel plenty of heat. That and the primal fear of fire got him writhing and screaming. Mason held him over the fire a minute, then he eased off on the line. Schliemann slowly swung away from the fire.

Mason walked over to Schliemann with his face next to his victim's. The man muttered, "Please, stop," over and over again.

"Valerius's real name and location."

Schliemann sputtered and shook, but he remained silent.

Mason pointed to a small stack of logs near the fire. "I can add a few more logs and get the fire really going."

"He'll skin me if I tell you."

"My first concern would be avoiding being roasted alive."

Schliemann glared at Mason. "They'll hunt you down. You'll wish you let those gunmen do their job."

Mason walked back over to the tag line. Simon pleaded,

"No, no," with more desperation with each of Mason's steps. Mason pulled on the tag line, bringing the terrified Schliemann back over the fire. He tied off the line, then picked up some logs and threw them into the flames. Sparks flew up and swirled in the wind. Some landed on Schliemann's naked body. The flames rose higher. The snow on Schliemann's skin began to steam. The thick hair on his chest and groin started to curl. Schliemann's screams echoed in the forest. His body twitched against the ropes.

Mason untied the tag line and let it go. Schliemann swung like a pendulum, relaxing as he moved away from the fire, then renewing his struggle when he came closer. Mason walked over and stopped Schliemann from swinging. The man's skin along the front side of his torso had turned pink. The odor of burned hair crept up Mason's nostrils.

"Fortunately for you," Mason said, "you're not well hung, or that thing would have turned black by now." He paused, letting Schliemann catch his breath.

Schliemann began to weep. The whole scenario made Mason sick to his stomach. He never wanted to be put in this situation, but them going after Laura, him being hunted for months on end, and living in the wild and on the run had drawn a dark curtain over his soul. He was now face to face with one of the orchestrators of that misery. All the deaths and the rage burned in him just as much as the fire had cooked Schliemann.

"Tell me, Max. Tell me, and this will all be over."

Schliemann gritted his teeth and glanced at Mason. Through his tears he mustered defiance.

Mason shrugged and moved for the tag line.

"Stop," Schliemann screamed. "Please."

Mason turned to face the man.

"I don't know his real name." Schliemann jerked his head to look at Mason. "I swear."

"You're one of his lieutenants, and you don't know his name?"

Mason turned back to the rope and pulled it taut.

"Please, you have to believe me," Schliemann said, his voice raspy from screaming. "The man is a master at hiding his identity. I've never met him face to face. It's always been through an intermediary, each time someone different." He kept pleading, "I swear, I swear. Not again, please."

"Location?" Mason demanded.

Schliemann took deep gulps of air.

Mason knew he was stalling, and he pulled on the tag line.

"Wait!"

Mason held him halfway to the fire.

"Vienna. He's in Vienna."

"Which zone?"

Schliemann remained silent.

"What zone, Max?"

Schliemann shook his head as if fighting with himself—talk, or die in agony. Mason tugged on the rope, eliciting another scream from Schliemann.

"All I know is he's in the international zone. That's all I know. I swear it. I don't know where. Only rumors."

"Valerius is American, British, Austrian?"

"I don't know! Please, please …"

Mason's instincts told him Schliemann was telling the truth. He'd get nothing more out of the man. Any more time over the fire and the man's mind would crack. Without a word, Mason went about extinguishing the fire and gathering his things. Everything he possessed resided in one backpack. During all that time, Schliemann muttered incomprehensibly.

When Mason was finished, he lowered Schliemann to the ground and kneeled next to him. “Unlike what you planned to do to me, I’m going to give you a chance to live.” He cut the rope attaching Schliemann to the overhanging branch, and then cut the knot binding his ankles and wrists together. He left the rope tying his feet together, and the one that bound his hands behind his back. Schliemann lay motionless on the snow. His heavy breathing created puffs of steam in the frigid air.

“Head straight downhill,” Mason said, “and you’ll find your chalet. You’ll have to crawl. You might make it. You might freeze to death. That’s more of a chance than you gave my friends.”

Mason stood and walked away. He headed up the slope, toward the peak. There would be endless peaks before he got to Vienna. Three hundred and fifty miles, maybe a week of walking. That is, if he survived crossing the Alps.

Then, if he made it to Vienna, the real danger would begin.

6

Mason's footsteps echoed in the empty street. He knew he was in the Russian sector of the southern outskirts of Vienna because of the posters plastered on the sides of buildings depicting Stalin or square-jawed Russian soldiers with propaganda slogans in Cyrillic. He kept to the shadows as much as possible and adopted the plodding gait of a down-trodden man—just another displaced person seeking shelter. Homeless wanderers were a common sight.

Like Germany, Austria was divided into four zones of occupation after the war, each held by one of the four conquering Allied armies, the Americans, the British, the Russians, and the French. And Vienna, like Berlin, was surrounded by the Russians and divided into four separate Allied zones, with the old city center, or Innere Stadt, policed and administered by an international alliance of the four powers.

He entered a quarter of the city where the buildings had been ravaged by fire or threatened to collapse. In addition to a year of bombing raids on the city, wherever the German forces or local militia had made a stand against the invading Russian army, the battle had left pockets of destruction. The majority of streets had been cleared of rubble, and much of that rubble had been expeditiously disposed of by shoveling it into the hollowed-out interiors of the ground floors of the buildings. It was past midnight. A cold wind hurried the clouds across the moon, which created sweeping patterns of dark and light that made the blackened skeletons of buildings appear to undulate. The scene brought up memories of his time in Munich as an army investigator, which inevitably stirred his thoughts of Laura.

Two blocks away, headlights appeared around a corner. Mason ducked into an alley. Two Russian-style jeeps passed, and Mason saw grim-faced Russian soldiers in both. A patrol, obviously, looking for stragglers. Or prey. While Mason worked at the army intelligence offices in Frankfurt shortly after the war, he'd heard stories of the raping and pillaging by the Russians on a massive scale. Though the worst of those atrocities had diminished over time, he was sure it still occurred with some frequency. Women out on deserted streets at this hour would be fair game in the eyes of the Russian predators. And a straggler like him could be beaten or thrown in one of the makeshift prisons.

Mason had spent quite a lot of money to buy a fake ID and a Soldbuch, which claimed he was Gregor Witt, a German ex-soldier of the Wehrmacht. He was fluent in German, but it was clearly of Bavarian origin, and though Austrian German was similar, he'd never be able to pass as a native. Walking around the streets of Vienna was dangerous for German ex-soldiers. Austrians resented their presence, at least those unable to slap down a wad of cash for safe passage. And the Russians were known to encourage, even pay in some instances, gangs of Austrian communist fanatics to patrol the streets looking for German ex-soldiers to beat or imprison. Or both.

Despite the risks, posing as an American would get him nowhere if he wanted to probe the network of local criminals in his search for Valerius, and faking a British accent or trying to speak French was beyond his capacities.

Mason waited for the sounds of the vehicles to fade, then he cautiously stepped back out onto the street. This process of prowling in the shadows and hiding from patrols had to be repeated several times before he decided he was close enough to the city center. The homeless and displaced persons used many of the damaged buildings as shelter, but Mason chose a five-story office building. No one else dared to enter a building where the upper floors threatened to collapse at any moment.

He navigated the large chunks of concrete and steel on the ground floor. The moonlight penetrated just enough to help him find a stairwell. The steps leading up were buried in rubble, but those leading down to the sublevel were clear. He pulled out his cigarette lighter and spun the flint wheel. With the feeble light from the flame, he descended the steps.

The lower level had suffered its share of damage, mostly from the enormous chunks of concrete and steel beams that had fallen from the levels above and pierced the sublevel's ceiling. The sound of water dripping seemed loud in the darkness. The furnaces stood like silent sentinels. The larger pipes for the main plumbing lines and heating system had collapsed in places, but the floor was reasonably navigable. The building groaned occasionally under the force of gravity.

Mason came upon a dry area and laid down his heavy backpack and a bundle of clothing wrapped in crude burlap.

There was enough wood around to build a fire, and once the fire burned on its own, he opened the bundle and set aside a folded clean shirt, trousers, and a suitcoat. He then removed items that one might say was plunder, but he considered it payback, items he'd acquired from the villas of Valerius's two hapless lieutenants: two gold watches; a carton of Lucky Strike cigarettes; and a swath of cotton containing women's jewelry, and rings, bracelets, and necklaces of gold and silver, some inlaid with precious stones. A wad of cash tied with a string was next, which was a collection of Italian lira, Swiss francs, and U.S. dollars. A handful of Swiss francs and U.S. dollars went into his pocket, and the rest he laid out next to the other items. Finally came a small leather pouch. He opened that and dropped nine diamonds of various sizes into his palm. He picked out the smallest, dropped that in another pocket, and put the rest back into the pouch.

He gathered up everything and wrapped it in a tattered shirt, then tied up the ends. It took him a few minutes, but he finally found a short section of ventilation pipe. He stuffed the treasure into the pipe and buried it in powdered concrete and shattered brick.

Returning to the fire, Mason let the heat warm his tired bones. The flames, coupled with his exhaustion and hunger, mesmerized him. The faces of those who had died by Valerius's assassins—friends, fellow investigators, good men—came into view. Laura's face replaced the rest. The details of her face were fading in his memory, but his heart still ached for her, and his soul felt empty.

From his backpack, he pulled out a long wood box and opened it. Inside was a seven-inch hunting knife along with a sharpening stone. He took his time running the blade across the stone. After several minutes, he tested the sharpness with his thumb. He then raised it to his neck. With precise strokes, he began to shave off his beard. Once that task was completed, he cut his hair close to the scalp. There was no way to make it neat and even, but that fit in with his plan.

IT DIDN'T REQUIRE TOO MUCH ASKING AROUND FOR MASON TO be directed to the most popular black-market spot in Vienna. Karlsplatz sat just outside the inner city, or Innere Stadt, and formed an elongated rectangle two city blocks wide and two short ones deep. The baroque church, Karlskirche, with its green dome and two imposing columns, anchored one side, while two wide boulevards and a wooded park bounded the opposite. The black marketers used both the plaza and the park, and it looked like a typical European open-air market, only these people weren't selling fruits and vegetables but their worldly possessions—silver serving pieces, furs, antique furniture, and jewelry—for enough to buy food and clothing.

The whole thing reminded Mason of his days in Munich, where starving residents sold their precious heirlooms and household goods for food or cigarettes, the main form of currency. Even the random destruction from Allied bombing raids was similar to Munich: sparing one section of buildings, then right next door, nothing but rubble or the empty shells of buildings. Vienna, too, had their troops of Trümmerfrauen, the women removing rubble and cleaning each individual brick, then neatly stacking them for reuse.

Inside the plaza, the marketers had set up makeshift booths or tents, or simply stood in the open, their coats open, displaying jewelry or watches. Their best customers were the American, British, French, and Russian soldiers. The police and military authorities looked the other way.

Mason kept his battered homburg hat low on his forehead as he crossed the plaza, even though the military policemen and soldiers were more interested in the items for sale or the young ladies than checking for identity papers. Mason had changed out of the rags he'd worn on the long trek and had donned a black suit and long black overcoat. The clothes were suitably tattered, and his shoes were appropriately scuffed.

This was the third day Mason had come to Karlsplatz. He'd chosen a particular copse of trees in the middle of the park. From his spot he had a good 360-degree view of the entire plaza. He leaned against a tree trunk and watched the people pass or eyed the vendors, old and young, men and women, and the children collecting discarded cigarette butts. After twelve years as first a detective, then an army intelligence officer, picking out the real bad actors among a crowd of minor transgressors came second nature to Mason.

A pang of nostalgia flared in his chest. Now he was a vagabond, a hunted man, a hunter of a devil, a man alone. His hands cramped, making him realize he'd balled his fists in his pockets with enough force to dig his fingernails into his palms. He yanked his hands out of his pockets and rubbed them against his trousers to release some of the tension.

Two British officers looked his way. Mason gave them a toothy smile and tipped his hat to reveal his jagged haircut. They lost interest, and Mason moved to another tree on the other side of the copse. The movement brought his gaze toward the southern edge of the plaza and a civilian walking with purpose and confidence. He looked to be in his midthirties, and even at fifty yards, Mason could tell he wore a tailored suit and a wool overcoat of the finest quality. With his head held high, he acted like he owned the place—no furtive glances at the soldiers or the occasional cop—and headed for another, younger man lounging on the rubble of a metro station entrance that had suffered a direct hit.

An American soldier passed close to the young man, and they made an exchange as deftly as two spies passing a secret message. The young man was obviously a drug dealer. Mason figured it was either cocaine, heroin, or amphetamine pills. Such substances had to be plentiful. Business would be good in a city full of the desperate, or bored soldiers with pockets full of cash. Idle hands …

The young dealer almost snapped to attention when he saw the well-dressed man approach. The two barely spoke before the young dealer slipped something to the older one. It happened fast, but Mason could tell it was a wad of cash.

Valerius—whoever he was—wouldn't let freelance dealers operate in his territory, and those two were probably low-level minions in Mr. V's enterprise. The fancy-dressed one said a few more words to the dealer and headed back the way he'd come.

It was as good a place to start in his hunt as any.

7

Mason gave the well-dressed dealer a few moments, then started after him. His quarry exited the park behind the Karlskirche, then made a zigzag pattern through several small streets. The man checked for a tail on several occasions, but Mason easily evaded his amateurish attempts at spotting one. Mason kept track of the turns and figured they were going in an easterly direction. And, sure enough, after ten minutes the man came upon Schwarzenbergplatz, a large plaza with a massive fountain and a semicircular colonnade commemorating the Soviet soldiers who were killed while taking control of Vienna. Typical of the Soviet penchant for the grandiose, and it also served as a symbolic thumbing of their noses at the other Allied powers.

The drug dealer crossed the plaza, which also demarked the boundary between the Soviet zone and the British. If there was any doubt of this, signs in Russian and English announcing the fact were plastered at intersections. Soldiers from each side stood guard and warily eyed each other.

The man headed for one of the small streets on the other

side, but a British sentry intercepted him. Mason stopped and watched. The sentry looked over the man's papers, then waved him to continue.

Mason had no choice but to risk the sentry. He'd paid good money in Bolzano, Italy, for a forged German Soldbuch—the essential piece of identity for every German soldier. A decent forgery that got him across several checkpoints in his trek through Italy and into Austria. But if Vienna was anything like Munich, he should have additional papers allowing him to be in Vienna, discharge papers or at least an *Ausweis*, a document giving him permission to travel.

"*Ihre papiere, bitte*," the sentry asked in heavily accented German.

While keeping his eye on his mark's progress, Mason pulled out his Soldbuch and handed it to the sentry.

Asking for his papers was the extent of the sentry's German, because he asked in English, "Is this all you have?"

Mason didn't have time to come up with a story. He said in English, "American. Undercover. U.S. Army CID." He pointed out the dealer with his eyes. "I'm following that guy."

"Do our investigation-branch lads know about this?"

Mason nodded and plucked the forged ID out of the sentry's hand.

The sentry appeared too surprised to say anything. Mason didn't wait for the man to find his tongue and walked away. But there was no sign of his quarry. He hissed a curse and quickened his pace. At the next intersection, Mason looked to his left and right, then spotted the minion walking east three blocks ahead. Mason had to risk being noticed and jogged down the street to close the gap.

Almost immediately, the man turned left, and Mason got to

the intersection in time to see that he had stopped at the front door of a townhouse in the middle of the row. He appeared to be fishing around in his overcoat pocket for the door key. At the same time, he checked his surroundings.

Mason ducked back around the corner. He took off his hat and ruffled his hair, which was already a chaotic mess from the hatchet job of a haircut. With an exaggerated smile plastered on his face and hat in hand, he turned the corner and trotted toward the man.

The drug dealer had his key in the lock and turned it to open the door, when Mason said in German, "Oh, sir. Might I have a word?"

The man spun around and jammed his hand in his overcoat, presumably where he had a pistol nestled in a shoulder holster. Mason acted as humble as he could and slightly off his rocker.

"You come any closer and you're a dead man," the drug dealer said. "Now, get out of here."

Mason held up a pack of cigarettes and took two steps forward. "I have cigarettes for sale."

"Not interested."

A step closer. Slow and easy. "But I have many cigarettes. I can't smoke them all, and you look like a smart businessman who has the means—"

Mason stopped speaking when the guy pulled out his pistol. He held it at his side and glanced up and down the street. Obviously, he hoped removing his gun would be enough of a dissuasion, but Mason just held up his hands and took another step forward. A gap of four yards now lay between them.

"I'm a businessman like you, and I have many cartons,"

Mason said and pointed down the street. “They are stashed just down there. Very cheap. I’ll let them go for very cheap.”

Mason took a chance and moved another step closer, betting the man’s greed would counter his caution. “And look,” he said and transferred the pack of cigarettes to his left hand, then hovered his right above his overcoat pocket. With his fingers spread, he reached into his pocket. “I have something very special in this pocket. It’s not a weapon.”

Very slowly, Mason slid his hand deeper into the pocket. The man tensed, lifting his pistol and aiming at Mason’s chest. Mason’s fingers slipped past the hammerless .380 pistol he had in his pocket and found what he was looking for. Slowly, he pulled his hand out and held up the diamond he’d put aside the night before. “A diamond.”

The man’s gun arm sank a few inches as he stared at the stone.

“I was in the army,” Mason said. “I was supposed to guard a general’s valuables.” He shrugged. “I seem to have misplaced some of the general’s diamonds and his mistress’s jewelry.”

As Mason said this, he shuffled forward. “I have more.” He continued to hold the diamond as if presenting it as an offering to a king.

The man’s eyes were locked on the stone. A diamond, even the small one between Mason’s forefinger and thumb, would bring in more wealth than he could make in four months of dealing drugs.

Two yards … Mason sprang forward. He latched on to the man’s pistol with his left hand, and with a twist, he yanked the gun from the man’s hand. With the same move, he jammed his right elbow into the man’s jaw.

The drug dealer never saw it coming. The blow stunned him, and he staggered backward.

Mason slammed the butt of the gun into the man's temple, then grabbed his lapels and shoved him into the open door. He didn't know if an accomplice was waiting, so he used the man's body as a shield as he pushed.

Mason kicked the door closed and, halfway into the living room, let go of the man's lapels. The man tumbled onto his back. Mason brought up the gun and crouched into a shooting position. The room was empty. No sound. Nothing moved except for the fancy-dressed dealer, who struggled to recover from the blow to his temple.

Mason put his right knee on the man's chest, forcing the air from his lungs. The dealer thrashed and kicked, trying to buck Mason off of his chest. Mason struck him across the chin, stunning him. He pulled the hunting knife out of his boot and held the point under the man's chin.

"Make a move, make a sound, and I'll pin your tongue to the roof of your mouth."

The man stopped struggling. He gritted his teeth and stared at the ceiling in an act of defiance.

"I'll only ask you once: Who is Valerius?"

The man's eyes shifted to Mason with surprise, and he shook his head.

"I'll make it easier for you to talk," Mason said and let off the pressure of the knife tip, then pressed the edge against the man's pulsing carotid artery. He slid the blade a fraction of an inch, and the sharp edge sliced into the dealer's skin just enough to draw a drop of blood.

The man let out a high-pitched moan, then found his voice. "I don't know who he is. I swear."

Mason believed him; if a midlevel lieutenant like Schliemann didn't know, then neither would a street-level thug. "Who do you work for?"

The drug dealer clamped his mouth shut and turned his eyes away. Mason cut a little deeper, not deep enough to hit the artery, but blood flowed from the gash. The man whined through his closed lips. His body shuddered.

"I said, who do you work for? If I cut much deeper, you'll bleed out in seconds."

Mason heard voices coming from the other side of the door. The man started to speak, but Mason clamped his free hand onto his mouth. Just as he glanced behind him, the door opened.

Two men stood at the threshold. They yelled out and went for their guns. Mason only had enough time to grab his .380 and flip on his back. He got off two shots. The men ducked behind the doorframe. The drug dealer spun around and grabbed for Mason.

The two at the door fired from their concealment. A bullet struck a chair near Mason's head. Another buzzed past his ear. Then one struck his attacker in the back. He collapsed onto Mason. Mason returned fire as he squeezed out from under the wounded man's body.

Mason clambered to his feet and fired at the doorframe to keep the shooters pinned. He dashed for the back of the house. The two men opened fire. Bullets impacted the return wall near the entrance to the kitchen. Others screamed past his ears. Mason dived behind the kitchen return wall and fired.

Except for the drug dealer's groans of pain, all fell silent. A standoff.

He was trapped and low on ammunition. He glanced

toward the back of the kitchen. There was a door, but it was barred and padlocked. To his left was the doorway to the dining room, where a picture window looked out onto a small backyard.

He fired his last round and then launched off the wall and raced into the dining room. With his head down and his left arm shielding his head, he ran straight for the window. Leading with his left shoulder, he smashed through the glass. He dropped the six feet and hit the ground and rolled. His shoulder flared with pain, but there was no time. He ran full speed to his right at the six-foot brick wall separating the property with its next-door neighbor. Summoning his army basic training, he leapt for the top of the wall. He grabbed hold and pulled himself up and over.

The two gunmen fired just as he swung his feet over the edge. He landed and ran at the back wall. A garden trellis aided him in scaling it, and he leapt into the backyard of a house on the street behind. He landed badly and twisted his ankle.

By this time the neighboring residents yelled or screamed. Someone shouted for the police.

I'm getting too old for this, he thought as he hobbled for the front yard and the street. Fortunately, that house had no walls, and he cleared the side of the house and turned randomly to his right. He ran as fast as his injured ankle would allow. Dogs barked, people yelled at him, while others ran for cover.

The direction didn't matter, just so long as he put distance between him and the shooters. Beyond the next intersection was a block of fire-damaged buildings. Maybe he could cut through one of those and exit on another street. He crossed the intersection and headed straight for a three-story burned-out shell of a building.

Just then, a group of twenty men stepped out to cut him off. They had grim looks, and their eyes were filled with hate. A few had knives, others held clubs or pipes.

Mason stopped and went for his pistol. Even if it was out of ammunition, they wouldn't know that. The gun was gone. He felt around, but his pockets were empty. It must have fallen as he leapt out the window or climbed one of the walls.

He turned to race back the way he'd come. Six more men blocked his escape. And beyond them, the two gunmen stood still, staring at him. There'd be no more chasing. No more shooting. Even they seemed reluctant to cross these men.

Mason tried running for an abandoned building, but in two seconds the men were upon him. The ones with pipes and sticks swung. Mason guarded his head. In one swift move, he grabbed a pipe from one of the assailants and attacked the closet man. That just infuriated the rest even more. They began to beat him relentlessly. They struck his back, his arms, his legs. Mason fell to the asphalt and curled up in a ball. Others kicked him in the ribs. Then he heard a distinct whoosh. He didn't know if it was a pipe or a heavy stick. It didn't matter. It found its way between his hands and struck the back of his head.

Mercifully, he remembered little else.

8

Mason's eyes popped open. He was lying on his back in darkness. Just before becoming fully conscious, the surrounding noises had infiltrated his dream: a soft rustling, random coughing, and a man, half crazed, yelling for his mother.

He became aware of hands on his head. He jerked away, thinking he was still on the street among the damaged buildings and the men beating him. The rapid motion caused every part of his body to send out shockwaves of pain.

A man's voice in German said, "Easy now. You'll open that wound again."

Mason tried to sit up, but his spinning head made him drop onto his back again.

"Do you want me to fix you up or not?" the man asked.

Mason turned his gaze to the speaker. The man looked to be in his midthirties, probably handsome at one point, but now the skin on his face was drawn tight across his skull. His eye sockets were two dark pools, which emphasized his pale, jutting cheekbones. He had a massive scar across the right jaw, and his right ear was shredded and scarlet—a recent wound.

"They really beat you," the man said. "Besides the massive bruises, you have two cracked ribs and a concussion. I don't know what kind of internal damage has been done."

That explained the pain in his chest with every breath. "Where am I?"

"You're in a bombed-out factory. A makeshift prison run by a gang of Austrian communists. More paid thugs than ideologues."

"What's your name?"

"Peter Kraus."

"You're a doctor?"

"I was a medic in the Wehrmacht. And you?"

"Gregor Witt," Mason said, using the name on his forged identity papers.

"You have a peculiar accent. A touch of Bavarian, but I detect something else."

"*Volksdeutscher*. I'm German-American, and I heeded the call to fight for the fatherland."

"And now look how far you've come, huh?"

Mason grunted a response.

"It's a shame you wandered into this sector," Kraus said. "Our captors are fanatics. They blame all Germans for what happened to them as communists and to Austria. Now they want revenge." Unconsciously his hand rose and hovered near his ear, then he stopped himself.

"They do that to you?"

Kraus gave a melancholy smile. "The worst of what they did to me isn't visible. Still, I can't imagine what my wife might say if I ever get home."

Mason lifted himself on his elbows. His side exploded in pain, but he had to see where he was. The room had been stripped of machinery and replaced by men sleeping or wandering around in the darkness. He figured there were close to three hundred men in a space 250 feet long and 100 feet wide. The roof, some thirty feet above their heads, had gaping holes, letting in a soft light from the moon. A few snowflakes had found their way through the holes and drifted down to land on the prisoners. A heavy mesh of barbed wire had been strung across the areas where bombs had blown open wide gaps in the walls.

Mason saw a man in ill-fitting black clothes carrying a submachine gun just outside a car-sized hole opposite of where he lay. Beyond the guard was a debris-strewn area of concrete, probably the parking lot and loading docks for the now-defunct factory.

"How many men guard this place at any one time?" Mason asked.

"At night, maybe twelve or so," Kraus said. "Heavily armed. They have three machine-gun emplacements at strategic locations." He furrowed his eyebrows at Mason. "There've been several escape attempts. No one has made it. If that was what you were thinking."

"I'm not going to stay here so they can take chunks out of me—" Mason stopped. "Sorry."

"No problem. It's just that you're not in any shape to make a run for it."

"All I need is to get a little of my strength back. Then I'll make …"

The whole room started to spin. His stomach contracted. He turned on his side and threw up some blood and bile that burned his throat. He spit out the remainder and dropped onto his back.

Kraus's face came into his field of view, but it spun as well, like he'd downed a keg of beer. He could just make out Kraus's words, telling him to get some rest while he worked on the rest of his wounds. Mason tried to say thanks, but his mouth refused to move.

MASON LAY ON HIS STOMACH AND LEANED ON HIS ELBOWS. He'd been in the makeshift prison for the past five days, and he was beginning to move about with less pain. The morning sun barely penetrated the heavy clouds, but it still provided enough light to take in his surroundings. He had a decent view of the courtyard beyond the barbed wire, since most of the prisoners were crowded around the two barrels containing the slop disguised as soup. For the first two days, he'd done nothing but sleep, but since then, he'd been able to study the defenses.

The courtyard was approximately forty by sixty feet, formed by the L-shaped factory—one leg housing the prisoners and the other to his right. To Mason's left stood a twelve-foot-high wall closing off the factory from the street and accommodated a gate secured by two equally tall wooden doors. The loading dock was to his right, with three bays for the section of the factory that was now an empty shell. One of the two machine-gun emplacements now occupied the far bay, providing easy coverage of the entire courtyard and access to the street.

Two guards stood by the doors of the courtyard entrance. Another two manned the machine gun, while two others meandered the yard. Mason couldn't see it now, but earlier he'd spotted the barrel of another machine gun sticking out of a ground-floor office window of the two-story building situated to the left of the prison area gate. The two machine guns together could sweep the entire courtyard, cutting down anyone who dared to make a run for it.

On the side opposite the courtyard, where the adjacent building formed an alley, there was a third and final machine gun that could cover any escape all the way to the street. That way was a death trap.

Any escape would have to be through the courtyard. But even if he could dodge machine gun bullets and guards, there was still the formidable-looking gate. Mason returned his gaze to the loading dock bays and into the burned-out warehouse. If only he knew what lay in wait in the dark interior.

The only thing in his favor was that none of the guards, as far as Mason could tell, were experienced soldiers or had been soldiers at all. They had no discipline, smoked constantly and complained of the boredom or the cold.

Kraus's legs came into his view. His new companion sat and held out a wooden spoon and bowl of soup and a piece of moldy bread.

Mason sat up with a little less difficulty than the first couple of days. A spasm of pain emanated from his cracked ribs. It froze his breath for a moment until the sensation subsided. He nodded his thanks and took the bowl and rotten bread.

"Be warned," Kraus said, "it tastes like the guards pissed in it before bringing it out."

"Thanks for that image."

Kraus smiled. "Glad I could help."

Mason dropped the black-and-green bread into the soup and crushed it with the spoon.

"That's disgusting," Kraus said.

"It's better to take it in one big gulp," Mason said and tipped the bowl to his lips and drank. His stomach lurched, but he managed to control the spasms and finish the soup.

Kraus grimaced with disgust.

"It was the only way I could eat the crap they gave us in the POW camp," Mason said, leaving out the part where he'd been a U.S. Army intelligence agent imprisoned in both a Nazi concentration camp and a prisoner-of-war camp near the end of the war.

"In Italy?" Kraus asked.

Mason nodded, lying.

"Did you try to escape there, too?"

"And do what? Link up with my outfit and fight for a lost cause?" Mason shook his head. "I decided to wait it out until the war was over."

Kraus looked away and fell quiet as he stared at his ragged boots. "I was with the 16th Panzer Division in Czechoslovakia at the end of the war. Most of the division—or what was left of it—was captured by the Russians. Fortunately, I was with the few who made it to the American lines."

Mason nodded knowingly. "Did the Americans treat you okay?"

"I survived. They let me go about four months ago. I was walking back to Linz, when I made the mistake of passing through Vienna."

"When did these bastards pick you up?" Mason asked, tilting his head at the guards.

"I lost track. Maybe three months ago. At the rate that prisoners around here disappear, I'm one of the old-timers."

"You seem to have Lady Luck on your side."

Kraus chuckled mirthlessly. "True, but it's only a matter of time before my luck runs out."

"Another reason to get out of here as soon as I can. What's the catch with these people? We were on the same side."

"They're communists, Gregor. They either escaped or were forced out of Austria when the Nazis took over. Now that they're back, they want to take revenge on anyone that caused their misery. Whether we did it directly or not."

"I imagine some of these guys are here for the Russian money, and some get a kick out of beating helpless men."

"Dirty yellow-bellied rats," Kraus said in English. He tried to mimic an American gangster.

It came out of nowhere and sounded so incongruous that Mason's jaw dropped.

Kraus chuckled. He went back to German, saying, "I'm a student of American gangster films. That was James Cagney in *Taxi*."

Mason just nodded, feigning a lack of interest. He kept a neutral expression even while he fought to suppress a belly laugh.

Most of the prisoners had found a spot to eat by then, and except for the sound of wooden spoons tapping against the sides of the bowls, the weight of desperate silence lay heavy in the air.

A horn honked just outside the main gate, and all heads turned toward the sound. All the spoons stopped clacking. Dread and alarm were in the men's eyes as two guards unlocked the gate doors and pulled them open. A troop transport truck and a sedan drove into the courtyard, both army green with red stars painted on the door.

With his back to the courtyard, Kraus continued to stare at the ground. His eyes were wide as if witnessing some horrible atrocity.

The two vehicles came to a stop, and a man hopped out of the truck cab. He wore a Soviet Army uniform with sergeant's epaulettes and barked orders, prompting a squad of soldiers to pile out of the back and line up along the side of the truck. The prison guards backed away in an apparent attempt to put more distance between them and the Russians.

Two young men climbed out of the sedan. They wore army-green uniforms and officer's caps and waited on either end of the sedan. Finally, a man in his late forties stepped out of the back seat of the sedan. The soldiers and officers snapped to attention.

Tall and lean, the man wore a black wool cape over his gray suit, and a tall cylindrical hat of wool over close-cropped gray hair. Mason had rarely interacted with the Soviets during or after the war, but he'd learned enough about the army to know that the *papaha* hat was reserved for colonels and above. So, even though the man was dressed in civilian clothes, he had to be high enough in rank to merit wearing that symbol of prestige.

The man wasn't a politician or political officer; his demeanor, his vigilant gaze told Mason he had to be in intelligence. It puzzled Mason that a high-ranking intelligence officer would bother visiting a prison full of ex-soldiers of the German army. What did he hope to find?

The officer nodded at the sergeant. The sergeant barked more orders, and the squad of soldiers, machine pistols at their hips, marched into the prisoners' area. The soldiers spread out in a line and stopped. Most of the prisoners averted their eyes or turned away.

The officer moved forward, one deliberate step at a time. As he did so, his gaze swept the crowd of prisoners like a probing searchlight. The prisoners were so packed in that the *papaha*-wearing man, and the junior officers who followed, had to step over arms and legs.

The officer said nothing, but the junior officers pointed fingers at seemingly random prisoners. The pointing prompted the soldiers to move out in pairs and grab each hapless prisoner. Some went quietly, while others begged to be spared.

Kraus looked up at Mason and whispered, "Don't look at them. Are you insane?"

Mason ignored Kraus and watched as the officer continued his slow pace, leaving the junior officers to harvest their victims; to what fate, Mason didn't know.

The soldiers had rounded up more than a dozen prisoners and dragged them to the truck when the officer's eyes locked onto Mason's. Mason refused to look away. He didn't cower. The man paused to study Mason. A faint smile formed on his thin lips, then he continued.

After another twenty feet, he stopped and said something in Russian to a prisoner. He spoke as if addressing an old friend. The prisoner said nothing. The officer said something louder, obviously not to the prisoner, because two more soldiers marched up and lifted the man to his feet. The prisoner remained calm as the two soldiers led him away, but then the prisoner said something loud enough in Russian for the officer to hear.

The Soviet officer whirled around. In that same motion, he

withdrew his Colt M1911 pistol from a holster under his cape. With remarkable speed and accuracy, the officer fired one shot, hitting the prisoner in the back of the head. The force of the .45-caliber bullet split the man's head in two.

Startled, the two soldiers jumped back, letting the now-dead prisoner fall to the ground. They recovered quickly, probably having experienced this before from their civilian-dressed commander, and left the dead man where he lay.

The Soviet officer holstered his pistol and started his walk back to the entrance. He stopped parallel to Mason and glanced at him once again. He said something to the junior officers, and they came at Mason.

With dread in his voice, Kraus said, "I told you not to look at them. Good-bye."

9

Mason continued to stare at the intelligence officer as the junior officers yanked him to his feet. A searing pain flared in his knees, hips, and rib cage, but he refrained from showing any discomfort. The junior officers led Mason toward the entrance, keeping a respectable distance behind their commander. While the soldiers loaded the selected prisoners into the back of the truck, the intelligence officer turned left and entered the office portion of the factory.

To Mason's surprise, the junior officers followed the man. The entourage moved down a short hallway serving several offices. At the end of the hallway, they mounted a flight of stairs to another hallway and more nondescript offices. The intelligence officer entered onc, and the junior officers followed. One of the Austrian guards sat at the desk, listening to the radio and smoking a cigarette. As soon as he saw the Soviet soldiers, he hastily stamped out his cigarette and fled the office.

The intelligence officer removed his hat and lifted off his cape, carefully posing both on a coatrack mounted to the wall.

He sat behind the desk and gestured toward a spot in front him. He said something in Russian, and one of the junior officers retrieved a rickety wooden chair from a corner and placed it opposite his commander. The other junior officer pushed Mason into the chair. Then the two men stepped out into the hallway and shut the door.

The intelligence officer said nothing as he pulled out a cigarette from a pack of Lucky Strikes and lit it. Finally, he looked at Mason and took something from his pocket. He tossed it on the desk. It was Mason's Soldbuch. He said in perfect German, "It's a good forgery, but a forgery, nonetheless. We see so many, but this one is better than most. You must've paid well to have this one done."

Mason said nothing.

The officer placed the .380 hammerless pistol on the table. "Your Austrian hosts found this when they captured you in the British sector. American made."

"What do you want?"

The man reached into his pocket once more and held up the diamond Mason had used to entice Valerius's minion. He laid that next to the pistol, then placed a pack of cigarettes next to it.

"My name is Colonel Leonid Konstantin."

"NKVD?"

"We're the MGB now. Who knows what we'll be called next month, but what's in a name? We're still the same organization. Our mission is the same. And I know you're not who you claim to be."

Mason's chest tightened. In healthier times, he could control his reactions, but despite trying, he felt the blood rush to his cheeks.

That elicited a smile from Konstantin. "Ex-German intelligence. No?"

Relief flooded over Mason. His real identity was secure. For now.

Mason's silence seemed to please Konstantin. "Tell me, why would you attack a lowly drug dealer? What did you hope to gain?"

"I didn't like his looks."

"You couldn't have been in Vienna for more than a few days. And the first thing you do is go after a low-level drug dealer—one among the many scum who infest this city."

"He just happened to be in the right place at the right time. For me, anyway."

Konstantin studied him as he puffed on his cigarette. "Normally, I would just shoot a man who dares to be so flippant. But there's something more to you than meets the eye, and that intrigues me." He paused. "I could use some unsavory methods to get an answer, but I might have plans for you instead."

"I won't be your spy."

"Yes, I think you will. The alternative is very unpleasant. However, a cooperative man—and a clever one with strong nerves and intelligence experience—is more valuable to me than a reluctant one."

"Or a dead one."

"Indeed."

Konstantin gathered up the Soldbuch, pistol, and the diamond, and put them in his suit jacket pocket. He tapped on the cigarette case so a few would stick out and held the case out to Mason. Mason took one and put it to his lips. The intelligence officer leaned forward and lit it for Mason. He then took one for himself, and a moment of silence passed between them. Mason knew the generous act and the silence that followed were intended to unnerve him. He had used the same techniques in interrogations. Despite that awareness, he found himself nervous about what might come next. His fate could be decided in the next few moments.

Konstantin looked at Mason and leaned back in his chair. "I know what information you demanded from the drug dealer."

"Whatever the dealer told you, he's lying to save his skin."

"Perhaps. Though it didn't work. He's dead." Konstantin held up his hands. "Not by me. He was a useful informant. No, a man of our mutual interest disposed of him."

Mason's stomach clenched. He didn't know what to think, and the stress and confusion made him lightheaded. *Valerius? Was he talking about Valerius?*

His shock must have shown through, because there was a look of satisfaction on Konstantin's face. "I don't know your reasons for finding this man—"

"Who is he?" Mason said, interrupting his captor.

Konstantin ignored the outburst. "Our interests in him are for very different reasons. Perhaps, if you work for me, and I see you merit the information, then I would reveal his name. But not before."

"Spy on my countrymen for you on the unlikely chance you give me a name?"

"I don't need another asset to spy on Germans. American intelligence is looking for German and Austrian ex-intelligence officers to spy on my comrades. You would make yourself available to their counterintelligence corps and report to us anything you discover." He leaned forward. "I know you won't leave Vienna without having your vengeance on Valerius. I can see that in your eyes."

Mason shook his head. "No deal."

Konstantin crushed out his cigarette, then drew out his monster of a pistol and aimed it at Mason's chest. He pointed it as casually, as devoid of emotion, as someone might point a finger. Mason resisted showing any reaction, even though his heart raced. The Russian had shot a man in the head without flinching.

Konstantin pulled back the hammer. Mason braced for the impact. The long trek for days with little food and a beating had taken its toll. His head spun from the effort. A voice inside his head begged him to take the deal. He'd have three square meals a day. Drinks and cigarettes. And he'd get to keep the blood inside his body.

Konstantin continued to aim the pistol at his chest, and the moments that ticked by seemed like hours. Finally, Konstantin pointed the barrel at the ceiling and gently returned the hammer back to its resting place. He put the weapon back in the holster. "With nerves like that, you'll make a good agent. I'll let you reflect on my proposal in that shithole down there. It might take a few days, but you'll come around. But don't wait too long."

Konstantin called out in Russian, and the two junior officers came in, pulled Mason to his feet, and shoved him out the door. They continued to shove him and strike him as they moved down the stairs and along the hallway.

It was obvious that Konstantin had given them instructions to rough him up—part of the man's persuasion tactics. He tolerated the abuse as best he could, knowing the guards were enjoying themselves, and he was sure they looked for any excuse to escalate the harassment.

But just before they exited the building, the junior officer at his back jammed the end of his truncheon into Mason's kidney, and he lost his control. He whipped around, bringing up his elbow as he did so, and slammed it into the guard's neck. Stunned and breathless, the guard fell against the wall. Mason got in two more punishing blows before the other officer hit Mason on the side of his head.

Mason's head spun. Blasts of light overwhelmed his vision. He was only aware of the officer's hands on his back, spinning him around and thrusting him out the door. Two of the soldiers must have joined in at this point, because a multitude of fists and truncheons struck his torso and head.

The beating stopped, and Mason uncovered his head to see why. In front of him stood the second junior officer. He had a sneer on his face as he peered into Mason's eyes. Then he jammed the truncheon into Mason's stomach. Mason fell to his knees and struggled to breathe, only to gag on his own blood.

He then heard Konstantin shout in Russian. His savior and tormenter decided he'd had enough. For now.

Two of the soldiers lifted him by the shoulders and dragged him on his stomach into the prison area. The prisoners scattered, making a path for the soldiers. They crawled or slid, as standing invited punishment. Mason had a worm's eye view and saw that most of the prisoners scowled at him.

The soldiers reached the middle of the defunct factory's floor and dropped Mason to the fouled concrete. Mason rolled onto his side and drew his knees up to his chest to ease the pain in his stomach and abdomen. No one came to his aid after the soldiers left the compound.

The spasms began to subside as he listened to the truck and sedan engines start up and drive away. Just below those sounds, some of the men in the back of the truck cried out in terror or begged for their lives. The sound of the vehicles faded as they drove out of the gate, and then the doors closed with a clang.

Kraus's feet came into view, then he squatted next to Mason. "Can you walk?"

Mason nodded, and Kraus helped him to his feet. He let Kraus guide him to their usual spot and take some of his weight so he could lie on his side. Then he noticed that the other prisoners had moved away and stared at him with anger in their eyes.

"They think you're spying on us," Kraus said in a whisper.

"Do you?"

"I don't know."

"And what would I have to report?" Mason said loud enough for the men around him to hear. "That the food is crap, and the latrines are overflowing?"

"Fear is driving them. Not reason."

The guards shouted commands, and the prisoners' attention was drawn to the main gate. Mason ignored the pain and sat up to watch two of the guards open the gate. Four civilians stepped in and handed over three men, presumably captured on the streets. Two were badly beaten and had to be dragged into the compound. The third was able to walk in on his own. One of the guards gave the man a halfhearted shove, though generally the guards handled him with deference; they neither shouted commands at him nor urged him along with their truncheons.

The third prisoner stood at six feet and had the build of a

middle-weight boxer. He showed no expression as his hands were unbound. He then walked with an air of confidence as he scanned the prisoners' faces. His gaze was focused like radar until it settled on Mason. He continued his sweep a heartbeat later but with less intensity. He had found his target.

Valerius had sent in one of his assassins. Now the hunt would begin.

10

Mason turned his attention to Kraus, who alternated his gaze between him and the new inmate, with a puzzled look on his face.

"He's here for you, isn't he?" Kraus asked in a lowered voice.

"Not much gets by you," Mason said with a tone of sarcasm.

Kraus furrowed his brow. "Who are you, really?"

"I'm nobody. Leave it at that."

"I would like to know if the man I treated is good or bad. Should have I left him to rot? If these are my last days, I'd like to know."

"These aren't your last days."

"You don't know that. But you seem to know they won't be yours. A spy would have a way out."

"I'm not a goddamned spy."

"Then who are you?" Kraus said it loud enough to cause the surrounding men to look their way.

Mason staring back made them turn away again. He lowered his voice. “I came to Vienna to kill a devil. And he’s just sent one of his assassins to kill me.” He peered into Kraus’s eyes and said, “You’ll live longer if we don’t stick around together.”

“I can help.”

“No, you can’t. I’ve been the cause of too many deaths. I won’t be the cause of yours.”

Mason stood. His muscles were stiff from the cold, and his ribs sent out electrical shocks of pain that threatened to freeze his lungs. He took a moment to glance at Valerius’s man. His would-be assassin looked straight ahead. The killer would bide his time.

Mason stepped over legs and torsos and found a place on the other side of the compound. He sat with his back to a column.

Now he would wait.

Mason had closed his eyes quite some time ago, but his mind continued to whirl. The half-moon was close to setting, and a cold breeze signaled it was a few hours before dawn. During the war he’d spent time in foxholes on cold nights, waiting and listening. Gauging time while peering into the darkness trying to see if an enemy patrol wandered close to the line. The cold, the vigilance, he was used to those, but he’d never gotten used to the waiting.

He heard footsteps, soft and slow, just under the snoring and moaning of the other prisoners. He constricted his muscles, ready to spring. When he opened his eyes, he saw the shadow of a man approaching. Then the dim light of the moon caught the man's face. Kraus.

Mason pulled him down, disturbing a few of the prisoners near him. He growled in Kraus's ear. "I nearly broke your neck."

"I wanted to see if you're still okay."

Mason released him. Adrenaline still pumped in his veins. The soldier's instinct to kill still raged in his head. It made him angry. He figured he might as well do something about it. He was sick of waiting, anyway.

He stood next to the column and waited for life to come back to his legs and the pain to subside. While he did so, the guards swept the compound with a searchlight. At this time of the morning, they passed the light only occasionally, and Mason figured the majority of the guards were fast asleep at their posts or in the small office building.

A moment later, the searchlight was extinguished. Mason moved forward, ignoring Kraus's high-pitched whispers of warning. He had a distance of forty yards to cross. He stepped carefully and quietly; waking his target wasn't his concern. Despite his closed eyes, the man would be sleeping with one eye open. His stealth was to avoid alerting the guards, and the fewer prisoners he disturbed, the better.

With each step, his heart beat faster, pumping adrenaline. He summoned all his training and fighting experience, plus a good measure of instinct.

Valerius's assassin sat with his knees pulled up to his chest, and his head was bent forward as if sleeping. But Mason saw his ears perk up as he approached. He squatted by the man's side, just out of arm's reach. The assassin remained as he was, probably surprised by Mason's bold move.

"I got tired of waiting for you," Mason said in German in a low voice.

The man lifted his head but stared straight ahead.

"I thought I'd come to you and get it over with," Mason said.

"I don't know what you're talking about."

"I see. You'd rather wait until I'm vulnerable and shiv me in the back. Make it easy on yourself."

"When I want to kill you, I'll do it to your face."

"I'm here now," Mason said. When he got nothing from his adversary, he said, "Or are you just a little bit afraid?"

In a lightning-fast move, the man lunged. A reflection of the light flashed off the metal in his hand. The blade sliced into Mason's overcoat.

Mason was ready and caught the man's arm before the blade reached flesh. He twisted his body into the man's torso and used the motion to slam his elbow into his opponent's jaw. Mason thrust upward in an attempt to plant his knee on his opponent's chest to pin him to the ground. But the man sprang into motion, countering Mason's maneuver. Both were on their feet now. The man was equally skilled, and they traded kicks and blows. Mason still had control of the man's knife arm, and he tried to dislodge the knife, but the excruciating pain in his ribs was slowing him down. In his struggle to disarm him, his opponent was getting in most of the blows.

The prisoners were on their feet and cheering, mostly for Mason's would-be assassin.

The man used his free hand to clamp onto Mason's larynx and squeeze. That was his first mistake.

Mason spun out of the choke hold, elbowing the man in the throat. At the same moment, he kicked the man's feet out from under him and threw him to the concrete.

Stunned, the man lay on his back. And after several debilitating blows to his face, Mason twisted the knife out of the man's hand.

His opponent still fought from his prone position with desperate kicks and swings. He growled and turned with his mouth open in an attempt to bite Mason's leg.

The adrenaline, the fury, turned Mason wild, and he landed blow after blow to the assassin's face.

A multitude of hands yanked Mason away. Several prisoners kicked and struck at him. A severe blow landed on the back of his neck. Another to the side of his head. His mind threatened to shut down. His sight narrowed to a dark tunnel. His ears rang.

But through the ringing and the din of the shouting prisoners, he heard the guards blowing their whistles. And just below that, Kraus yelling something. He looked to his right and saw Kraus fighting off assailants. He, too, was on the receiving end of angry blows.

Mason body-slammed one man away from Kraus, then flipped another on his back. He took a defensive stance and readied the knife to slash the next man who dared attack him or Kraus.

The prisoners backed off to form a tight circle. Mason's would-be assassin lay at his feet, holding his damaged throat as he spat up blood. Kraus was on his knees, out of breath and pressing a hand against a bleeding wound to his forehead.

Mason couldn't hold them off for long—the prisoners had

bloodlust in their eyes. Mason, it seemed, would be their way of venting their fear and pain.

Gunfire erupted. Over the heads of the prisoners, Mason could see nightsticks raised and then coming down upon the prisoners. As the crowd began to disperse, Mason caught glimpses of the guards firing their pistols in the air as they beat the prisoners.

The guards' poor training worked to Mason's advantage: they had spread out, overly confident of their ability to cow and intimidate. They had isolated themselves among a crowd of frenzied men.

A guard charged Mason with his nightstick up. Instead of retreating, Mason moved forward, trapping the guard's nightstick arm, then landing three precise blows that put the guard on the ground.

Mason looked back at Kraus, who appeared to pick up on this daring tactic with a nod. The dozen prisoners who had just witnessed Mason taking the guard down turned and attacked the other guards. Possessed with the chance of freedom and whipped up to a frenzy, the close to three hundred prisoners overwhelmed the six guards. In less than a minute, the mass of men charged for the open gate and the courtyard.

Mason grabbed Kraus by the arm and yelled over the noise of the riot, "Follow me."

Mason and Kraus ran for the open gate behind a wall of charging men. Sporadic shooting erupted. Then a machine gun opened up. Still the mass surged forward out into the open courtyard. Mason and Kraus stayed low and had to leap over the men who had fallen.

Mason took a sharp left just outside the gate. Kraus

followed, and several men, seeing the folly of running blindly into machine-gun fire, did the same. Mason glanced back as he ran and saw men either throwing themselves against the main gate or charging the two machine guns. Mason led the others along the fence and out of view from the machine gunner firing from the office building's ground floor. As he approached the door to the two-story office building, an officer charged out with his pistol at the ready. His face distorted in alarm when he saw Mason and the others running straight at him.

Mason rammed into him, pushing him into the hallway. With two quick blows, he had the officer on the floor. He ripped the pistol from the stunned officer's hand and let the men behind him finish him off.

To Mason's right was the door to the ground-floor office, where the machine gun raked the crazed prisoners. While he was taking down the officer, others burst through the office door and descended upon the machine-gun crew. Gunshots where followed by screams, then all fell silent.

Mason looked back to make sure Kraus was safely behind him, then he saw that other prisoners had taken note of Mason's tactics, and now more men streamed into the hallway. He ran for the exit leading out onto the street. An iron rod blocked the door and was fixed in place by a heavy padlock.

The prisoners behind were crushing him and Kraus against the door. Then a guard opened fire from the top of the stairs. Several men groaned or collapsed. Mason turned and fired. The guard fell down the stairs, and Mason yelled for someone to see if the dead guard had any keys.

After a moment of fighting off the crush of men, someone

threw a ring of keys over the prisoners' heads toward Mason. He caught them and inserted the first key. Nothing.

Back at the door to the prison yard, gunshots rang out, and the fifty-plus men crammed into the hallway started to cry out or fall where they stood: The guards in the courtyard had seen what Mason and the others were doing and now fired into the backs of the desperate men.

Mason finally found the correct key and unlocked the padlock. He flung the iron bar aside and opened the door. He half expected more guards to be waiting in the street, guns ready, but when he dashed out the door, the street was empty.

He took Kraus by the shoulder and pulled him to the left to avoid the possibility of running into any of the guards that might come out by the main gate. Behind him, he heard a multitude of boots on pavement along with heavy breathing as they steamed out onto the streets and ran in both directions.

Helping Kraus slowed Mason down, and other escapees surged ahead. That alerted the machine gunners at the end of the narrow alley, and the gun opened up. He and Kraus had no choice but to take the chance of crossing the stream of bullets. Mason poured on the speed. He felt a ripping at his overcoat, but he and Kraus made it across.

Mason, Kraus, and four others turned right down a small side street, then another, trying to put as much distance between them and the prison.

"Mason," Kraus hissed.

Mason turned and realized Kraus had fallen behind. He was out of breath and leaning on his knees.

Kraus pointed in another direction. "That way. It's the fastest way out of the Russian zone."

Mason changed course and let Kraus lead the way. Two

other prisoners stayed with them, while the others chose their own way to safety. Half the Soviet army and all the Austrian communist militia would soon be out hunting for them. And this time they would shoot on sight.

Mason poured on the speed.

11

Mason and Kraus ducked behind a wall inside the lobby of an abandoned hotel. Just as they managed to conceal themselves, another patrol of Soviet soldiers rode past on their horses. The other prisoners who'd followed them for the past ninety minutes decided that two had a better chance at concealment and had gone in another direction.

Mason peeked around the corner. He had a clear view of the intersection of the small street they were on and a wide boulevard. All was clear.

He signaled for Kraus to follow, and they dashed across the boulevard and entered the street on the other side. He estimated that they had maybe two hours before dawn, but they were running out of options. Their idea was to avoid the city center and sneak into one of the British zones that lay on either side of the Soviets, but each time they tried to approach the border between the two zones, Soviet soldiers or roving groups of militia had cut them off. Consequently, they'd been forced to go closer to the heart of the city.

Mason and Kraus reached the end of the small street and

paused behind a pile of rubble to catch their breath. An hour and a half of sprinting after the melee at the prison had left them both beyond exhausted. Mason's muscles burned, and it felt like his ribs were constantly digging into his side.

Kraus pointed to the next side street across another wide boulevard. "If we keep going that way, we'll end up in the Innere Stadt. Too many patrols. We'll be trapped."

Mason looked out to the boulevard as he weighed their options.

"Our only choice is to go south," Kraus said. "I'm betting most of the patrols are covering the borders to the British zone. Maybe they won't expect us to go deeper into the Soviet one."

Mason ducked back behind the rubble. "I didn't come all this way just to run back into the countryside. I need to link up with the Americans."

"What's so important that you'd risk being shot on sight? The war is over, you know."

"This is personal. You should go the other way and get home. Be with your wife and kids."

Kraus looked back from where they'd come. "Back that way?" He shook his head. "I won't make it alone. I think I have a better chance sticking with you."

Mason didn't want to be responsible for another person's death. He'd lost too many already. He looked at Kraus, determined to tell him to get lost, but Kraus looked frightened. He couldn't leave the man helpless.

"Who has control in the city center?" Mason asked.

"All four have combined power. The patrols are in American jeeps: one American who always drives, one British, one French, and one Russian. Like a joint police force."

"Then our only chance is to get into the city center."

"Are you sure about this?"

"No," Mason said and took off running.

THIRTY MINUTES BEFORE SUNRISE, A SLIVER OF THE HORIZON had already turned from black to inky blue. From inside a bomb-damaged building, Mason and Kraus observed a group of five militia who were posted at a choke point next to the wide boulevard known as the Ringstrasse, or ring road, that circled the old part of the city.

Mason and Kraus had been watching the group for the past twenty minutes. During that time, the militia group had made several moves to change positions, but each time, the guy who seemed to be in charge would consult someone via his handie-talkie, and they would return to their former position. Something was up. Maybe they'd been spotted, and their pursuers were closing in. It was now or never.

"We have to move," Mason said.

"Those are Austrian militia. They won't respect the border."

Mason shifted his position. His cramped and exhausted muscles complained. He didn't know how much energy he had left, and he was in healthier shape than Kraus. They would have to run for their lives and cross six lanes of the Ringstrasse to get to the Innere Stadt. Eighty yards over open ground.

The roar of an engine echoed in the dawn's silence. Mason and Kraus looked to their left and past the waiting militia. The vehicle's headlights indicated it was on the ring road and coming at them at a good clip.

"Russian, you think?" Mason asked.

"I don't know."

When the vehicle got closer and the sound of the engine became clearer, Mason smiled. "I'd know that sound anywhere. That's an American jeep."

Kraus scrambled to his feet next to Mason and peered into the distance. "The Russians don't use American jeeps. Maybe it's one of the inner-city patrols."

The jeep passed the militia and headed toward Mason and Kraus. It got close enough for Mason to see distinct silhouettes of the occupants: four men, two wore caps and two wore different shaped helmets.

"Are you ready to make a run for it?" Mason asked Kraus. "This might be our only option."

Kraus's face was taut with fear, but he nodded. They broke into a run. They scaled a pile of rubble and exited the building. Mason sprinted across the sidewalk at a diagonal trajectory to intercept the speeding jeep. He leapt over a barbed-wire barrier set up by the Russians. Right behind him, Kraus miscalculated and cried out as he stumbled.

The jeep was almost abreast of them. Mason rushed back to help Kraus to his feet, and they raced across one lane of the road, then two.

The jeep sped past them. The MPs hadn't noticed two men running wildly for them, and Mason cursed their carelessness. They would be gone in a moment. Mason had to risk being spotted by the militia. Shooting off his pistol might provoke the patrol to open fire … "Hey!" he yelled and waved his hands.

The jeep kept going. The men in the patrol apparently couldn't hear him over the roar of the engine. But the militia, eighty yards behind them, did.

As Mason and Kraus poured on the speed, the militia yelled for them to stop. They turned into the lane directly behind the jeep and waved their hands in hopes they might be seen in the rearview mirror. Mason's leg muscles cramped. His broken ribs felt like they were slicing into his side with a red-hot blade. Behind him, Kraus heaved in air, his footsteps unsteady. The jeep continued, putting distance between them.

Gunfire erupted to their rear. A bullet screamed past Mason's head. Another struck the pavement ahead of him. Mason had a decision to make: continue or make a dash for the inner city.

He was about to turn left for the city center, when the jeep braked and made a quick U-turn. Their hope renewed, Mason and Kraus yelled and waved their hands at the men in the jeep.

Mason looked back and saw the militia men had stopped their pursuit. They stood there watching helplessly. Or maybe the militia was waiting for them to be arrested and returned to the Soviet authorities.

Mason turned back to the approaching jeep. Its headlights blinded him as it came to a stop twenty feet ahead. Out of breath and praying his gamble would pay off, he raised his hands.

The four military policemen climbed out of the jeep. They were silhouetted by the headlights as they stepped forward and stopped a few feet from the front of their vehicle.

"American," Mason said breathlessly in English. "I'm an American." Keeping his hands high, he took slows steps toward the policemen.

Mason got within ten feet when the American MP said, "Hold it right there."

The British MP said, "You look about as American as Adolph. Show your ID."

The Russian MP said in broken English, "These men are German, and they escaped from one of our prisons."

"Goddamn it," Mason said, "I'm an American. Mason Collins. I was a CID investigator in the five-o-eight police battalion." As he said this, he could feel Kraus's eyes on him.

The American and British MPs moved toward them. The American MP said, "Five-oh-eighth, huh? Where were you stationed?"

"Munich, then Garmisch-Partenkirchen."

The Russian MP growled, "These men must be returned to my commanding officer."

Mason nodded to Kraus. "This man was working undercover for the CIC. Both of us should be handed over to the American authorities."

The American and British MPs stopped in front of Mason and aimed their flashlights into both of their faces.

"Sergeant, I insist," the Russian MP said.

"I'd ask you who's the top homerun hitter for the Yankees," the American MP said, "but you German agents can be pretty clever."

"Sergeant, I haven't been up on baseball stats for over a year. Plus, I hate the Yankees. I'm a Cubs fan."

"We'll see what the post commander has to say," the American MP said.

Mason nearly passed out with relief.

12

Flames as high as his head surrounded Mason. It was as if he were in a black void filled with fire. He shielded his face from the intense heat. He wanted to run, but his legs refused to move. Somewhere within that inferno, he could hear groans and mournful wails of pain. A woman's voice …

"Laura!"

He couldn't get a fix on her location. The woman's moans kept changing, and he turned one way, then another, his panic rising to a fever pitch. "Laura!"

A hand grabbed his shoulder from behind. His spine turned to ice. He looked at his shoulder. Blackened fingers sank deep into his flesh. He cried out and jumped.

Mason woke up seated in a wooden chair flailing his arms and legs. The light hurt his eyes, but his sight quickly recovered.

He was in a small windowless room. The chair faced a table, where he had laid his head. He looked to where those blackened fingers had touched him and saw someone standing over him.

Through his sleep-induced haze, he recognized the man immediately.

Mike Forester, an old friend, wore a devilish grin. "You look like roadkill, buddy. And you smell worse."

Mike Forester and Mason had worked together in the army's G2 intelligence corps during the war. Mike had joined the CIC, the U.S. Army's Counter Intelligence Corps, when Germany had surrendered, and had even helped Mason during his investigation into a brutal killer in Munich.

Still trying to clear the cobwebs from his brain, Mason said nothing as he shook Forester's hand. That's when he noticed the clock on the wall—half past noon. He'd put his head down on the desk at eight thirty a.m., after the MPs took him and Kraus to the shift commander's office. They'd taken Kraus to another room, and then an MP sergeant had grilled Mason for a half hour.

"Where've you been?" Mason asked. "You get lost on the way over?"

"I'm a little busy saving the world from communism," Forester said. He lit a cigarette and handed it to Mason. Mason accepted it and took a long drag. It was the best sensation he'd had in what felt like a long time.

Forester lit one for himself. "I'll have them bring you some food," he said and walked to the door.

"And a gallon of coffee," Mason said.

Forester opened the door and said something to a person waiting outside it. He returned to the table and sat.

"Where's my companion, Peter Kraus?"

"The one you claimed worked undercover for us?"

"It was the only thing I could think of to convince those MPs to bring us in and not turn us over to the Russians."

"To answer your question, one of my officers is talking to him now."

There was a knock at the door, and an MP brought in a tray with a plate and a carafe of coffee. He put the tray on the table and left. After a quick thanks, Mason attacked the sliced ham, cheese, fried potatoes, and slices of dark bread.

Forester watched him for a moment, then asked, "The last time I saw you was before you were transferred to Garmisch. I read about you breaking up that crime ring."

The mention of that time—ten months ago, though it seemed like years—made him think of Laura. He fought back the lump growing in his throat. "A lot of bad road after that."

"I heard tales about you leaving a trail of broken bodies from Augsburg to Marseilles. Rumor was, you were in Tangier. So, what are you doing in Vienna?"

"Looking for the man who put out a contract on my life. That trail of bones I left behind belonged to his assassins. A lot of good friends were murdered or put in the hospital." He looked up at Forester. "Mike, I think he has Laura."

"Laura? Your ex-sweetheart?"

Mason nodded. "So far, they've failed to get to me, so he's been going after everyone associated with me, or whoever helped take down that crime ring. His men burned down Laura's house. The investigators found her husband's body, but she's missing. Mike, you've got to help me find out if she's been kidnapped, killed, or on the run. You've got to find her—"

"Whoa, slow down. Who's the guy you're after?"

"I only know his code name: Valerius."

The name made Forester's face drop. "Valerius?"

"You've heard of him?"

Forester glanced at the floor, clearly troubled.

"What a minute. You know who he is, and you're not going to tell me?"

"You're not in the service anymore, Mason." Forester held up his hand before Mason could argue further. "I *can* tell you that we know of the existence of Valerius, but not his identity. And because you're an old friend, I will tell you to lay off trying to find this guy because—"

"Yeah, I know. He's as dangerous as they come."

"That's right."

"I'm going after him anyway."

"No, you're not. You left the army—"

"I was told to get out or face a court martial."

"Regardless of how or why, the fact is you—as a civilian—aren't even authorized to be here. The Russians want you, and so do the Austrian authorities for attacking one of their citizens."

"A drug dealer working in Valerius's organization."

"That's what you tell a judge. Not me."

"You'd turn me over to the Austrians?"

"If you don't drop this? I just might. Command doesn't want to upset the apple cart. They're trying to get the Austrians back on their feet and build a democratic government. Which, of course, the Russians don't want. They want a puppet organization loyal to Stalin. So, if we start usurping their limited authority, it could upset the delicate balance."

"You sound like a bureaucrat. You bucking for a promotion?"

"Mason, the war is over. It's time to start thinking about the future."

"The Russians don't seem to think it's over. You're the one

who told me we're in a standoff with them. Espionage is the new battleground."

Forester crushed out his cigarette and stood. "I'll get you out of here. In fact, I'll see you get on the first ship back to the States."

He turned to leave, when Mason said, "Do you know a Leonid Konstantin? Russian intelligence chief?"

That stopped Forester. He turned and waited for Mason to continue.

"When I was in that prison, he picked out a dozen or so men from a crowd of three hundred and had them hauled off in trucks to God only knows where. While making his selection, he picked me out of the crowd and took me into an office for interrogation. He knew why I attacked that drug dealer. Konstantin assumed I'd been in German intelligence, and I wasn't about to correct him. He offered me information on Valerius in exchange for becoming one of his agents."

Forester said nothing as he lit another cigarette, but Mason knew the man's expressions and could tell his mental wheels were turning.

"Now, why is a high-ranking Russian intelligence officer so interested in Valerius?" Mason asked. "He knows, or claims to know, his identity. He even claims to know that Valerius executed the drug dealer I roughed up. And why offer that information to me? Was he hoping I'd go after the man after setting me loose as one of his agents?"

Forester still hadn't said anything.

Mason continued, "My guess is, you guys don't know who Valerius is because you haven't got anybody who's been able to get close to him. So, I've got a proposal: You set me up as a —I don't know—a private citizen. An American banker or charity official. And see what I can dig up. The first day I got here, I got closer to him than any of your officers or agents."

Forester tapped the table with yet another cigarette. "Or maybe you take Konstantin up on his offer."

"No. He wants me to spy on Americans. Expose your German and Austrian assets. I won't do that. Even if you have me feed him false information, the setup would take too long. Because in the meantime, he's still hunting anyone associated with me. Valerius might have Laura."

"Say I agree to your proposition, and we put you out on the streets; you're just as likely to wind up dead or recaptured."

"Not if we do our jobs right. You give me foolproof credentials and let me do the rest. I stay off the books in case I'm arrested or killed. Nothing that could get back to you."

Forester thought for a moment, then shook his head. "I don't like it. The people you'd be going up against are smart. They've managed to keep us in the dark for months. That means they must have their fingers in everything, including military government officials, local politicians and judges, and the police. Then there's Russian intelligence with their moles and agents everywhere. And you usually go in guns a-blazin'. Regardless of whether or not you're on the books, it could come back and kick us in the balls."

Mason leaned forward. "Valerius is a big fish, and I bet you want him bad. And it seems to me you have very few options. I'm your best bet right now. And you know if you try to get rid of me, I'll just come back."

Forester lit another cigarette—a chain smoker of the first degree. Finally, he said, "It's going to be a few days to set you up. In the meantime, we have to get you out of sight and make like we've sent you packing."

"I need something from you in return."

"Oh, here we go …"

"See that Kraus gets home, outside Linz. Get the Austrians to drop the murder charges against me. And use every resource the CIC's got to find out what happened to Laura."

"That's it?" Forester asked with a tone of sarcasm.

"I think your boys can pull that off."

"Are you sure I can't talk you out of this?"

Mason shook his head. "You know me better than that."

"Yes, I do, and I know you're heading out on a suicide mission."

13

Mason stood under the shower, letting the hot water wash away the filth. It'd been over a month since he'd bathed in anything other than the icy water in a steam or river. He lifted his head and let the water splash on his face. He felt invigorated, and the shower seemed to wash away some of the pain. Though it did nothing to soften his rage.

He turned off the water and stepped over to a towel rack. As he dried himself, he caught a glimpse of his face in the mirror. He hardly recognized the man in the reflection. Being clean-shaven with his hair chopped short just highlighted his hollow face and thin body. The sight elicited a flashback to his time in the two Nazi prison camps. Though his present condition was nothing compared to the emaciated wreck he'd become before liberation, it still brought the horrors and pain to the forefront of his mind.

He shook off the images and checked his wounds from his latest beatings in Vienna. The swelling and bruising had started to subside. The pain in his ribcage had eased to a dull ache.

"Could be worse," he said to his reflection, then leaned in. "Could be better."

He was in a bathroom with four open shower stalls, usually reserved for hospital staff, but Forester had seen to it that he received the VIP treatment. Forester had supervised his transfer from the international command center to the U.S. Army hospital, taking care to create a ruse for anyone who might be watching from the shadows. Two U.S. MPs had led him out of the command center in handcuffs, stuffed him into Forester's sedan, and taken a circuitous route to the hospital under guard.

Mason finished toweling off, then put on clean pajamas. The hospital-issued garments were stiff from too much detergent, but they still felt like the finest silk when he slipped them on. He then put on a robe, exited the bathroom, turned down two corridors, and entered a semiprivate room.

Kraus was sitting on one of the two hospital beds. A nurse leaned over him as she dressed one of the multiple festering sores on is back. Kraus looked up and smiled through the thermometer stuffed in his mouth. His hospital gown billowed over his emaciated frame. His washed face revealed skin bordering on gray punctuated by violet and crimson bruises.

The nurse was around thirty and attractive. Her ample body pressed against her uniform in all the right places, and Kraus stole several glances of her and then would shyly look away.

To Mason, it looked like love at first sight, and he took pleasure in watching the woman after being around filthy, scrawny, lice-infested men.

The nurse finished dressing Kraus's wound, then plucked the thermometer from his mouth and checked it. "You've got a fever. A hundred and one."

Puzzled, Kraus looked at Mason, who said, "Thirty-eight and a third degrees."

Kraus nodded that he understood.

Without looking at Mason, the nurse said to him, "Have a seat on the bed. I'll look you over once I'm done with him." She dropped the thermometer in a metal tray with alcohol. She said to Kraus, "I'll be back in a few minutes."

Kraus watched her cross the room and looked at Mason only when she was out of sight.

"How long has it been?" Mason asked.

"The last time I was on leave to see my wife and daughter," Kraus said in English. "1943."

Mason raised his eyebrows. "You speak English?"

"I studied medicine for two years at King's College in London. My father had to cut my funding when Germany took over Austria in the Anschluss. Actually, my French is better than my English."

"I guess the CID and CIC decided you're not a communist spy."

"I thought their questions would go on forever," Kraus said, then a serious expression formed on his face. "You fooled me with your sad German Soldat story. Where did you learn to speak such good German?"

"I was born in Augsburg. I was a very young boy when my father died in World War One, and that's when my mother took my sister and I to the U.S. We lived with my grandparents, who only spoke German."

Kraus scratched at one of his sores as he nodded. "My father was never the same after fighting in the trenches."

A moment of silence passed between them, then Mason said, "You'll be happy to know that Forester as agreed to get you home, courtesy of the United States Army." He expected Kraus to show his joy at the news, but Kraus returned a frown.

"I want to stay here with you," Kraus said.

"You mean hang around to see more of that nurse," Mason said jokingly.

Kraus looked serious. "No, I mean to help you with … well, whatever you're working on."

"You don't want any part of what I'm going to be doing. Go home and be with your wife and kids."

Kraus glanced at the door, then leaned forward and lowered his voice, "I know it's going to be dangerous."

"You don't know that."

"Yes, I do. They went out of their way to sneak us out of the MP station and take us here. They could've pushed me out the door or taken me to an Austrian hospital or turned me over to the police. They treated me kindly. Not like an ex-Wehrmacht soldier. They gave me hot food and Schnapps, like the meal the army served to soldiers before a big battle. It's something dangerous. You saved me from certain death at that prison, and now I want to return the kindness."

"You treated me and brought me back to life. We're even. Go home."

"What are you going to do out there alone? Your German is Bavarian not Austrian. I know this city. I know the people. I speak English, French, and a little Czech. I can be your eyes and ears."

"Peter, I'm going after the leader of a dangerous crime organization. He's responsible for the deaths of a half dozen of my friends, and at least that many were put in the hospital because of him. He either killed, abducted, or is hunting the woman I love. I won't stop until he has me killed, or I bring him down."

"I assumed it had to be something like that."

"And what brought you to that conclusion?"

"I have the impression you don't do anything small."

"Except saving your skinny carcass."

"American humor used to relieve the tension or change the conversation. I have made a study of American humor, but I still don't understand it."

"The point is, now that you have the opportunity to go home, take it."

Kraus looked away.

Mason noticed how deflated he looked and said, "You're afraid, aren't you? Afraid your wife will see that big scar on your face and bolt. She'll still love you—"

He stopped when Kraus looked at him with profound sorrow in his eyes.

"My wife and daughter were killed in a bombing raid in Linz," Kraus said. "My mother died when I was young. My father died shortly after he buried my wife and child. My brother froze to death on the eastern front. I have no one to go home to. I lied to you about my family because sometimes I pretend they're still alive. It's all I have left."

"I'm sorry, Peter."

"Don't be. Let me be a part of this. If this man is ravaging my homeland, my people, then he deserves to be brought to justice. I may not be as strong or as good a fighter, but I have faculties that you lack."

The nurse returned with the doctor. While the doctor examined Kraus, the nurse turned her attention to Mason. Little was exchanged except for the doctor or nurse giving them instructions. The nurse changed the dressing for the gash on Mason's head, and said, "Whoever sewed you up did a nice job."

Mason tilted his head toward Kraus. "That's his handiwork."

After some probing and questions about Mason's symptoms, the doctor said, "I should have some X-rays done, see if you've suffered any internal injuries."

"No X-rays, doc."

"I can't diagnose much without them. You could be walking around with a damaged organ.

"I'll be fine."

"Suit yourself. Nothing we can do about the rocks in your head, anyway."

With that, the doctor left, passing Forester on the way out. The nurse told Kraus to take the antibiotics and pain medication she'd brought him and to rest in bed for at least a week. Kraus nodded at her with a puppy-dog smile.

Forester stepped forward as the nurse left. "You both still look like a couple of cadavers." He held up an envelope and said to Kraus in German, "Your travel papers. You'll head out with a convoy at 0700 tomorrow."

Mason answered in English, "Change of plans. He's going to work with me."

Forester looked from Mason to Kraus. "The doc says my blood pressure is already too high. Is this some kind of plot to make me pop a blood vessel? I went over a couple of heads to get this man away from the Russians and Austrian police. An ex-Wehrmacht soldier, no less." He said to Kraus, "Now you want to go out there with his cowboy and get yourself killed?"

Kraus said in English, "I appreciate all your efforts, and

I'm sorry to have caused you any trouble, but I would like to help Mr. Collins."

Forester looked at Mason with surprise.

"Yeah," Mason said, "he speaks English and French."

Kraus added, "And a little Czech and Russian."

Mason shrugged at Forester. "He could be a good asset."

Forester lit a cigarette while studying both of them. He rolled it between his fingers as he thought. Mason remembered Forester as a man who liked to take risks and made quick decisions, but either age or the pressures of command had changed him.

Finally, Forester said, "He'll be your responsibility. Civilian or not, I'll put you behind bars if I find out you've shared classified material, and then he shares it with someone else. He operates on a need-to-know basis."

"Understood," Mason said.

Forester turned to go, then stopped as if remembering something. "I'll change the paperwork. Both of you be ready to leave at 0900. You'll be catching a plane to Salzburg. We do all this in plain sight. You'll get prepped there, then return here on separate flights."

Mason pointed at Forester's cigarette. "High blood pressure."

"They're my arteries. You just worry about how you and your new friend are going to stay alive."

14

Mason and Kraus emerged from a U.S. Army Air Forces C-47. They descended the few steps down to the tarmac of the Salzburg airport and into a drizzling rain. They were dressed in civilian clothes, trench coats, and fedoras. While the other passengers, a mix of military brass and civilian administrators, walked the short distance to the terminal building, an army MP met Mason and Kraus and directed them to a waiting sedan.

They were barely settled into the back seat of the car when the driver hit the accelerator and sped toward a side gate flanked by MP guards. The guards waved them through, and the driver took a two-lane highway that cut through the flat farmland outside Salzburg. Kraus stared out the side window in the direction of the old city, but a bank of low-altitude clouds obscured the view.

In less than fifteen minutes, the sedan approached the gates to the headquarters for the USFA, or United States Forces, Austria. The main gate was bounded by two granite columns, which were then flanked by rectangular structures pierced by pedestrian-sized gates and topped with what looked like Nazi eagles. Guards posted by the columns checked the occupants' papers, then waved the driver through. Before them were two long driveways bordering a manicured lawn. At the far end of the driveway stood a grand baroque palace.

"Schloss Klessheim," Kraus said as he peered out the sedan's windshield. "I visited it with my family when I was a boy. It's appropriate that the conquering army is using this palace. Hitler received Mussolini and other fascists here, and there was a failed attempt on his life when the palace was hosting an exhibition."

"A damn shame they didn't succeed," Mason said.

The driver eased the sedan next to the left set of stairs leading up to the palace entrance. A private met them as they climbed out of the sedan, and he directed them to a side entrance formerly used by the servants. They entered an open space filled with desks, with a hallway at the opposite end. Typewriters clacked. Uniformed clerks entered or exited offices bearing fistfuls of papers. The saying goes that an army marches on its stomach, but Mason knew a modern army couldn't move anywhere without first generating truckloads of paperwork.

Mason and Kraus followed the private to the end of the hallway and into a modest-sized conference room. A rough-hewn table and century-old chairs dominated the center of the room. A chalkboard and a handful of file cabinets lined one of the eighteenth-century stone walls. The private asked them to wait, then he left them alone.

Mason walked around the room, looking out the shallow rectangular windows that revealed little but the dreary autumn sky. A wooden floorboard creaked in a quick rhythmic pattern, and he turned to the noise. It was Kraus's right leg bouncing like a piston, and the man stared at the door as if unaware of the annoying sound, or his leg.

"Nervous?" Mason asked.

Kraus glanced down at his leg and stopped it from bouncing. "I just want to do the right thing and not make mistakes. My father always told me that if I can't do something right, then don't do it at all."

"Relax. You'll be fine."

A uniformed man without a branch insignia or rank came into the room without knocking. "Gentlemen," he said with a brisk nod. He stopped at the head of the table near the blackboard, then tossed two manila envelopes on the table, one in front of Kraus and the other on the opposite side for Mason. Mason sat, opened the envelope, and pulled out its contents.

"I am Agent Sam Boyd. These are your new identities." He looked at his notes and pointed to Kraus. "Your name is Philippe Bossart. Swiss banker. French speaking. You'll see your history, your connections, your credentials." He pointed to Mason. "We made you an American charity organizer named Martin Anderson. The family has money. Baltimore. You have a reputation as a gambler and ladies' man." He stopped and looked up at the ceiling as if weary of the absurdities of his job. Kraus wiggled his eyebrows at Mason.

Boyd turned his attention back to his notes and picked up where he left off. "… a ladies' man. You two represent a charity called the International Fund for a Democratic Austria."

"Here, here," Kraus said.

Boyd lifted his eyes off the page to look at Kraus. "You're Swiss in this case, not Austrian. Your goal is to get investors to build infrastructure in Austria and make a load of cash for potential clients."

"And ourselves, of course," Kraus said.

"Now you're getting the idea."

"My father was a banker—"

"We know. We checked up on you. Your background will give you a leg up—"

"I don't understand."

"An advantage," Mason said, clarifying.

Kraus nodded.

Boyd pocketed his notes. "You'll be briefed more in Vienna. Flight leaves tomorrow morning. You have until then to memorize your files. Know it backwards and forwards. I don't know your assignment, but if Major Forester got the CIC to hustle this, it must be high-priority and high-risk. You slip up just once on this stuff and—"

"It'll be curtains," Kraus said in a bad imitation of a thirties gangster.

Boyd looked at Mason. "Where did you dig up this guy? Berlin burlesque?"

"He's a student of American gangster films," Mason said.

"I hope he does a better imitation of a Swiss banker," Boyd said and then turned to Kraus. "Because tomorrow's your first test. You'll be on a flight to Vienna with a baker's dozen of other businessmen and politicians from the U.K., U.S., and France. That's at 0830." He said to Mason, "You fly out at ten hundred hours, then you're on your own. We'll have clothes and toiletries packed in suitcases brought in here, and clean suits to put on for the trip. In the meantime, you'll stay here overnight and, most importantly, out of sight. The Soviets have got spies spying on spies. They've got kidnapping rings targeting just about anyone they think is a threat. Hell, they kidnapped a half-dead Russian soldier out of the army hospital thc other night, right under everyone's noses. Good luck, gentlemen. You're going to need it."

With that, he headed for the door, only to stop when someone knocked.

A private entered and said to Boyd, "Sir, Major Forester is on the phone, and he wants to speak to Mr. Collins. Says he has news on the person you've been looking for."

Mason shot up from his chair and followed the private to an office across the hall. The receiver was off the hook and lying on the desk. Mason snatched it up.

"What have you got for me?" Mason asked.

"We tracked down Laura—"

Mason couldn't wait for the rest. "Is she all right? Where is she?"

"She's hurt, but doing fine, according to the doctors—"

"Doctors? What happened? Where is she, Mike?"

"If you'd clam up for a moment, I'll tell you." When Mason said nothing in response, Forester continued. "She's in Innsbruck, at a medical university. First, she's recovering just fine, okay? She's been there for almost five weeks, so she's healing."

"From what?"

"She has second-degree burns on portions of her body and is a little banged up."

Mason felt like someone had just slugged him in the stomach. He felt like hitting something, anything. He felt like slamming down the phone and running out of there.

"Before you do anything stupid," Forester said, "listen to me. I've got a plane ready for you at the airport. You'll be carrying a diplomatic pouch that has to get to the French officials there. Innsbruck is in their zone, and having you do this was the only way to bypass all the red tape and get you in there fast. You deliver the pouch, then you'll have only a short time to go to the hospital before you have to get back on that plane to return to Salzburg. You okay with doing that?"

"I'll be back, Mike. I'm not about to miss the opportunity to make Valerius pay."

15

In the hospital corridor, Mason showed his travel pass to the French gendarme of no more than twenty who stood guard by the door. The young guard scanned Mason's ID and travel pass, then nodded. Mason knocked lightly on the door, waited, then entered a semi-private room. The only light came from two bedside lamps. The first bed had rumpled sheets, though it was vacant. The fabric screen dividing the two beds was drawn closed.

Mason hesitated a moment, steeling himself for what he might find. He then crossed the room and stopped at the foot of Laura's bed. She was asleep. Bandages covered the back of her neck. Her hair was short and tousled, and where the hair had been burned away, new growth was coming out curly and black with tinges of gray. The top sheet came up to her shoulders, revealing more bandages wrapped around her right shoulder and back. A black-and-purple bruise poked out from the white bandages.

Mason's chest constricted. His heart pounded. He took a

deep breath to calm his rage and stepped over to a chair placed next to the IV drip. "Look what they've done to you."

As he settled into the chair next to Laura, she stirred and opened her eyes. She gave him a weak smile, though the rising of her cheeks squeezed out tears. Mason stood and bent over to kiss her on the cheek.

"You're a sight for sore eyes," Laura said. "Though it looks like you've been to hell and back."

"I kind of have, but you look as beautiful as ever."

"Liar."

"How are you doing?" Mason said, then immediately regretted asking such a stupid question.

Laura looked away. "They killed my husband. He was burned alive. They were trying to get me, not him, but I'm still here. How do you think I'm doing?" She turned to look at Mason. Her face was twisted with sadness, but her eyes flared with anger. "And don't you feel guilty. This wasn't because of you. He died because of my article."

"Laura, no one's to blame but Valerius and the killers he sent after us." He wanted to add that he'd make them pay for what they've done, but it would just sound hollow.

They both fell into silence, Laura twisting her sheet as she looked at some invisible horror, and Mason watching her hands as he tried to keep his rage in check.

Laura shifted her position, then winced in pain.

That prompted Mason to ask, "Looks like a pretty nasty bruise. Did they attack you while you were getting out of the house?"

She shook her head. "That happened later. I thought they'd be waiting for me if I ever made it out of that inferno alive, but

I guess they figured they'd finished the job, because no one was out there when I managed to get through the front door. I don't remember how long I ran, but about halfway down the hill, someone passed by and picked me up. They wanted to take me to the police station, but I wanted to slip out of town without anyone knowing if I was dead or alive. I knew that was the only way to get them off my trail. I was hoping they'd be watching the town and roads leading to Munich, so I asked a friend to drive me south. But then at the Austrian border, someone must've been watching. Just as we got over the border into Austria, we were ambushed. My friend was killed, and the car slid into a tree. My shoulder took the brunt of the impact, but I managed to drive away. A French patrol picked me up and brought me here."

Mason looked at her, amazed at her bravery.

Laura furrowed her brow. "Stop looking at me that way."

Mason decided it wasn't the time to tell her he was still deeply in love with her.

Laura softened her expression, perhaps reading what was on Mason's mind. "What are you doing in Austria? The last I heard, you left for France and ended up in North Africa."

"It's a long story."

"I'm not going anywhere, but I get the feeling this visit isn't going to last very long. You haven't let go of your hat, and you're sitting on the edge of the chair like you're ready to make a fast exit."

"I found out who's been sending out assassins to kill me, you, and anyone in Garmisch CID involved in taking down the crime ring."

"He's in Austria?"

"Vienna. I only know his codename, Valerius, and he's got the biggest criminal operation in the region."

"And you're going to try to take him on all by yourself? You can't do that, Mason. I lost Richard. I don't want to lose you, too."

"I've got some help. A friend. Mike Forester in counterintelligence. You met him once while we were still together in Munich."

"You're going to need more help than that, if this guy is as big as you say he is."

"I have a couple of other people," he said, lying.

"If you take this man down, someone will just fill the void. And good people will die. Again."

"Laura, I've got to do this. If I do this right, that'll be the end of it."

"I wish that were true."

"It's the only way to save whoever's left on Valerius's kill list. And maybe bring some justice to those who aren't. I may as well be dead if I don't do this."

Laura tried to sit up, and Mason helped her. The muscles in Laura's cheeks quivered as if she suppressed a flash of pain.

"How are the burns?"

"Tolerable. It's been almost five weeks, but they're still giving me some trouble. I'm on some kind of pain medication and something to help me sleep. I've had some problems with an infection, but another round of penicillin seems to be doing the trick."

"Did the doctors say when you might get to go home?"

Laura averted her gaze and shrugged. "Soon, I guess."

"You should stay away from Garmisch. It's still too dangerous."

Laura snapped her head toward Mason. "I have to bury my husband."

"Have his parents tried to contact you?"

Laura nodded. "Just enough to let me know that they blame me for his death. And that they're taking his body back to Bristol." She wiped a tear. "Where his brother is buried."

Mason refrained from saying anything.

"Yeah, I know," she said, as if reading Mason's mind. "Seems like the most fitting place."

Mason couldn't talk about where she might go after being released, losing her again.

Laura must have sensed again what he was thinking. She looked at him with sad eyes. "Do you have to go back to Vienna?"

Mason nodded.

"Maybe you can look me up when this is all over."

Someone knocked on the door, and a nurse entered. An orderly was with her. The nurse said to Mason, "We're are going to change her bandages. You can wait outside."

Mason took Laura's hand. "I have to go. I could only get here courtesy of the CIC, and they want me back tonight."

Laura pulled his hand to her lips and kissed it. Mason leaned in and kissed her on the cheek.

"Let me know where you decide to go," Mason said.

Laura wiped a tear and drew in her breath to say something, then stopped. "I will."

Mason forced himself to stand. He paused and looked down at her, then he turned and headed for the door.

"And promise me you'll stay in one piece," Laura said just as he reached the door.

"I promise," Mason said. He smiled at her and left. He could hardly put one foot in front of the other as he walked away from her room. And he hoped to hell he could fulfill that promise.

16

Mason returned to Vienna on a Pan American Airways flight. The Lockheed Constellation had picked up several other businessmen and politicians at Salzburg to add to the mostly American and British passengers already on board from the U.K. and the U.S. Some of the passengers were in uniform and some in business attire, and all of them had turned the plane into a party. Mason kept to himself and couldn't stop thinking of Laura. A few came up to him, mostly having had too many cocktails. Mason had his alias story down tight and seemed to convince the curious that he was legitimate. From what he overheard of their conversations, Mason figured that, while some of them approached their missions in Austria with good intentions, the majority were there to boost their careers or make money.

Fortunately, the flight lasted only an hour and a half—fortunately because by then, quite a few of the passengers had become curious about the quiet man in row ten. The plane landed at Tulin, the U.S. Army Air Forces' base for Vienna. He deplaned and walked to the small terminal building with the others. This time, there was no CIC officer or other contact on the tarmac to meet him, and he understood why when he got in line to go through passport control: entry was controlled by the Austrian border police and supervised by a single MP sergeant. If the Soviets had planted as many local assets as Forester and Boyd claimed, then any one of the airport employees could be working for the other side, surveilling who was coming and going, or were on the lookout for Soviet designated targets.

Mason handed over his "Martin Anderson" passport. The Austrian border cop took his time with the document. He eyeballed Mason before stamping one of the pages, where some clever CIC forger had already placed entry stamps for England, France, and occupied Germany. Mason retrieved his passport, collected his suitcase, then crossed the terminal lobby. He kept a relaxed demeanor, though his eyes scanned the people in the busy terminal.

There was a man getting his shoes shined, and a shoeshine boy, both of whom took more interest in those who walked past than the man's shoes. There was a woman sitting at the bank of chairs, and a man in civilian clothes reading a newspaper. Mason caught a middle-aged man glance at him, then go back to scrutinizing the candies at the store counter. He wore a cheap overcoat and tattered hat, and most tellingly, he had no suitcase or briefcase.

Mason exited the terminal and walked into the crowd of passengers meeting their drivers or awaiting taxis. Some of his fellow travelers were in the taxi line. One of the Americans he'd met on the plane offered to share a cab with him, but Mason declined. He slipped through a line of waiting customers while keeping his head down and the brim of his hat pulled low. Using a phalanx of porters with carts full of luggage, Mason ducked past them, strode over to the exterior wall of the terminal, and tucked behind the return wall by a window to partially conceal himself from anyone exiting.

Sure enough, the middle-aged man in the cheap overcoat emerged from the terminal at a quick pace. He rose up on the balls of his feet and rocked to his left and right as he strained to peer over the heads of the crowd. A second man similarly dressed rushed up to the cheap-overcoat guy. They talked. Were they Soviet assets, and did they recognize him? Was his cover already blown?

Mason slipped behind the two men and the crowd, then went to the end of the taxi line. He tapped on the window, but the driver shook his head and pointed to the head of the line. Mason pulled out a wad of cash and waved it at the driver. He didn't know how much he had plucked out of his pocket, but he was sure it was more than the guy could make in a week.

The taxi driver pointed his thumb at the back door. Mason jumped in, and the taxi took off.

As it passed the now-angry crowd and other drivers, Mason looked out the rear window. The guy in the cheap overcoat spotted him and waved. An old Buick pulled up to the curb. The two men pushed through the crowd and jumped into the car.

Mason's taxi took a turn, and he lost sight of them. He turned back to the front. Maybe they were following him, maybe someone else.

He couldn't do much else but settle in for the ride.

THE TAXI DROPPED MASON OFF IN FRONT OF THE HOTEL Bristol, a stately, turn-of-the-century building of seven stories. It was just after twilight, and the hotel lights glittered in contrast to the bombed-out shell of the once-exquisite Wiener Staatsoper, the Vienna opera house that sat across from the hotel on Kärntnerstrasse. The street had been hit by a series of bombs, and like Munich or Frankfurt, some buildings had been spared, while many others were now in ruins, the same randomness of calamity, the fickleness of bombs.

Mason looked to his right and spotted the battered BMW 326 that had been following his taxi since the airport. It slowly passed him and pulled over half a block up the street. He was tempted to walk over to his followers and ruin their evening, but he had to uphold his cover of a mild-mannered businessman. Instead, he walked toward the hotel's entrance.

A doorman opened the door for him, and Mason entered the opulent interior. The space was covered in intricate details, from the chandeliers exploding in crystals to the carved marble and wood, and art nouveau fixtures. The lobby was abuzz with well-dressed civilians and men in uniforms laden with brass and medals. In less than twenty-four hours, he'd gone from primitive campsites and wretched prisons to glittering excess, and it jarred him. The CIC had apparently spared no expense in amplifying his cover as a successful businessman and charity organizer to the wealthy.

He walked up to the reception desk and gave a somber-looking man his name. While the man checked his ID and travel papers, Mason kept an eye on the entrance. An elderly couple entered, both a little tipsy and chatting in British accents. They walked past him and toddled up the stairs. No one else entered. He scanned the lobby's lounge behind him and saw three men who kept a wary eye on things. Who they worked for, or which intelligence group for which country, Mason had no idea, but with so many top-brass military government officials and influential businessmen, the hotel was surely a hotspot for spies.

The receptionist handed Mason his papers along with a room key. Mason signed the register with the signature he'd developed for his cover. He lifted his suitcase and headed for the bank of elevators.

Halfway there, a tall, thin man with gray hair and a time-ravaged suit stepped forward. "Mr. Anderson?"

It took Mason a split second to react to the name. He pivoted to face the man, who jutted out his boney hand.

"My name is Gunther Bauer," the man said and tipped his homburg hat. "I am the Viennese liaison for the International Fund for a Democratic Austria."

Mason shook his hand, and Bauer made a slight bow at the same time. The man made a deft move, almost imperceptible, and deposited what felt like a slip of paper into Mason's hand.

"I heard you had arrived," Bauer said, "so I decided to meet you at the hotel."

"I look forward to us working together," Mason said as he palmed the paper.

"I as well. Our first opportunity will be the charity ball in two nights. In the meantime, I would like to offer my assistance in enjoying our lovely city."

"Perhaps tomorrow," Mason said.

Bauer tipped his hat, made a slight bow, and headed for the exit.

Mason crossed the short distance to the bank of elevators and stepped into one that was waiting. He told the elevator operator to go to the fifth floor. Just as the operator started to close the doors, a young man in a tailored suit slipped in and stood in front of Mason. He asked for the fourth floor, and the operator put the car in motion.

The man immediately turned to Mason and grinned, holding out his hand. He smelled of cigarette smoke and moth balls.

"Hello," the man said in English with an Austrian accent. "My name is Felix Strotheim. I like to know better people with whom I stay in the hotel."

Mason kept his hand to his side and said with a curt smile, "Martin Anderson."

"American, yes?"

"Yeah. From Baltimore."

The man furrowed his brow as he peered at Mason's face. "Did you have accident?"

"A car accident just before catching the plane for Austria."

"I hope you are feeling better."

Mason said he was, then Strotheim put a hand to his chest. "I am a great follower of American baseball. But I can't remember which team is in Baltimore."

"We only have a minor league team. The Orioles."

"Ah, yes, of course."

The operator opened the elevator door and announced the fourth floor. Strotheim tipped his hat and said good-bye as he stepped out. The operator glanced at Mason before closing the door and renewing their ascent.

Mason felt sure the guy was checking him out, but from what intelligence agency? *Hell*, he thought, *even the elevator operator could be working as an intelligence asset.*

The operator opened the door and told Mason they'd

reached the fifth floor. Mason exited with a nod to the operator and turned right. As he walked down the hallway in search of his room, he told himself he would have to shake off the feeling that everyone in the damn town was a spy.

He found his room, unlocked the door, and turned on the light before entering. Like the lobby, no surface in the room had been left undecorated. The plush carpet silenced his footsteps as he crossed over to the window overlooking the battered and scorched opera house. He looked down to the street. The car that had been following him was still in the same spot. After closing the curtains and dropping his suitcase on the bed, he looked at the piece of paper Bauer had handed him. The note bore only an address and a time of eight thirty p.m. He committed the info to memory and popped the tiny note into his mouth, chewed it, and swallowed.

There was a soft rap at the door. Mason went over and opened it. Kraus stood on the other side.

Before Kraus could speak, Mason put a finger up to his lips. He said, “Monsieur Bossart, come in.”

A little puzzled, Kraus entered.

Mason leaned over and whispered in German, “The rooms could be bugged.”

Kraus’s eyes popped wide, though he recovered enough from his shock to respond in character. “These are lovely rooms, are they not?”

“Yes. You don’t see this kind of place in Baltimore.” As he slipped on his overcoat, he said, “Before we start working on our presentation, I’d love to go for a walk and see some of the city. It’s my first time in Vienna.”

“Yes, of course,” Kraus said a little too loudly at the ceiling.

Mason moved toward the door. "Shall we?"

"Yes," Kraus said theatrically. "That would be lovely to go for a walk."

Mason ushered him out the door before he could say anything else.

17

Mason and Kraus said nothing as they took the elevator down to the ground floor. Mason helped himself to a map of the city from the stack on the concierge's desk as they passed. When they exited the hotel, Mason glanced in the direction of the BMW that had followed him. It was gone. Whoever had followed him probably left after verifying that Mason, as Martin Anderson, had checked into the hotel and gone to his room. Or they had left someone behind to watch for him, somewhere in the shadows.

No telling how many intelligence services were working the same area: The U.S. alone had the CID, CIC, and Army intelligence; then the successor to the defunct wartime OSS, the Central Intelligence Group, and their fledgling clandestine branch, the Office of Strategic Operations. And that was just one country. There were three others with high stakes in Austria: France, Great Britain, and the Soviet Union. Within each was a cadre of intelligence agencies with their assets, snitches, informants, and freelancers.

Mason consulted the city map like any tourist would, then

led Kraus on a route that took them deeper into the center. The curfew for locals had gone into effect an hour after sunset, so the streets were relatively quiet except for soldiers and civilian officials.

Mason constantly checked their surroundings for tails. At least half the city was still without electricity, so they wandered down darkened streets and past burned-out buildings that loomed over them. A patrol of mixed MPs stopped them and asked for their papers, then let them proceed.

Mason took several unnecessary turns and backtracked on occasion to make sure they weren't being followed. Kraus looked nervous and breathed with his mouth open, but he kept up with Mason and imitated his vigilance.

"Do you really think our rooms have listening devices?" Kraus asked in English.

"I'm not going to bet that they don't. Assume your telephone is being monitored, and you're being watched, too."

Kraus glanced behind him, then left and right.

"It's not too late to back out," Mason said.

Kraus shook his head and pointed to the next street. "That's it."

They turned left and began looking for building number 101. As they approached the 100s, a car door opened ahead of them. A very large man stepped out. Mason stopped and braced himself for a fight. Kraus came to a halt close to Mason's side.

"Mr. Bauer sent me to fetch you guys," the big man said with an American accent.

Mason weighed his options. He glanced at the building numbers to see how close they might be to their destination in case they had to make a run for it.

The man said, "There's no 101, if that's what you're looking for." He opened the rear passenger door. "If you guys want to pop in, I'll take you where you want to be."

Mentioning 101 was the only confirmation the guy knew what he was talking about. Mason didn't know why, but his slight Brooklyn accent reassured him. He moved toward the car while watching the big man for any false moves. Kraus stuck close to Mason's shoulder as they walked up to the open car door.

The big man tried on a smile, but it still looked menacing. Mason looked inside. The back seat was empty. Then he noticed the size of the '39 Opel's interior.

"How many guys did it take to squeeze you behind the wheel?"

The big guy produced a genuine smile this time. "I manage."

Mason and Kraus got in the back seat. The big guy managed to fold himself into the front, causing the car to dip to the left. He held out two blindfolds.

"You got to put these on. Sorry."

Mason tied on his blindfold. "This isn't going to look suspicious at all, two blindfolded guys sitting in the back of your car."

"Don't worry. I'll get you there."

Mason tried to keep track of the turns and stops, the sound of the tires when they drove over cobblestones or asphalt, but the city had too many twists and turns. Plus, the big guy could have taken a circuitous path, just in case Mason was doing exactly that.

In a little over ten minutes the car stopped, and the big guy cut the engine. Mason had no idea where they were, except that they hadn't stopped at any checkpoints, meaning it was very likely they had remained within the perimeter of the old city.

"Please keep your blindfolds on until I say otherwise," their escort said. "I'd hate to kill one of you for peeking."

The big guy got out of the car, which sprang back to level. The back door opened, and Mason heard shuffling as the man helped Kraus get out. Mason slid over. Strong, meaty hands guided him out onto the pavement. He could detect the faint odor of smoke and burned wood just under the metallic tinge of concrete dust stirred up by the wind.

They were apparently very near ruins, but that could be anywhere in Vienna. Their escort guided them down eight concrete steps. He then knocked lightly on a wooden door.

The moment of truth: either they'd walked into an elaborate trap, or they were, as Mason hoped, at a secret CIC location.

Someone answered the door, and without a word, the big guy guided Mason and Kraus inside.

"You can take off your blindfolds now," a man said.

Mason took off his blindfold and blinked against the light of two dim table lamps. His eyes quickly adjusted, and he saw Bauer leaning against the back of a ratty sofa. He said nothing, apparently waiting for them to get oriented.

They were in a cramped studio apartment with a living room, a dining area, and a corner kitchen. It smelled of mildew and was furnished in early twentieth-century decrepit. "Cozy," Mason said.

"Sorry about the blindfolds," Bauer said and led them to a round table near the kitchen, while the big guy stayed by the door.

"Only Major Forester and Sebastian there—" Bauer pointed at the big guy.

"Sebastian?" Mason said to their escort.

Sebastian just shrugged.

Bauer continued, "Only they and I know about this place. We'd like to keep it that way." He sat at the table and waited for Mason and Kraus to join him. When they were all settled in, Bauer said to Kraus, "What I am about to share with you and Mr. Collins should never be repeated to anyone. Do you understand?"

When Kraus nodded, Bauer said in Austrian German, "I read the intelligence report on you. You're not a communist, a Nazi, or a criminal. So, I'm going to trust you'll keep your mouth shut and do what Mr. Collins tells you. Or I will personally kill you."

Kraus nodded. "You speak like a native Austrian."

"I am a native Austrian. I immigrated to the U.S. in the twenties. But I've come back to help my country. You do anything to screw that up and I'll—"

"Take it easy on him," Mason said. "He volunteered. And if he tries to go to the other side, I'll kill him myself."

Kraus gave Mason a nervous smile. "You'll be fitting me for a cement overcoat."

Mason chuckled. "Nice try, but that's a Chicago overcoat or cement shoes."

Bauer got up from the table and stepped into the kitchen. He opened one of the cabinets, which concealed a built-in safe. He retrieved something inside, returned to the table, and set two file holders in front of Mason.

The folders were bound together by a thick rubber band. There was a handwritten note attached to the front file. There was no name, but Mason recognized Forester's scribble. "*Our latest—and only—intel on Valerius. I advise you to memorize and destroy.*"

"If you have intel on him, then that means you have a pretty good idea who he is. Is that the case, and you're not telling me?"

"Like you, that name keeps coming up whenever we or CID bust up a dope ring or nab a racketeer," Bauer said. "All we have we've pieced together from a multitude of interrogations and investigative operations. Which is to say, we don't have much." He pointed to the folders. "Those folders contain the limited information on who we think are Valerius's lieutenants." He said nothing more and took his time removing a cigarette from his pack and lighting it.

Mason supposed Bauer was waiting for him to open the first folder, so he removed the rubber band and opened it. The top document was an eight-by-ten black-and-white photo of a middle-aged man with tussled hair. His neck was slightly bent, and he looked down—presumably an enlarged surveillance photo of the man leaning forward to get into a car. His facial features were unremarkable: probably handsome and athletic in his youth, but age and alcohol had rendered his face puffy and wrinkled.

"Franklin Wentworth," Bauer said. "American. He's the third son of a mining tycoon, and his brother is a U.S. representative. He's heavily connected. And best we can determine, he bought his way into a top position in the U.S. military government."

"What makes you guys think he's connected to Valerius?"

"We can't prove anything, but we know he's been making piles of money while he's been here. And it's definitely not from his government salary. He makes regular trips to Switzerland, Italy, the American zone in Germany."

Bauer nodded at the file. "There are reports in there on his movements. He was associated with most of the big players in the crime ring you busted in Germany, but nothing stuck to him. Or he wriggled out using his connections. We did arrest a couple of what we suspect are his underlings for extortion, prostitution, smuggling, but nothing we can tie directly to Wentworth."

"Does CID have anything on him?"

"This is our case."

"Yes, but this is the same problem I ran into in Germany. Each investigative department pisses on their territory and refuses to share."

"Let's say this one goes under the heading of counterintelligence. So, yes, it's our territory."

"Valerius is involved in espionage? He and his cronies are spies?"

"If we knew that, we'd have rounded them up by now."

"That's why Forester bent over backwards to get me in the field. You guys think he's spying for the Soviets."

"That's classified and definitely above my pay grade."

"And you haven't picked up either of these guys because you're hoping they'll lead you to Valerius."

Bauer looked away, suddenly finding his cigarette fascinating. Mason used the silence to review the reports on Wentworth. They just echoed what Bauer had told him, except for a single paragraph stating that Wentworth was known to pal around with some Soviet army brass and local political bigwigs.

Mason closed the top folder and open the second. This time

the eight-by-ten black-and-white photograph showed a man with a jutting chin, high cheekbones, and deep-set eyes. His hair, dyed charcoal black, was slicked back, and the creases on his face hooked downward following the contours of a frown as if they'd formed from a lifetime of bitterness.

"Emile Gruber," Bauer said. "Austrian national. Gruber's probably an alias, as we believe he was the leader of a prominent crime syndicate in Vienna before the war. When the Nazis took over Austria, he fled to the U.K. claiming to be an anti-Nazi politician and requested exile. He gained access to high levels of government—probably using funds he managed to bring with him or deposited in Swiss banks—to buy his way in. He lobbied for Austria to be considered the first victim of Nazi aggression."

"Hitler was Austrian. How is that supposed to work?"

"We doubt Gruber had anything to do with the policy, but the Allied powers decided to designate Austria the first national victim of Nazism."

"You believe that?" Mason asked Kraus.

Kraus blinked a couple of times, then finally got his mouth to work. "Austrians are not Germans. We speak the same language, but we are different people."

"You didn't answer the question."

"For the majority of Austrians who had dreamed of German reunification, no. But there was a large minority who were adamantly against it. I was one of them."

Mason still didn't get how Austria had pulled off getting victim status, but he decided to drop it and turned back to Bauer. "What have you got on Gruber?"

"Nothing we can arrest him for. He's linked up with a few of his former syndicate friends—the ones who survived, anyway—and we believe they've reformed their former network of black-market operations, narcotics, and extortion. We're fairly certain Gruber's also organized a kidnapping ring, working with the Soviets and more radical Austrian communist elements, grabbing targets in the American, British, and French zones."

"Let me guess, every time you get close, the evidence and witnesses go missing. Or someone is able to quash the investigation."

"That's about right."

"Is Gruber's network part of Valerius's empire?" Kraus asked.

Bauer nodded. "His kidnapping work for the Russians makes him a good suspect for espionage."

Mason leafed through the rest of the documents on Gruber. The earliest reports on both lieutenants were a little over five months ago. Both men moved and operated in the open. They seemed untouchable and acted like it. The irony was that made them vulnerable in Mason's eyes.

"Obviously they've been protected by Valerius," Mason said, "which means Valerius has got to be a big shot with one or more of the Allied forces' organizations. How is it that after months of investigation, you guys still haven't identified him?"

"You talk about the CIC and CID not cooperating. That's nothing compared to the lack of sharing intel between four different countries. And this isn't the only investigation going on in Austria. The Soviet espionage operations are running rings around us. Plus, almost all of our most experienced agents were sent back home. And the replacements have never had any intelligence experience, or all they had was a three-month crash course. Some of them are just now learning the ropes. I know it sounds like an excuse."

"No," Mason said, "I ran into the same problem with the CID in Germany."

"You two are on the invitation list for a fundraiser for orphaned and poor children," Bauer said. "Everyone will be there. Make the most of it." He nodded at Sebastian, who retrieved a box from the living room and brought it over to the table. From inside he pulled out two Walther P38 pistols, a small Minox camera, and an envelope of cash—a mix of U.S. dollars, British pounds, and Swiss francs.

After laying everything out on the table, Sebastian held up a tiny cardboard box. "You guys want cyanide pills?"

Mason just stared at Sebastian, though he heard Kraus swallow hard.

Sebastian laughed. "Just kidding." He opened the top and pulled out a black leather pouch. "Lock-picking tools."

Kraus let out an audible breath he'd been holding.

"Ever thought of performing on vaudeville?" Mason asked.

Sebastian laughed again. "I like a little levity from time to time. But seriously, those guys get ahold of you, you might wish you had some on hand."

"We'll pass. But I'll take extra ammo, a Ka-Bar knife, binoculars, and a blackjack. Maybe some knuckle dusters, if you have those."

"Jesus, Mason," Bauer said, "are you planning on close combat?"

Mason nodded. "Close and dirty."

Sebastian looked at Bauer, who nodded. Sebastian rifled through several kitchen drawers to find what he needed and put everything on the table.

"A kitchen any homemaker would be proud to have," Mason said.

Sebastian laughed and pointed at Mason. "That's a good one. A little levity."

Mason looked at the array of weapons laid out on the table. If he had to use them, very little levity would be involved.

"If we find out anything, how do we get in touch?" Mason asked.

"You don't," Bauer said. "One of us will periodically check up on you. I don't have to tell you that if you get caught or killed, we can't claim you work for us."

Bauer walked them to the door. They shook hands, and Bauer wished them luck. Mason knew luck would be the most important tool in their arsenal.

18

Mason and Kraus wore blindfolds again while Sebastian drove them back toward the hotel. About halfway to their destination, Sebastian told them they could remove their blindfolds.

Mason did and saw they were on the ring road. The street was empty of traffic except for an occasional jeep or small convoy of trucks.

Sebastian took a roundabout way into the city center before pulling up two streets short of the hotel. "You kids have a good night. You might see one or both of us at that fundraiser."

Mason and Kraus got out, and the car pulled away. Their pockets weighed heavily with the weapons, and Mason carried a leather satchel with the binoculars, camera, and two boxes of ammunition.

"What if we get stopped and searched?" Kraus asked.

"We're just out for an evening stroll."

"Bauer didn't give us that much information. I don't see what we can do that they haven't already done. There's just two of us."

"There are a few things we can assume. If those two lieutenants have been followed for a few months without our friends finding a direct link to Valerius, it's obvious there's no direct contact between him and his lieutenants. Or at least they only meet in public settings with lots of people. And they probably exchange messages through go-betweens or surreptitious drops. Following them won't get us far."

"There can't be that many people in Vienna who have such power and still remain incognito."

"That's my thinking. The most logical thing would be to build files on anyone with that kind of power, but we don't have the time or the resources."

"Then just what are we supposed to do?"

"Go for the throat."

"I don't like the sound of that."

They turned the corner, and the hotel was up ahead. Mason used his arm to stop Kraus, and they retreated back around the corner. The black BMW that had followed him from the airport was again parked near the hotel, about fifty yards past the front entrance.

"What is it?"

"My tail is back."

"Tail? What do you mean?"

Mason ignored Kraus's question and peered around the corner at the car's rear window. An army truck moved along the street in the opposite direction, and its headlights lit up the parked car's interior for a moment. No one was inside.

Mason stepped out from the corner and looked at the hotel entrance. He expected to see someone suspicious keeping watch, meaning one of the occupants of the car, but only the doorman stood outside. On the taxi ride from the airport,

Mason had seen the silhouettes of two individuals. If it was the same two from last time, both had to be inside. At least Mason hoped they were.

"Come on," Mason said and moved toward the parked car.

"Where are we going?"

Mason didn't respond as he took long strides down the sidewalk. The doorman spotted them and shifted positions to hold open the door for them, but Mason kept walking with Kraus in tow. He approached the car as if it belonged to him and tried the driver's door. It opened.

"Idiots didn't even have the brains to lock the damn thing."

Kraus hissed, "What are you doing?"

"Shut up and get in."

Mason climbed into the car, and Kraus did the same. Once behind the wheel, he bent over and felt underneath the dashboard. He found the correct bundle of wires and said to Kraus, "Keep a lookout for the two goons."

"How am I supposed to know which ones are the goons?"

"They'll be the ones running for this car. Probably with guns aimed at us."

Kraus hissed a curse and turned in his seat to watch the rear. Mason yanked on the wires, exposing them. He pulled the main switch wire and crossed it with its companion. The engine started. Mason jammed the in gear and took off down the road.

"Those guys are going to lay eggs when they see their car is gone," Mason said.

"You're crazy, you know that?"

"You think you can get me to Sonnenfelsgasse?"

Kraus thought for a moment, then pointed at the next intersection. "Turn right."

Mason did so.

"Where are we going?" Kraus asked, his voice a pitch higher from fear.

"Do a little recon."

"Sonnenfelsgasse is where Wentworth lives."

"That's right."

"It's almost eleven. Aren't we going to look suspicious driving up to his house?"

Mason glanced at Kraus. "You worry too much."

"Somebody's got to do it."

KRAUS CALLED OUT THE BUILDING NUMBERS AS MASON slowly drove down Sonnenfelsgasse. When Kraus called out the number eighty-four, Mason pulled the car to the curb and shut off the engine.

"There it is," Mason said, pointing to a building five doors down from where they'd parked.

Wentworth lived in an ornate nineteenth-century townhouse with carved statues of two gargantuan naked women supporting the portico. The second-floor balcony sported equally naked, though much smaller, men, women, and flying cherubs.

Mason got the binoculars out of the satchel to get a better look at the place. Under the portico and just in the shadows, he spotted two men keeping watch. After a brief search, he spied another man seated on the wide cement railing of the balcony.

The men smoked cigarettes with one hand and held their coats tight against the evening chill with the other. The man on the balcony spent a few moments looking their way before standing to stretch, then pacing the confined space. Most of the interior lights were extinguished except for one room on the ground floor, where the light leaked through a gap in the heavy curtains.

"Heavily guarded for a diplomat," Mason said. "Wouldn't you say?"

"If I learned anything from gangster films, it's that the bosses are always heavily guarded. I don't see what you hoped to accomplish by coming here."

"Looking for the best way to break in."

"Tonight?"

"It'll be better when Wentworth is out of the house. Probably fewer guards then."

"Can I have a look, please?"

Mason handed over the binoculars, and Kraus used them to scan the house. Mason expected him to comment on how the place looked like a fortress, that trying to break in would be folly.

Instead, Kraus said, "Most of these buildings have inner courtyards that share a common space and are divided by walls or fences. If you can get access by one of the other buildings, the rear would probably be a little easier way to get in through the back." He handed back the binoculars.

"Then that's what we'll do."

"We?"

Mason said nothing as he put the binoculars back in the satchel, started up the car, and made a three-point turn to drive back the way they'd come. At the end of the street he made a left, then another left, and parked the car in front of the apartment building on the street behind Wentworth's townhouse. He surveyed their surroundings for patrols or pedestrians. Satisfied, he pulled the Walther P38 pistol from his overcoat pocket and checked the magazine.

"Arc you planning to shoot your way in?"

"No, but I might have to shoot my way out," Mason said and then put the blackjack in his left overcoat pocket and the pistol in his right. He slipped the Ka-Bar knife nestled in its sheath down the back of his pants.

Kraus watched this with a look of dread.

"I advise you to check your weapon," Mason said.

Kraus pulled out his pistol, and though his hands shook from nerves, he handled it like an expert. Mason got out of the car and pushed the door closed as quietly as he could.

Kraus got out and did the same. "What am I supposed to do?"

"Watch my back."

19

Mason and Kraus crept to the large exterior doors of an apartment building that Kraus estimated shared the same rear courtyard as Wentworth's townhouse. After a glance down the street, Mason took a knee and worked the lock with the lock-picking tools. In a matter of seconds, he was able to turn the lock's tumbler, and the door's bolt clicked back.

They slipped into a dark corridor. To the left was a narrow staircase leading to the upper floors. The door just off to the right of the main doors had a sign indicating the occupant was the building's concierge and displayed the hours that he or she was available. A dim light, probably from a candle, glowed through the laced curtain of the single window.

At the end of the corridor was another massive door. Kraus closed the main door and eased the bolt back in place. Despite his care, the bolt made a loud click as it settled into place. Mason held his breath as he listened for any stirring inside the concierge's apartment. After a long moment they headed for the doors at the other end of the corridor.

Once they were through, they found themselves in a

rectangular courtyard the size of a large living room. Bicycles and trash cans occupied the cement area, while a small vegetable garden took up the rest. The surrounding apartment buildings rose up on all sides, but only a few windows glowed with candlelight. Either the electrical grid had not been repaired in this block of buildings, or the cost of electricity was too steep for most of the residents. In stark contrast, the lights in Wentworth's building shined bright. Somewhere a baby cried, and a couple talked loudly, the sounds echoing in the courtyard.

A seven-foot brick wall divided the two properties, and Mason figured Wentworth had ordered the barbed wire strung along the top.

"Not very neighborly of him," Mason said as he calculated the distance he'd have to run and jump to get a good handhold on the wall. It was the barbed wire that would make the climbing more difficult. Behind him, Kraus made a rustling sound, then Mason's partner walked a bicycle up to the foot of the wall. He made a gesture for Mason to climb on. Kraus steadied the bicycle while Mason mounted the bike's frame. It was easy enough to hoist himself to the top. He leaned over and helped Kraus climb, and together they assessed the rear of Wentworth's house.

The backyard consisted of a flower garden along the brick wall, a manicured lawn up to a patio, and limestone stairs that led to a small porch and the rear entrance. The porch light was on, as well as a light in the kitchen. Another light was on in an upstairs window, which Mason figured was one of the bedrooms. He was surprised there wasn't someone posted to watch the rear, either through negligence or the guy was on a break.

"You stay here," Mason whispered. "I'll need to get out fast, so when I come running, you give me a boost up."

Kraus nodded, and Mason stepped gingerly over the barbed wire and jumped into the garden. His landing hardly made a sound on the soft soil, but he still paused to see if someone came to investigate. All was quiet.

He crept across the lawn and mounted the stairs. At the back door he picked the lock and eased back the bolt. It clacked open, making too much noise. He paused again.

A light went on near the back door. Mason squatted beneath the door's paned window. He pulled the blackjack out of his pocket and held it with his left hand and brought the pistol out with his right. At that same moment, a thought came to him, and his chest constricted with alarm. If the guard peered out the window, he might see Kraus perched on the wall. He jerked his head around, but Kraus had disappeared. He let out a breath of relief and readied himself.

Footsteps approached the door, then a hand turned the doorknob. Mason coiled his legs, ready to strike. The door opened, and Mason lunged forward.

Surprised, the guard was slow to react. Mason jammed the barrel of the pistol into the spot just below the guard's sternum. The shock to the web of nerves paralyzed the man's lungs. He let out a chirp as he tried to take in air.

Mason swung a swift left hook with the blackjack into the side of the man's skull. His legs went limp, his knees buckled. Mason grabbed onto his jacket lapels as he collapsed, trying to break his fall. The man hit the floor, but with less of a thud than he might have had in a freefall. Blood oozed from the place of impact. He was out cold. He might wake up. He might not. If he did, he was sure to have a debilitating concussion.

Mason went to the kitchen and found a dish towel. He tied the checkered towel around his face to hide everything but his eyes; not the mask of choice for the most discerning criminal, but it would have to do.

He stepped up to a doorway leading to the dining room. The dark room extended to the front windows. All was quiet. He slipped across the room and turned right into a vast foyer that was elegantly appointed, with a broad marble staircase that split at a landing halfway to the second floor. Each set of stairs led to separate hallways. He had no floorplan, and he didn't know if Wentworth's kids or wife were in the house, where the bedrooms were, if there were more guards waiting in another room. He began to question his hastiness at invading the house without a floorplan, or a plan of any kind. His best bet was to try the room where he'd seen a light from the backyard.

Halfway up the first flight of stairs, Mason heard movement on the porch just on the other side of the front door. He stopped, crouched near the railing, and watched. One of the guards could come in at any minute to pee or grab a sandwich. Silhouettes moved across the curtained windows on either side of the door. Mason crouched, ready for another fight, but no one entered.

Mason got to his feet and headed up the stairs two at a time. The only sound was the shuffling of his shoes on the carpeted steps. At the landing, he took the right side of the stairs and detected the faint odor of cigarettes when he reached the top step. There were two doors on the right and one on the left of the short hallway. Light leaked from underneath the door to his left, the rear-facing room and the source of the cigarette smoke.

He turned the doorknob slowly and opened the door just enough to squeeze through. He had his pistol ready as he entered. The room served as a study, with bookcases lining wood-paneled walls. A massive carved oak desk faced the door, but Wentworth wasn't sitting behind it. Instead, the man sat in a highbacked chair. He faced a fireplace, his back to the door, his head bent as he read a book. The only light in the room came from a floor lamp near the chair and a hanging lamp above the desk.

The noise of the crackling fire masked Mason's steps as he crossed the parquet floor. A wall clock ticked the passing of time. He stopped just behind the chair and stuck the barrel of his pistol against the man's skull. "Don't move. Don't make a sound."

Wentworth sucked in his breath and dropped his book. An instant later, he seemed to have regained his composure and took a drag on his cigarette while continuing to stare at the fire. "If you've come to rob me, you're making a very big mistake."

"Valerius sent me."

Upon hearing the name, Wentworth's hand froze, leaving the cigarette to hover in mid-arc. "You're American," he said and turned to look at Mason. He tried a patronizing smile. "A misinformed American to boot. I don't know anyone named Valerius." He tried acting cool, but his eyes kept glancing at the barrel of the gun.

"Are you sure you want to play it that way? I have orders to put a hole in your head if you don't cooperate."

"And what does this Valerius individual want with me?"

"He knows what you've been doing. He says if you don't stop, there won't be any talking next time. Just a lot of screaming on your part."

Wentworth's smile disappeared, and his forehead began to bead with sweat. "I don't …" He trailed off. His eyes jerked back and forth in their sockets as he tried to think above the panic. "Maybe he uses a nom de guerre …"

Mason said nothing, knowing the silence would compel Wentworth to keep talking.

"I would like to set up a meeting with Mr. Valerius to find out what I'm accused of," Wentworth said. "I can assure him everything I've done is exactly to his wishes."

Still Mason said nothing.

"He shouldn't accuse me of something without hearing my side of the story," Wentworth said in a pleading tone.

"You're saying he's wrong?"

"No, no. Not like that. There must be some misunderstanding."

From the moment Mason pointed the gun at Wentworth's head, he'd been trying to find a way to get the man to reveal Valerius's name. But asking outright would tip off Wentworth, and Mason didn't have time to wrench it out of him. He was also struggling with the impulse to put a bullet in the man's head and be done with it, but killing him would eliminate one of only two viable leads. Not to mention the ethics of committing cold-blooded murder.

Time was ticking.

Mason decided on another tactic. "He knows you've been skimming off the top, operating side ventures—"

"I've done none of those things," Wentworth said, raising his voice.

Mason pushed the gun barrel harder into Wentworth's head. "You speak in anything louder than a whisper again, and I will splatter your brains all over that nice rug." He paused to let that sink in. "If you're not doing those things, then a man under you is. Get your house in order, or Valerius will."

Mason took one step back. "Don't move until you count to one hundred. You let out a peep before then, and I will come back for you."

Mason backed out the door. He lowered the hammer on his pistol and rushed down the stairs and through the house to the kitchen. He got as far as the manicured lawn when he heard Wentworth yelling for his guards.

While racing for the back wall, he hoped Kraus was waiting to give him a boost, or his hunt for Valerius would be over real quick. He took a running leap for the wall and got a fingerhold on the top. As he struggled to scale the wall, he whispered loudly, "Kraus!"

Shouts and heavy footsteps came from inside the house.

From seemingly nowhere Kraus appeared, wide-eyed and breathless. He leaned over and hoisted Mason to the top. Just as they climbed over the barbed wire and jumped off the wall, the back door of Wentworth's house banged open.

Mason ripped off his mask. "Where were you?"

"I heard someone running and thought maybe one of the guards was coming for me."

The sound of several men tromping across the lawn prompted Mason to take Kraus by his overcoat and pull him along. They ran through the hallway, blew out the front door, and dashed for the car. Kraus dived into the passenger's seat. Mason got behind the wheel a moment later. He started the engine, put it in gear, and hit the accelerator. In the rearview mirror, he saw two men burst through the apartment building's main door.

Mason hoped the men got a good look at the license plate,

and Wentworth had someone on his payroll who could look up the owners. That might throw them off track and stir up a little trouble for the guys who'd been following him.

Things were going to get interesting. Dangerous, but interesting.

20

Mason sat with his back against the wall. He was at a table situated near one of the hotel restaurant's windows that let the gray light of morning enter the room. He sipped his coffee while waiting for a plate of eggs. Men in suits circulated, chatting or glad-handing, or they sat at tables draped in fine linen tablecloths with porcelain dishes and silver dinnerware. Some were there with their wives or mistresses, some in groups. A few sat alone, as he did, staring into their coffee. Some of those nursed a hangover. There were generals and colonels, as well as members of the military government. Mostly American, some British.

His eggs arrived just as a man in a tailored suit approached his table. Mason had already shooed away another guy wanting a favor, so he forced a smile but remained seated.

"Paul Cantrell, United Aluminum," the man said and stuck out his hand.

Mason shook it. "Martin Anderson."

"Yes, I know," Cantrell said and pulled out a chair. "Listen,

I'd like to talk to you." He pointed at the chair. "You mind?" The man didn't wait for a response and sat, giving Mason another reason not to like to him.

"I'll get right to the point—"

"Good 'cause my eggs are getting cold," Mason said, interrupting.

Cantrell didn't blink an eye at that and continued. "A democratic Austria is all well and good, but they're talking about nationalizing their industries, and my company—hell, most of us here—are hoping they'll embrace a more free-enterprise approach. I hope you can see your way—in your limited capacity, of course—to persuade them to our way of thinking. The American way of thinking. I don't see them forming a viable democracy with those kinds of socialist inclinations. What's your opinion on the matter?"

"My opinion is that my coffee and my eggs are getting cold. And I get real ornery when that happens. Go peddle that crap to someone else."

Cantrell held his breath for a moment before letting out a nervous chuckle. Mason ignored him as the man got up from the table and walked away.

From the next table over someone said, "Not very professional of you."

Out of the corner of his eye Mason saw Kraus sitting at the next table. He must have taken the table while Cantrell was giving his pitch.

"I need at least three coffees in me before I get anywhere near professional," Mason said while staring into the room.

"Did you sleep badly?"

"My sleep isn't what you need to be worrying about."

"Well, *I* couldn't sleep thinking about how careless you

were last night. You put us both in danger. If you'd been caught or killed, then where would your investigation be?"

"Neither of those things happened."

"And you didn't have to burn that car last night. We could have just left it somewhere and walked away. But you had to stuff that dish towel into the gas tank and light it. We barely had time to get out of there before it went up in flames."

Mason snapped his fingers as if trying to remember something. "You know that scene in that movie *The Public Enemy*, where James Cagney smashes that grapefruit in that girl's face?"

"What does that have to do with anything?"

"I wish I had a grapefruit right now."

The waiter came up to Kraus's table, and Kraus ordered coffee and fruit.

When the waiter left, Mason said, "You don't like the way I handled things? It's your turn. You're going to approach Gruber. Give him a similar message to the one I gave Wentworth."

Kraus said nothing. Mason poured another coffee from the carafe. He was about to take a sip when someone else stepped up to his table.

"Mr. Anderson. Good morning."

Mason recognized the voice. It was Bauer. Mason looked up and gave him a cursory greeting.

"We seem to be out of sorts this morning," Bauer said.

"He hasn't had enough coffee yet," Kraus said.

"Good. Then I'd like to propose we visit a typical Viennese coffeehouse and talk over our strategy for the upcoming fundraiser."

Mason stuffed the rest of his eggs into his mouth and rose

from the table. Kraus made a move to get up, but Bauer subtlety shook his head.

Mason turned to Kraus as he put on his overcoat. "He's taking me there to declare his undying love for me. Three's company."

Mason followed Bauer out of the restaurant. In case someone was following, they exchanged innocuous banter about the fundraiser as they exited the hotel. Mason wondered how the coffeehouse would be any different, but he figured Bauer knew the place wasn't bugged, and the employees were discreet.

Once they were well past the hotel, both of them fell silent until they reached a coffeeshop four streets away. The place was packed to the gills, but the manager nodded to Bauer and led them to a corner booth with a reserved sign on the table. The manager removed the sign and left them to squeeze into their seats. Mason looked longingly at a waiter who passed with a tray full of coffees and pastries.

"Relax," Bauer said. "They'll get to us. Eventually."

"What's so important that you took me away from my eggs and coffee?"

"We know that was you at Wentworth's last night."

Mason was surprised, but he didn't show it. "You want to get to the point?"

"That was a boneheaded move."

"My partner would agree with you. But I know the only way to get things moving is to stir the pot. Forester gave me free rein. I have to do it my way."

Bauer stared at him for a moment, then said, "Well, it worked. Whatever you said made him so paranoid he got care-less and made phone calls he probably shouldn't have."

"You bugged his phone?"

"We patched into his line a couple of weeks ago. We've been monitoring his calls since then, but he's been very careful. At least until last night."

"Did he call Valerius?"

Bauer shook his head. "We don't know for sure, but it doesn't seem so. However, he did make two ill-advised calls. One to an Austrian deputy police commissioner, blaming him for any discrepancies of the money flow."

"The deputy commissioner is on Wentworth's payroll?"

"That would be my guess. That's something we didn't know. We'll put a tail on him."

"I assume the second call was to someone higher up."

"By Wentworth's conciliatory tone, it had to be. A Stephen Flannigan. He's OMGUS. Director of their regional government coordinating office."

OMGUS stood for Office of Military Government, United States, the governing arm of the American occupation zone.

"Jesus," Mason said as he watched another waiter pass with another tray of coffee. "That means he has political contacts with the other Allied powers, the Soviets, and all the local Austrian politicians. You have any idea how high up he is in the Valerius hierarchy?"

"Only that he appears to have more access to the top. Wentworth didn't mention anyone by name, but he begged Flannigan to pass on his claims of innocence to their mutual friend. He kept repeating himself. Pathetic to hear."

"What did Flannigan say to that?"

"Just that he didn't appreciate the call, and he told Wentworth to pull himself together and get off the phone."

"Valerius will hear about it, but we'll need to put more pressure on his organization before he comes to the surface."

"Don't push too hard, or he'll see the ruse."

"I'm not done pushing, but I'll take that under advisement."

"You keep getting results, then we won't stand in your way," Bauer said, then he hooked a waiter by his arm and pulled him over to the table. He ordered two coffees and two apple strudels. When the waiter left, Bauer fell silent and fidgeted with one of the menus.

"You got something to get off your chest?" Mason asked.

Bauer could barely look at Mason. "Your sweetheart, Laura Talbot? She disappeared from the hospital."

Mason grabbed the small table with both hands, making the wooden tabletop groan under the pressure. "You guys were supposed to be keeping her safe."

"We have no real jurisdiction in the French zone, but the French authorities agreed to set up a rotation of gendarmes to guard her room twenty-four hours a day. And we asked the hospital staff to watch out for her, too."

"How could someone get past so many people to snatch her up?"

"Mason, we don't know that someone kidnapped her. She could have snuck out of there—"

"She was on pain pills and antibiotics when I saw her."

"The French are combing the area. We even took one of our agents off another case to help look for her."

Mason's mind whirled as he weighed his options: stay in Vienna and continue the hunt for Valerius, or drop everything and go looking for her. But where? How? He shot up from the table. "I need a phone."

Bauer called after him, "Mr. Anderson, the most reliable phone is back at the hotel."

Mason waved a thanks and rushed out of the café.

21

Mason found a phone booth near the Bristol Hotel men's room. After talking to the operator and fiddling with the occupation schillings, someone picked up the phone and said, "Five-oh-eighth."

"I need to speak to Chief Wilson, right away."

The man on the other end of the phone asked, "Who are you, and what do you want?"

Mason gave him his name and former rank. "I was stationed in Garmisch. Wilson was a fellow investigator, and I need to speak to him now."

A moment of silence passed before the man said, "Sir, Mr. Wilson was killed in an automobile accident two days ago."

Mason rubbed his forehead to ease his rising tension. "There was a master sergeant," Mason had to think for a moment before recalling his name, "Camden. Bill Camden. He was in command of the MPs when I was there."

"Yeah, he's still here."

"Then get him on the phone. It's important."

The headquarters operator told him to hold on. Mason

paced as far as the phone cord would allow. Valerius had managed to get to every investigator involved in the crime-ring bust. The only one spared was the supervising officer of the small CID contingent at that time, Patrick Densmore, who had been transferred back to the States. Mason was trying to think of who else might become a target, when he heard someone pick up the receiver.

"Mr. Collins? This is Sergeant Camden. Mr. Wilson told me about your last call. What have you got for me?"

"You know Wilson's death wasn't an accident," Mason said.

"That's what most of us believe, but we don't have any proof."

"Listen, you know the fire at the reporter's house …"

"We still haven't found any trace of Mrs. Talbot."

"CIC tracked her down. She was at a hospital in Innsbruck, but either she was kidnapped, or she left on her own. If that's the case, she could be in Garmisch or headed that way to bury her husband."

"I haven't seen her, but we'll all keep a lookout."

"If she shows up, sit on her. Don't let her go anywhere. You got that?"

"Sure, I'll try, anyway. She's a pretty tough cookie, if I remember."

Mason smiled at the thought despite his rising panic.

"I hate giving you more bad news, Mr. Collins, but Mr. Abrams, your ex-partner, was stabbed multiple times two days ago. He's in a hospital up in Frankfurt. He's barely hanging on, the last I heard. You watch out for yourself. Okay?"

Mason wanted to bang the receiver against the phone, but two army officers came out of the bathroom and eyed him before moving on. He waited until the two men passed, then said, "I'm going to stop them, Bill. I'm going to send them to hell." He hung up the phone and took deep breaths to calm down and get back to being Martin Anderson. How long could he keep up the businessman façade and not go for someone's throat? That time was getting shorter by the hour.

THE RESTAURANT AMADEUS WAS SITUATED NEAR Michaelerplatz and the Hofburg Palace on a narrow street with bars, restaurants, and small boutiques. Mason could feel the barrel of his Walther P38 sticking in his back and weighing heavily against his belt.

He knew from the CIC surveillance reports that the Amadeus restaurant was Gruber's favorite. On most days Gruber would go for a lunch of wiener schnitzel and sauerkraut. What a good little Austrian he was. Mason stood across the street from the restaurant and under an awning to stay out of the rain. He'd arrived early. Usually Gruber and his bodyguards got there precisely at noon, so he still had a five-minute wait. Just enough time to plan what the hell he was going to do when Gruber got there.

After getting off the phone with Sergeant Camden in Garmisch and learning of more murders and attempted murders, he'd stormed out of the hotel with no particular plan in mind until his thoughts of revenge brought him here. No, not revenge. Gruber had done nothing to him, personally, but killing or maiming Gruber stood a good chance of bringing Valerius out into the open. With his blood up, getting Valerius outweighed any morality, even self-preservation.

He tilted his head back, trying to cope with the rage that boiled up with no way to relieve it. He closed his eyes and tapped the back of his head against the wall.

"Are you ill, sir?" a man said in German.

Mason looked down and saw an old man in a worn homburg hat and a moth-eaten suit. Then man looked at him with such concern that a scintilla of his rage dissipated. "No, I'm fine. Thank you."

The old man smiled and nodded before toddling off with the aid of his cane. Mason's tension returned when he saw a black Mercedes coming up the street. He turned away to block his face and watched the street using the reflection in the shop window. The Mercedes came to a stop in front of the restaurant. The driver and another bodyguard got out of the car and surveyed the surroundings before one of them opened the rear passenger door closest to the street.

Mason turned to get a better look. He lit a cigarette and pretended to be waiting for someone, glancing at his watch and then gazing toward the end of the street. Gruber emerged and checked the street for himself. He wore a black trench coat over a gray tailored suit. One of the bodyguards held open door to the restaurant, and the two of them ushered Gruber inside and out of the rain.

If he was going to do it, Mason knew now was the time. He pushed away from the wall. He could feel the pressure of the gun in his belt. He felt the knife in its sheath strapped to his ankle. With his right hand at the small of his back, he stepped out onto the street.

Hands from behind grabbed his coat and pulled him back onto the sidewalk. Mason whirled around, his fists ready to strike. Then he saw it was Kraus, and his partner looked madder than he'd ever seen him.

"Are you crazy?" Kraus said in English. "Get out of here."

"You're lucky I didn't put you in the hospital."

"You're lucky I was here to keep you from going to prison or getting hanged."

Mason seized Kraus by the shoulder of his coat and drove him to the doorway of a boarded-up building. "What makes you think I was planning on doing something that would land me in prison?"

"I could see it in your eyes. Not to mention, I can see that pistol bulging out of the back of your coat."

Kraus was right, leaving Mason without a good response. Instead, he furrowed his brow and asked, "What are you doing here?"

"You wanted me to approach Gruber, and that's what I'm doing."

"I wanted you to threaten him, like I did Wentworth."

"That's not going to work twice, and you know it. Keep your enemies closer. Remember? That's how I get to him. And the first step is to appeal to his greed. That's why I'm here: to have lunch with him. Now, get out of here before they spot you and tie us together."

Kraus shoved him away with a strength that surprised Mason. His partner gave him one more sneer before crossing the street and heading for the restaurant.

Mason lifted his head and let the cold rain fall upon his face, hoping that might cool his temper. Maybe it was that he'd become aware of the stares from the people, or the old man's kindness, or Kraus's admonishment. Whatever it was, he threw his cigarette on the ground and stomped it out. He turned, putting his back to the restaurant, and walked away.

MASON IGNORED THE SOFT AND STEADY RAIN. HE'D JUST traversed the busy Stephansplatz, and the sidewalk on this main artery was busy with pedestrians. Most were locals dressed in their threadbare clothes; some, who'd been lucky enough to find work, now searched for a place to spend their lunch breaks. Many just wandered aimlessly to forget their ever-present hunger.

Mason cut a path through them, too lost in his dark thoughts to bother dodging passersby. Maybe someone was tailing him. Maybe not. He didn't care. The walking helped to calm him; he needed a clear head and to be on his best behavior for the fundraiser that evening.

He turned left on a small street, where a series of bombs had landed. Some shops were open, but many of the buildings had been gutted, and the street-level shops were boarded up. Halfway down the block he spotted a Russian officer heading his way on the same side of the street. Something ticked in Mason's brain, and that sensation usually signaled danger. He looked carefully at the approaching officer. At this distance he couldn't be sure, but the officer's face seemed familiar. He tried to stay with a group of pedestrians to conceal himself and stole glances between them.

When the officer got within thirty feet, Mason could see the man's face clearly, and his heart kicked into high gear. It was the junior officer under Konstantin's command, the one who had beaten him at the makeshift prison. The man would surely recognize him.

Still, Mason kept on walking. If he did an abrupt about-face or crossed the street, it would draw the man's attention; he had a better chance to conceal himself in the crowd. He continued to look straight ahead as if the man were just another stranger, but out of the corner of his eye, he watched the officer's posture and gait for a sign the officer recognized him.

The Russian slowed his pace, as Mason had done, and he now walked with his back rigid. Mason stole a glance and saw that his eyes were full of recognition.

Just as the officer passed, Mason cut a sharp left and crossed the street. He reached the other side and began walking in the opposite direction at a brisk pace.

Mason continued on his side and matched the officer's speed. He had studied a map of Vienna and knew the officer was heading for the Russian commissariat, the main police and administrative building, which lay in that direction. The officer would get to the commissariat and report him before Mason could make it back to the hotel. Even if he could make the safety of the hotel, there would be an all-out effort to track him down. His anonymity would be lost. His cover blown. He had no choice but to stop him.

The officer glanced back at Mason and began walking faster. Mason ducked into a side street is if that were his intention all along. He then stopped, turned, and peered around the corner. The officer continued his quick pace and turned right.

Mason ran across the street and rushed up to the next corner. The Russian was now on a narrow street and had only three streets to go before crossing Heldenplatz and reaching the commissariat.

Mason rushed across the narrow street, keeping his head down as he followed the man. He ducked behind a pile of ruins when the officer glanced back. He crossed the street a moment later. Mason came out from the rubble and caught a glimpse of the Russian turning left.

Mason poured on the speed while calculating his next move. The corner building was a burned-out shell. Perfect cover. He ran inside and had to jump over fallen beams and dodge piles of bricks, pipes, and concrete. He kept a parallel course, or at least what he hoped was the same course. If the man indeed was going for the commissariat, he would turn left again at the next intersection.

Mason knew what he had to do. As he bolted around the blackened piles, he seized the blackjack with his left hand and pulled out the Ka-Bar knife with his right. Through gaps in the building's walls, he caught a glimpse of the officer. He had to get ahead of him. The dim light and the rubble threatened to slow him down, and he had to jump blindly over obstacles while trying to be as silent as possible. Finally, he saw a blackened opening that had once been a doorway to the street. He reached it and prayed the officer hadn't crossed the street. If so, it was all over before it really began.

While Mason was tucked just inside the doorway, a few pedestrians passed, then he heard quick footsteps coming toward him. He coiled his muscles. When the officer took one step past the doorway, Mason lunged.

He wrapped his left arm around the man's throat. The officer tried to fight back, and tried yelling, but Mason had too much pressure on his throat.

As Mason dragged him inside, an elderly lady froze not ten feet away. She screamed and then yelled, "*Polizei! Polizei!*"

The Russian threw his elbows and kicked. Undeterred, Mason dragged him deeper into the ruins. The going was slow and difficult, and the man fought for his life.

Mason struck the back of his skull with the handle of his knife. Stunned by the blow, he struggled less, his arms swinging wildly. Mason gave him another blow. The officer's legs folded underneath him.

Mason heard more people yelling for the police. He had to go deeper.

He slipped on a muddy spot on the concrete, and the Russian managed to twist out of his grasp. The man ran, but he was disoriented by the savage blows to his head and stumbled in the wrong direction, away from the street and safety.

Mason ran after him. The officer screamed for help in Russian. He turned to face Mason and went for the pistol still in its holster.

Fury and panic drove Mason. He plunged the blade of the Ka-Bar into the man's chest. He turned the blade and pushed it beneath the man's ribcage, aiming for the heart. He pulled up on the blade to widen the already gushing wound. The officer's eyes popped wide. His mouth opened, but nothing came out. Blood gurgled in his throat, and he collapsed.

Mason froze, watching as the officer's life slowly left him. He felt sick. He'd killed before, but somehow this felt like cold-blooded murder.

Loud voices and heavy footsteps brought Mason out of his stupor. He didn't need to look back. He knew there would be MPs or Austrian police searching for him. He ran into the shadows of the ruins.

22

The water from the faucet ran hot, scalding Mason's hands. Even with no trace of the Russian officer's blood remaining, he still kept rubbing soap into them, lathering, then rinsing. Finally, he stopped and leaned on the bathroom sink. He avoided his reflection in the mirror; he couldn't look at himself. Images of the Russian's face, twisting in death, kept playing over in a loop.

There was a knock at the door. Mason straightened and listened. Another knock. He looked toward the room, taking note of everything. He already cleaned the knife and tucked it away, out of sight, along with the blackjack and pistol. He'd already ditched his bloodstained overcoat in another ruined building on his way back and wiped the blood off his shoes.

He walked into the room and stared at the door. The knocks came harder.

"Mason? You in there?"

It was Forester.

"Yeah, hold on a minute," Mason said, put on a T-shirt, and

went to the door. He threw the lock and opened it to see Forester standing in the hallway.

"Jesus, buddy," Forester said, "you should get your hearing checked." He stepped in and then moved aside. "I picked up a stray."

Laura stepped in from the hallway. "Surprise," she said with a flat tone.

Mason was stricken dumb while a riot of emotions welled up: relief, shame, love.

She, too, remained where she was, and her eyes were filled with her own emotions of sadness and relief. She looked as beautiful as ever, wearing a blue beret and a sky-blue wool overcoat with the collar turned up to hide her burn scars.

Mason moved toward her, and she did the same. They embraced. Mason held onto her tightly.

"I thought they may have taken you," Mason said softly into her ear.

"I'm sorry I didn't let you know."

They broke the embrace, though Mason held onto her by the shoulders and waited for more.

"I started feeling vulnerable just lying there," Laura said, "so I sent word to a smuggler I knew from my reporter days. I'd heard he lived in Innsbruck and asked if he could sneak me out of the hospital. He surprised me one night by showing up in my room, undetected, and gave me one chance to make it out then and there."

Laura stopped and furrowed her brow with concern. "What happened to you?" she asked. "Are you okay?"

Mason's face was betraying him, and he desperately wanted to change the subject. He looked at Forester, "Thanks, Mike, for doing this."

"I didn't do anything except bring her here. She just showed up at my door."

Mason returned his gaze to Laura.

"I couldn't stay at the hospital," she said. "And I knew you were here on another suicide mission. Sneaking out was easy. Getting here, not so much."

"You must be bushed," Mason said as he led her deeper into the room. "Have a seat on the bed."

Laura pulled away from him and backed up to put some distance between them. "I'm fine. Mike was nice enough to give me a room here. I'll freshen up later. But only after you tell me what happened."

"Nothing that seeing you wouldn't fix."

She gave him a skeptical look. "I'll get it out of you one way or another."

"No, you won't. You've got to get out of Vienna. It was crazy coming here."

"I told her the same thing," Forester said.

"I'm not going anywhere. I'm here to help you. Make sure you don't screw things up." She put a finger against Mason's lips when he opened his mouth to say something. "It's not up for discussion." She glanced at Forester, then turned back to Mason. "I'm working for the CIC now."

Mason looked over Laura's shoulder and glared at Forester. "What the hell are you doing saying yes and putting her in danger?"

"I asked for it," Laura said.

"Hell," Forester said, "I said yes to get *me* out of danger. Your new partner is as hardheaded as you are."

Laura scowled at Mason. "You say no again, and I'll put *you* in the hospital. This Valerius killed my husband and almost killed me. He tried to kill you and may very well succeed. I would very much like for you and me to stay alive."

Forester cleared his throat. "I'll leave you two to hash this out. I've already briefed her, so I'll go and make the final arrangements for tonight." He said to Laura, "You'll have what you need delivered to your room. The delivery man will declare a package from Minneapolis. Don't open the door for anyone else."

"Don't forget a pistol I can fit into an evening bag."

"You got it," Forester said and left.

She turned to Mason, who had a hard time finding his voice. She smiled and walked to him and didn't stop until her chest touched his. "I'm going to be your date this evening. I heard you're supposed to have a reputation as a gambler and a ladies' man, Mr. Anderson."

THE TELEPHONE RANG IN MASON'S HOTEL ROOM. MASON answered it, and the front desk informed him his car was waiting downstairs. He hung up and tugged on his shirt collar and bow tie. The tuxedo shirt the CIC had furnished was a half size too small, making the veins in his neck pulse against the tight collar and emphasizing just how fast his heart was beating. It was showtime, and a lot was riding on getting everything right at the fundraiser, but that wasn't the cause of his pounding heart. Laura was his main concern; she was going to expose herself to considerable danger by showing up at the event.

He put on his overcoat and stepped into the hallway. Kraus

must have received the same call, because he, too, exited his room.

"You look very sharp in that tuxedo, Monsieur Bossart."

Kraus bowed. "The ladies will swoon at the sight of us, Mr. Anderson."

Mason glanced down the hallway expecting to see Laura, then he remembered he had no idea which room Forester had reserved for her.

Mason and Kraus went down to the lobby and scanned the space. Laura had her back to Mason, but he could recognize her figure anywhere. Three men in army uniforms had her cornered. She talked to them in English with a light French accent, something that made her even more attractive—if such a thing were possible.

Mason didn't know her cover name, so he stayed where he was. She must have sensed his presence, because she glanced back and saw him. She excused herself and came toward Mason and Kraus.

Flushed with blood, Mason's torso warmed at the sight of her. She wore a wig matching her dark brown hair, topped by a green sequined tiara. The wig draped across her shoulders and covered the burns on her neck. Her silk dress was a deep emerald green and was topped with a bolero jacket with multi-colored rhinestones. She was stunning.

Mason became aware of Kraus elbowing him and asking out of the side of his mouth, "Who is she?"

Laura came up and kissed Mason on both cheeks—French style. "*Bon soir*, Monsieur Anderson. Aren't you going to introduce me to your friend?"

Mason came to his senses. "Yes, this is Monsieur Bossart."

Kraus, as Mr. Bossart, bowed, and they exchanged pleasantries in French—or at least Mason assumed they were pleasantries. Mason remembered she spoke French and was engaged to a French soldier before the Germans invaded France.

"Shall we?" Mason asked as he gestured toward the door.

As the three companions exited the hotel, Kraus asked Laura in English, "So, what brings you to Vienna?"

"Didn't Mr. Anderson tell you? I'm his girl du jour."

A driver in a chauffeur's uniform opened the back door of a black Cadillac limousine.

"This is for us?" Mason asked the driver.

As Laura walked past Mason, she said, "Don't act so surprised. You're supposed to be a rich guy."

Kraus still stood on the sidewalk and had a puzzled look on his face.

"I'll explain in the car," Mason said and waved for him to get in.

Bauer was waiting for them in the back, dressed in a tuxedo. When the driver drove away from the hotel, Bauer said to Kraus, "I see you met Mademoiselle Vallier."

Mason briefly explained their relationship to Kraus, and why Valerius was after both of them. After mentioning the attempt on her life and the loss of her husband, Mason checked on Laura, but she looked grim and determined.

"There is this something I didn't tell you," Bauer said. "The venue? It's been changed to the Hofburg Palace, in the *Neue Burg*, or new palace. Which also happens to be in the Soviet zone and will be crawling with Russians."

"Oh dear," Kraus said.

"You just happened to forget to tell us that part?" Mason asked sarcastically.

"It was supposed to be at the Grand Hotel," Bauer said. "That hotel houses Soviet brass and officials, but at least it's here, in the international zone. For some unknown reason it was changed at the last moment. Security will be tight, but we're hoping our targets will feel more relaxed." He held out his hand. "I'm afraid you'll have to leave your pistols with me."

With angry stares, Mason and Laura handed over their guns.

Bauer took the pistols, then held out his hand again and wiggled his fingers at Mason. "The knife, the blackjack, and whatever else you have hidden in your tux."

Mason surrendered the knife and blackjack, then held up his hands indicating he had nothing else. Bauer looked at Kraus.

"I'm only armed with my wits," Kraus said.

"Well, that makes two of us," Laura said. "But I worry about Mr. Anderson."

Mason leaned forward. "Monsieur Bossart, if you don't mind, could you please pull mademoiselle's knife out of my back."

"We don't have much time," Bauer said and opened a notebook. He held it so Mason, Laura, and Kraus could see an array of photos, two to a page. "We expect at least half of the military government officials to be there, from all four Allied powers, and a bunch of Austrian officials." He pointed to a man in a U.S. Army colonel's uniform with a ruddy face and gray hair. "That's Flannigan. I don't need to tell you to watch for who he interacts with." Bauer turned to pages near the back and pointed to a man with unremarkable features except for puffy eyes and gapped front teeth. "That's Schumacher, the Austrian deputy police commissioner."

He handed the book to Mason, who put it on his lap so the others could see.

"Memorize as many of the faces and names as you can," Bauer said. "Maybe we'll get lucky."

"You really think Valerius will be there?" Laura asked.

"No idea."

"Valerius could be Austrian for all we know," Mason said. "It would explain how he moves and operates so easily in the Soviet zone."

"It's always a possibility," Bauer said.

"You're just a bundle of good news," Laura said to Bauer as the limo pulled up in front of the Neue Burg wing of the Hofburg Palace.

23

The Neue Burg section of the Hofburg Palace had all the trappings of ornate late nineteenth-century, neo-baroque architecture, with its multitude of columns in relief and arched doorways, and it was crawling with statuary. The grandeur of its façade, though, looked to be in serious need of repair and was spoiled by huge Soviet flags and a giant poster of Stalin.

Mason, Laura, Kraus, and Bauer joined the line of guests waiting to clear the Soviet army guards, who checked purses and patted everyone down. A female Russian soldier checked Laura, and two male soldiers checked the men. They all cleared the guards and moved into a large hall of marbled walls and floors.

As they joined the queue to enter the ballroom, Mason asked Laura under his breath, "How are the burns?"

"They're tolerable. The silk lining helps, but they're itching like crazy."

"Are you going to be okay in there?"

Laura kissed him on the cheek and drew him close. "Remember we're supposed to be the lustful couple."

Mason was about to say something, but Laura pulled him past a phalanx of Russian guards and peering eyes and into the lavish corps de logis. All four of them stopped to take in the scene. The corps de logis was a ballroom-sized space surrounded by marble columns and rose up two additional levels. The whole thing was graced by a decorative glass ceiling the same size as the floor. Flags of Austria and the four Allied powers hung from the second-level balconies, while thousands of candles glowed in floor-standing candelabras, and the Russians, of course, didn't miss the chance to hang another large portrait of Stalin.

"Up until recently," Bauer said, "this was used as a field hospital. Now, the Russians use it for fancy parties."

A children's choir was at one end of the ballroom, singing a classical piece Mason recognized but couldn't recall the name of. The celestial sounds echoed off the high ceiling. The two stories of balconies served unseen rooms that wrapped around all four sides. Chairs had been set up in the center of the ballroom, but most of the elegantly dressed guests stood and talked quietly in groups or circulated, making sure they were seen.

As the group moved forward, Kraus was stopped by an Austrian official with a ceremonial sash. As they talked, Bauer mumbled his excuses and peeled off for another spot underneath the balcony. Mason and Laura continued on to a group of guests standing in a horseshoe shape listening to the children.

The children ranged from six to sixteen, girls and boys, and Mason caught Laura staring at them. Her smile showed her delight, but her eyes reflected a melancholy air.

"Did you and Richard think about kids?" Mason asked.

"We tried. I miscarried about six months ago."

"I'm sorry."

She said nothing and continued to stare at the children.

"Valerius, or one of his confederates, might recognize you, you know," Mason said.

"Let them. And I hope their little penises shrivel when they realize I'm still alive."

That wasn't what Mason hoped to hear, but he loved her courage. He offered his arm. "Why don't we go for a stroll?"

Laura took his arm, and they began to move past clusters of guests: women in evening gowns and men in tuxedos or uniforms laden with medals. They went only a short distance before Mason squeezed on Laura's arm so she would follow his gaze.

"Wentworth," Mason said. "One of Valerius's lieutenants."

"The one you scared half to death?"

Mason nodded while observing the man. Wentworth stood with a woman Mason presumed was his wife. She was talking to him while he nervously glanced around the room. He downed a flute of champagne, then plucked another from a tray held by a passing waiter.

"We should definitely keep an eye on him," Laura said. "It looks like he's about to soil his expensive tux."

Mason noticed that a number of the men were looking at Laura. Most of them had desire in their eyes, though a few seemed to be studying her face, as if wondering who she might be.

"Doesn't your cover's job require you to gab with the bigwigs?" Laura asked. "Get money out of them?"

"I'll let Bauer do the talking," Mason said and nodded in Bauer's direction, who had cornered two British Army officers. "He seems to be a natural. Besides, I have a ladies' man reputation to uphold, and I've got the most beautiful woman in the room on my arm. I think my cover's intact."

They made a few turns and accepted a waiter's offer of champagne.

"It appears Monsieur Bossart is getting along well," Laura said.

Mason turned to look at Kraus. He talked to Schumacher, the deputy police commissioner and a reputed Valerius coconspirator. Then, to Mason's surprise, Gruber stepped up to Kraus and the commissioner. Mason worried that Kraus would shrink at facing two of Valerius's lieutenants at the same time, but to his credit, Kraus continued to smile, nod, and talk.

"Those two look awfully relaxed, considering Gruber has such an infamous reputation," Laura said.

That prompted Mason to survey the room. "They seem to feel untouchable here. That makes me think the man who calls the shots is here, somewhere …"

Mason looked up to the arched balconies. A few couples talked as they watched what was happening below. There were uniformed guards at various spots. Three of the arches had curtains drawn with gaps just wide enough for discreet surveillance. And he wondered if Valerius observed the fundraiser from a high perch, imagining himself a god looking down from Mount Olympus.

Mason was so absorbed in scrutinizing the rooms above that he nearly bumped into Flannigan. He only avoided a collision because Laura squeezed his arm to let him know of their proximity. Colonel Flannigan talked with three other men. By their uniforms, they were a British major, a French colonel, and a Soviet lieutenant colonel.

Flannigan noticed Mason and, particularly, Laura. Out of

the corner of his eye, Mason also noticed a tuxedoed man stiffen at Mason's approach. In all likelihood, one of Flannigan's bodyguards.

It was too late to make an about-face, so Mason plastered on a smile and extended his hand. "Well, you four could fill in as the four men in a jeep."

Flannigan smiled, as did the rest. Mason introduced himself and Laura. The man took a keen interest in Laura as he kissed her hand and said, "*Enchanté, mademoiselle.*"

Laura made a slight bow. "You men are ignoring the lovely children's choir. Shame on you."

More chuckles and grins. Mason launched into his sales routine per his Mr. Anderson cover, asking the men to be generous for the funding of the orphaned children, and to give a thought to what his organization is doing to promote democracy in Austria.

Flannigan listened with a fake smile planted on his face. He cut an imposing figure: 6'4" with the body of an aging wrestler who had put on pounds but never lost his muscle mass. While Mason pitched his foundation, Flannigan glanced over Mason's shoulder, and his expression turn murderous.

It lasted only an instant, but Mason had noticed. It was time to back away and see what might happen next. Mason and Laura made their excuses for moving on while expressing hopes of meeting again.

Once they were out of earshot, Laura said, "Did you see his face when he looked over your shoulder? It chilled my blood."

Mason led Laura to a spot underneath the balcony where they had a discreet yet clear view of Flannigan.

Bauer joined them and asked Laura, "Enjoying yourself?"

"The children's choir is wonderful."

In a quieter tone Bauer asked, "Get anything from Flannigan?"

"Yeah, to step back and watch the fireworks," Mason said and subtly pointed his chin to a man who stood on the opposite side of the ballroom about thirty feet from Flannigan's group. Wentworth. "And there's the man to light the fuse."

Wentworth stood alone by one of the columns and stared at the colonel. His chest heaved from nervous breathing, and he appeared to have trouble figuring out what to do with his shaking hands. A moment later, he clamped his jaw and marched toward Flannigan's group.

Flannigan said something to the three officers, then he stepped away and headed for an area free of guests. Wentworth intercepted him just as the colonel turned to face him. Wentworth seemed to shrink under the tall man's gaze. Flannigan flashed a warning with his eyes, but the shorter man ignored him.

Wentworth launched into a mini tirade, shaking his fists, demanding something unheard across the ballroom. His tirade was cut short by something Flannigan said, and Wentworth's face melted into one of pleading. Then Flannigan uttered only a short phrase, but it was enough to make Wentworth retreat to a safe corner.

Flannigan stood still as he watched Wentworth depart.

Mason had a hunch. "I'll see you two in a few minutes," he said to Laura and Bauer. He peeled off as his two companions hissed demands of where he was going.

Mason remained under the balcony as he headed toward the ballroom exit. He gambled that, after the confrontation with Wentworth, Flannigan would want to report the man's indiscretion. The gamble paid off, because after Flannigan checked his surroundings, he turned and headed for the exit.

To avoid being noticed, Mason maintained a leisurely pace as he passed behind the columns, but he quickly lost sight of Flannigan when the man entered the passageway. Mason increased his speed but was still a few seconds behind Flannigan when he stepped into the passageway. In front of him was the double-doored exit. To his left and right were staircases leading to the upper rooms. Which way?

He looked to his left just in time to see Flannigan's foot on the landing as he turned to climb the second set of stairs. Thankfully, the passageway was busy with late-arriving guests and those who'd had enough of children's choir music. There were a couple of Russian army guards keeping an eye on things, and they failed to notice Mason take the stairs.

As casually as he could, he climbed the marble staircase. At the top of the first flight, he came to the next level and a long, rectangular room. There were buffet tables and bars for guests who milled around, but no Flannigan. Mason made quick strides to a second set of stairs and took them two at a time. He reached the top and entered a smaller space that ended in a wide hallway. He saw Flannigan enter the hallway at the other end of the room.

The hallway provided access to private rooms, all on the left with views of the ballroom below. Flannigan headed for the third door, where two armed guards in Russian uniforms stood on either side. He stopped at the door to straighten his bowtie—a nervous gesture, it seemed.

Mason hustled down the hallway, causing the guards to turn toward him with their hands on their holstered pistols.

Mason did his best to ignore the threat. He waved his

hands and said, "Oh, Colonel Flannigan," as he trotted up to the colonel.

Flannigan looked alarmed when Mason stopped next to him. The guards put their hands on his chest to stop him, but it was too late; Mason was able to glance into the room before turning his attention back to the colonel.

"I'm sorry if I'm intruding," Mason said in an excited tone. "But I forgot that I wanted to invite you to an important conference with Austrian and military government officials next Tuesday. I'd love for you to attend."

Mason stole a second glance into the room. Two men in tuxedos sat among a group of Soviet army brass, drinks in one hand and cigars in the other.

Flannigan stared at Mason as if waiting for the real reason Mason had followed him to a room under armed guards. Mason kept his expression friendly, his eyes wide with seeming candor.

One of the guards said something to him in Russian. Flannigan held up his hand to signal he would take care it. "If you value your health, you'll leave now."

Mason feigned shock. "I'm sorry. My enthusiasm gets the best of my better judgment sometimes." He gave a slight bow, then turned and walked away.

Halfway across the rectangular room, he turned and saw Flannigan was still staring at him.

Mason held up a hand. "Hope to see you Tuesday," he called out and headed for the stairs. He concentrated on listening for pursuing footsteps, but there were none, and as he descended the stairs, he tried to assess what he just saw in that room: Flannigan was going in there, hat in hand, after Wentworth's tantrum, then his look of alarm when Mason got close enough to peek into the room.

He mentally ran through the images of all the people in Bauer's photo album. The Russian generals were unknown to him, but the two men in tuxedos seemed familiar. The first one was in his sixties, thin, and with a face like forty miles of bad road—jagged features, high cheekbones, pale blue eyes, and thin lips. Mason couldn't remember the man's name, but he was definitely a brigadier general in the adjutant general's office. Just a few rungs beneath the top American in Austria, General Clark.

The second was in his mid to late forties, with dark brown hair and a chiseled face that could have been handsome except for the high, protruding forehead that overwhelmed his deep-set eyes. In that room, he'd held himself with an aristocratic bearing and a relaxed confidence, like the other men were his guests.

Mason reached the bottom of the first flight of stairs. The face … he knew that face. He imagined leafing through Bauer's photo album he'd examined in the limo, one page at a time. Then, on the last page, that face stared back at him. A U.S. State Department heavy-hitting diplomat. His name was like something out of a Revolutionary War Who's Who …

Then it came to him: Hamilton Carver.

What were those two doing with Russian generals? Was either of them Valerius?

Mason bounded down the last flight of stairs, sidestepping three men who were on their way up. One of the men stepped in front of Mason. The other two filed in behind. Mason was about to shove the man in front and make a dash for it, but then he felt something small and solid being pushed into his back.

“You will come with us,” the possessor of the pistol said in English with a heavy Russian accent. “You are on our territory. I could shoot you, and there would be no questions. But then my boss will be very disappointed.”

The man in front turned and began to go down the steps. A prodding from the pistol convinced Mason to do the same. He’d wanted to find out who Valerius was. Now he might find out the hard way.

24

Strong hands shoved Mason into a chair. His abductors had put a hood over his head and driven around, seemingly in circles, so he had no idea where he was aside from the footsteps echoing in a wide space with hard surfaces. He could smell machine oil and hints of diesel fuel. Pungent enough to overcome his captors' reeking body odor.

Someone from behind yanked the hood from his head. Instead of facing the barrel of a gun or a vat of boiling oil, an empty chair was placed just a few feet from him and turned his way. To his right was a small table accommodating a shaded lamp. It reminded Mason more of a setting for an interview or a fireside chat than an execution site or torture chamber. Beyond this tableau, and in the deepening shadows, were machinery and tools for an auto repair shop. Only there weren't any automobiles. Maybe they planned to torture him by torque wrench or scissors jack.

There were at least two guys close behind him—he could hear their breathing—and clouds of cigarette smoke wafted in his direction. Mason's heart pounded, but he wasn't about to say anything, certainly not a plea for his life.

Off to his left, he heard hard shoes on the concrete floor. Mason continued to look straight ahead. The walker came into his field of view accompanied by musky cologne. He had smelled that cologne before, so he wasn't surprised when Colonel Leonid Konstantin eased himself into the facing chair.

Not Valerius but the Russian sadist. His goose might be cooked either way.

Konstantin said in German, "You look sullen. I hope bringing you here didn't cause you too much inconvenience."

"Not as inconvenient as what you plan to do next."

"My next move is up to you." He paused, obviously to let Mason stew on that thought. "You're a very resourceful fellow, Mr. Anderson. Though let's not pretend that Anderson is your real name. You had me convinced you were German. That impresses me. Your escape from the prison, however? Not so much. Any half-witted man could have recognized the serendipitous circumstances and run."

Mason said nothing as he wondered how much Konstantin knew about who he really was, or his mission. Still, if Konstantin knew he was working with the CIC, the man would have had him killed already.

"We retain German and Austrian assets who have penetrated your intelligence agencies—you must know this, of course—but to recruit an American to work for me … an American not motivated by greed or compromised for his sexual proclivities, but a man motivated by revenge—"

"Justice," Mason said, interrupting.

Konstantin chuckled. "Call it what you like," he said and took time to light a cigarette. He then held out the pack.

Mason wanted one badly, but not from the Russian.

Konstantin shrugged and put the pack in his coat pocket.

"Can you get to the point?" Mason said. "I have a fundraiser to go back to."

"You're not tied to the chair. You can walk out of here. I won't stop you. But we're past curfew for private citizens and deep in the Soviet zone of control. You won't get far. Either the Austrian gangs or the police will pick you up. And when they do, I'll let it be known that you murdered a Soviet intelligence officer. Then, even the western Allied police will be looking for you."

Mason's chest constricted, and his stomach flipped over. Did he know? But how? Or was he fishing? They had almost certainly found the Russian officer's body and determined he'd been murdered. He would have done the same thing in an interview—throw out the bait and see who bites the hook.

Mason managed to control his reaction and keep a neutral expression. "You've got it all wrong," he said. "I'm an American businessman. A charity organizer. And I certainly didn't murder anyone."

"Don't test my patience."

A moment of silence passed between them, then Konstantin said, "My offer still stands—"

Mason interrupted. "I know who Valerius is." He didn't, not really. He gambled and chose one … "Hamilton Carver."

Konstantin paused, his expression neutral. "Let me sweeten the pot, then."

A flash of electricity coursed through Mason. The man hadn't denied it. He'd guessed correctly and now knew Valerius's identity. He wanted to jump off of the chair and run, but he also wanted to hear Konstantin's offer. "Let's hear it."

"If you want to go after him, I'm offering assistance."

That took Mason by surprise. "What's the catch?"

"I give you help, and you give me information. It's that simple."

"It's more complicated than you let on. I know that because you had your goons kidnap me and take me to an empty repair shop. You didn't want to do this in your office. You didn't want anyone else to know."

Konstantin smiled. "Yes, that's true. There are too many eyes and ears at headquarters. Especially when I don't know who to trust."

"Go on."

"We have reason to believe Valerius—a.k.a. Carver—is receiving Soviet classified documents from a traitor and handing them over to American intelligence."

That news felt like a blow to Mason's guts. Konstantin must have noticed his expression, because he said, "Ah, something that you didn't know."

"Why don't you just kill him? Or, I tell you what, you capture him and bring him to me. I'll do it for you."

"Because we need to know who's passing him these documents."

Mason was too busy processing this information to answer. He wanted to take his revenge out on a valuable U.S. intelligence asset.

"Carver is being shielded by some high-powered Soviet officials," Konstantin said, "because they're profiting off his criminal organization. As long as they continue to profit, Carver will be able to stay in business."

"Even if they know he's selling Soviet secrets?"

"You are not so naïve. Greed trumps patriotism. That is, as long as those secrets don't compromise *their* positions."

"In other words, if you raise too much of a stink, you could go before Carver does."

"The only way to stop him is to have proof, and the perpetrator or perpetrators are caught."

"And how do you expect me to find the guilty party when he or they are Soviet top brass?"

"Use that resourcefulness of yours, Mr. Anderson. You work your end of the pipeline, and I'll work mine."

"To stop a valuable U.S. intelligence asset from supplying Soviet secrets to my government?" Mason shook his head. "I won't betray my country."

"I don't have to tell you the consequences if you refuse to cooperate. Others who were associated with you in the past may die. And consider this: Carver is betraying your country by running a powerful criminal enterprise. Austrian citizens suffer starvation, shortages of medical supplies, or worse, because of tainted and diluted medicine. What is more valuable to you? Tidbits of intelligence or countless innocent lives? When would it be too high a price? The death of ten children? One hundred adults?" He leaned in. "Think about it. You can have your revenge, and you not only save innocent lives but save your own." He sat back in his chair and stubbed out his cigarette. "Perhaps even the life of that lovely woman on your arm this evening."

Mason wanted to launch across the gap and strangle the man.

Konstantin smiled, and said in English, "You see, Mr. Anderson? I have you—how do you say—over a barrel." He seemed to be enjoying Mason's predicament.

"Be happy, Mr. Anderson," Konstantin said, reverting back to German. "You're still alive. Unharmed. That stunt you pulled to get a glimpse of Carver could have ended very badly for you."

Konstantin nodded to someone Mason couldn't see, and Mason braced himself for what might come. Maybe a little taste of the alternative if he said no. Instead, a young muscle-bound man walked up and placed a bottle of vodka and two shot glasses on the table. Konstantin poured the liquid into the glasses and held out one for Mason. When Mason accepted the drink, the Russian raised his glass. "To our successful partnership."

Mason had yet to say yes, but Konstantin was confident he would agree to the deal.

He downed the liquid knowing he just made a pact with the devil.

25

Mason endured another drive through Vienna with a hood pulled over his head. The hood stank from someone else's sweat and tobacco-tainted breath.

"Maybe I'll carry an extra hood around with me," Mason said.

The driver in Konstantin's employ said nothing. He drove like a maniac, and his wild maneuvers threw Mason from one side of the back seat to the other. His speed should have gotten the attention of the MP patrols, but either the guy led a charmed life, or Konstantin's car was known to all and was considered untouchable.

Konstantin had told the driver to take Mason anywhere he wanted, and Mason opted to go back to the Hofburg Palace in case Laura or Bauer or Kraus had waited to see if he showed up after vanishing earlier.

The driver slowed and said in German, "You can take off your hood." His clean accent meant he wasn't Russian but German. Surprisingly, not even Austrian.

Mason removed the hood as the driver rolled up to the

palace's Neue Burg wing. It was two a.m., so the street and park were empty. He got out of the car and stood in the driveway. The car drove off. The cocktail conference had finished hours ago, and he was left alone apart from the two Russian Army sentries at the wing's entrance. No one ran out to greet him. No one waited. And he didn't feel it was wise to try to get past the guards of a Russian-occupied establishment to see if anyone was in the building.

Mason shrugged and said to the guards, "I guess I'm too late for the party." He turned and started walking toward the inner city. All his nerves were firing, his mind and body on high alert to the danger. One of Valerius's assassins could come charging out of the shadows. Or he would feel the impact of a racing bullet followed by the sharp crack of a rifle.

Mason crossed the Ringstrasse and got within two blocks of the Bristol Hotel when another sedan pulled up beside him. He tensed, again. Had Konstantin changed his mind? Running wasn't an option, so he turned to the car that idled at the curb. He leaned over and saw Sebastian, the beefy driver who had taken Kraus and him to the CIC safe house.

"You gonna get in or what?" Sebastian said through the open passenger window.

Mason breathed a sigh of relief and climbed in the front seat. "I wondered if anyone cared if I was still alive."

"Me, I don't." With that, Sebastian hit the accelerator.

"Thanks. That's touching." Mason pointed at his head. "No hood?"

"Not this time."

Sebastian took a circuitous route while checking the rearview mirror every minute. He drove fast enough that anyone who tried to follow would be forced to keep up, making the tail obvious.

With the old city behind them, they came up to a U.S. MP checkpoint. They were waved through and entered the American zone. Mason breathed a little easier after seeing signs for the army PX and post office. They passed the enlisted men's club and the Vienna headquarters for U.S. Forces, Austria.

Several blocks later, Sebastian pulled up in front of a townhouse in the middle of a row of identical structures.

"How many safe houses do you guys have?" Mason asked.

"We change them all the time."

"Evicting the Austrians who lived here?"

Sebastian shrugged. The two men got out and approached the house. The front door opened as they climbed the steps to the front porch. Laura stood at the door. Her expression flashed from relief to joy to anger, then back again.

She met him at the top, and they hugged. Mason's tension fell away as he held her, allowing his exhaustion to fill the void. The driver excuse-me'd his way past them.

Laura broke the embrace, and her expression went back to anger. "Where have you been?"

Mason saw Forester and Kraus standing in the living room. "Can we talk inside?" he asked and stepped into the living room.

Sebastian hung up his overcoat and said to the agents, "I found him wandering near the Bristol Hotel."

Laura closed the front door and stood next to him with her arms crossed.

"I know who Valerius is," Mason said to the group. "Hamilton Carver."

"The State Department diplomat?" Forester said in a surprised tone. "What makes you so sure?"

"At the fundraiser, I followed Flannigan upstairs, and he led me to a room with two guys in tuxedos who were palling around with a room full of Soviet brass. I only got a glimpse before Flannigan threatened me with bodily harm. He looked genuinely scared when he realized I'd followed him."

"That doesn't prove anything."

"No, it doesn't. And I had no idea who they were until I stepped away and was able to ID the two civilians thanks to your photo album. But before I could get to you, I got picked up by Russian intelligence."

Laura sucked in her breath, Forester stiffened, and Kraus turned away as if reeling from the news.

"Look," Mason said, "I've been through the ringer. I'll tell you everything, but first I could use a stiff drink."

After Forester poured Mason a scotch, they settled into chairs in the living room. Mason was still rattled by the experience and had to lean forward to keep from fidgeting in his chair. As he swirled his drink, he glanced at Kraus. "Peter knows him. We both had run-ins with this guy before, at the vigilante prison camp. A Colonel Leonid Konstantin."

Kraus leaned forward and put his head in his hands. "*Scheisse*."

Mason went on, "He's head of the MGB, the ministry for state security, or pretty near the top."

"No," Forester said, "he *is* the top in this region from what we've been able to gather. That's a serious guy."

"I watched him put a bullet in a prisoner's head just for a cross word. He's as serious as they come."

"What did he want with you?" Kraus asked. "Does he know who you are?"

"Originally, he thought I was German ex-intelligence. I don't know why—maybe the forged papers. Maybe by the look in my eyes. But now he knows I'm an American, though only by my cover identity, Martin Anderson."

"Sounds like he believes you are, or were, American intelligence," Forester said.

"That seems right. He wanted to make a deal in exchange for letting me live. At the prison, he offered to give me Valerius's identity if I spied for him." He saw Forester scrutinizing him, and he held up his hand. "I turned him down, and they made it tough on me. I think if I hadn't escaped, I'd be dead or in some gulag somewhere. Peter and I both would be. The point is, when I threw out the idea that Carver was Valerius, Konstantin didn't deny it."

"Mason, that's not reliable intel."

"Wait until I'm finished. He didn't want me to be an asset. He wanted me to find out who is passing Soviet secrets to Valerius—or Carver—or whatever you want to call him."

"Oh, come on, Mason," Forester said.

"He believes Valerius is receiving Soviet secrets and handing them over to us," Mason said.

"If this guy was receiving Soviet secrets, I'd know about it. Period. I don't know what Konstantin's motive is, but he's dead wrong."

"You said it yourself, Russian intelligence is running rings around us. And Konstantin was absolutely serious. Maybe Valerius is handing them over to someone else."

"Konstantin is suckering you to try to get you on his side. They lie, cheat, or steal to turn someone into an asset."

"Is that what you do, Mr. Forester?" Kraus asked.

"Hell yes," Forester said. "We might not be shooting at each other, but this is still a war. Spies instead of soldiers. In that game, you do anything to win." He looked at Mason. "Including making up a story like that. He knows how to play on your emotions. And he's hoping you want Valerius so bad that you would turn traitor to do it."

Forester stood and scowled at Mason. "Maybe I should send you home. You're so emotionally tied up that you're liable to make bad decisions."

Mason had to raise his voice to match Forester's. "Look into it, would you? I want Konstantin to be wrong, so I can kill Valerius without regret."

"Mason," Laura said with a shocked tone. "I want revenge as much as you do, but murder?"

"I don't want this to end in murder either," Kraus said.

"Ruin his life," Laura said. "Put him in jail to rot, but not that."

Mason was too heated to answer. He stared straight ahead. Laura was right, but he still wanted to see Valerius die. *What's happened to me?* Mason wondered. *I was a cop. I'm still a cop.*

"It's hard sometimes to forget you're not a soldier anymore," Forester said with enough self-reflection that it broke some of the tension. He finished his drink and laid the glass on the table. "I'll look into it, but no more talk of murder. Meanwhile, stay clear of that Russian."

"I doubt he's going to give me that choice," Mason said. "I'll observe Hamilton Carver, but I'll keep my distance." He looked at Laura. "I promise." Though he wasn't entirely sure he would keep that promise.

"No," Forester said, "I'll look into Carver. You take Flannigan. See what shakes out."

"Wentworth's the weak link," Mason said. "He'll break first."

"Fine. Kraus is chumming it up with Gruber and the deputy police commissioner." He said to Kraus, "Keep that up."

Kraus nodded. "Wentworth's behavior last night made the deputy commissioner nervous, and he was nervous even before that."

"I'll stick with you," Laura said to Mason. "Keep you out of trouble. Also, I do have some contacts with a couple of smugglers from that series of articles I wrote about the black markets. They might have some information on Carver's organization."

"Okay," Forester said, "but don't get overanxious. We move carefully and methodically."

Mason said nothing, but only to avoid saying that he had no intention of heeding Forester's warning.

26

Mason and Laura strolled around Stephansplatz, a large rectangular plaza that served as the heart of Vienna. Anchored by St. Stephen's Cathedral, or Stephansdom, the perimeter was defined by burned-out shells of once-stately buildings now covered in scaffolding. They stopped occasionally at one of the stands set up to sell hot chocolate or pastries, with one enterprising fellow even selling miniature flags of the four Allied powers.

The plaza had been cleared of the locals trying to sell their wares for food, and the orphaned children running up to passersby to beg for coins or picking up cigarette butts, because, heaven forbid, the dignitaries gathered for Hamilton Carver's speech would have to tolerate the unwashed masses. Carver was at a podium giving a talk about a new Austria and all the great things the Allies were going to do to make that happen. The podium stood on a dais with the roofless, burned-out cathedral as a backdrop. Sitting on chairs behind Carver were representatives from the four powers along with elected Austrian officials.

"This is his third speech in a row," Mason said to Laura. "The dedication to the reconstruction of the bridge, one speech at an Austrian political rally … He meets with fifty-odd people every day. Any one of them could be working for him, taking orders, passing messages. Any one of them could slip him documents. Not to mention that he travels with a large entourage and numerous professional-looking bodyguards."

"We've only been tailing him for two days," Laura said. "And we're supposed to be following Flannigan."

"A day of that was all I could handle. He's not the source, and he's either at home or in his office."

"You were a cop. You should be used to boring stakeouts."

"I've been a cop long enough to know that we won't get anywhere this way. They're too careful."

"Mike has a team working on it. We're not alone."

"If we don't get some results soon—"

"Stop whining or go home," Laura said.

Mason chuckled despite his frustration. He stopped and looked at Laura. "You've spent the last few days just keeping me in line. You're the only person I've ever met who could do that without pissing me off. Maybe my grandmother, but that's it."

"I'll take that as an apology."

"If I keep misbehaving, do you promise to stick around to keep me on the straight and narrow?"

They looked at each other for a moment. Warmth spread across Mason's chest, but Carver's voice, booming across the plaza, broke the spell.

Mason clamped his eyes closed to keep his disgust under control. "Nothing like that asshole's voice to ruin a romantic moment."

"Is that what this was? I couldn't tell."

Mason smiled at her humor, even as Carver's droning voice drilled into his skull. He took Laura's hand. "Come on. I've got to get out of here."

"Where are we going?"

"Someplace where I hope to get quicker results."

Laura eased the Buick Forester had requisitioned for them next to the curb. Down the street was Wentworth's townhouse. Mason took out the binoculars.

"You sure this is a good idea?" Laura asked, though it sounded more like a warning.

"No," Mason said as he focused the lenses and scanned the front of the townhouse. He wasn't sure if he saw correctly and scanned again. He put down the binoculars. "The guards are gone."

"Did he have guards the first time you spooked him?" Upon Mason's nod, Laura said, "He's probably just out. If he's that scared, he could have taken his guards with him."

"Or he's skipped town."

"Or maybe the guards are inside, taking a break from the cold."

"Could be," Mason said as he lifted his pistol out of its holster and checked the magazine.

"I know what you're planning, and it's a bad idea."

"This is just for self-defense."

Laura pulled the snub-nosed .38 revolver from her purse and put it in her pocket.

Mason watched her and said, "What are you—"

"To keep you in line," Laura said and got out of the car, prompting Mason to do the same.

"What's the plan?" Laura asked.

"Sometimes the best way is right through the front door."

They crossed the street and approached Wentworth's while scanning the area for trouble. It was Sunday, so there was only a handful of people out on the street. None were close enough to worry about, and most appeared to be out for an afternoon stroll.

Arm in arm, Mason and Laura ambled up to the wall that separated the townhouse's small garden patio and the street. They stopped at the cast iron gate. Mason pulled out his lock-picking tools and leaned over as if using a key. In several seconds he had the gate unlocked, and they entered. Laura closed the gate behind her.

They crossed the patio, and Mason attacked the locks to the front door. There were three, so it took him several minutes to pick all of them. A couple pedestrians passed by, but neither of them paid attention to the nicely dressed couple entering their townhouse in in the middle of the day.

Mason finally got the better of the heavy deadbolt, and it clacked back. Mason signaled for Laura to get to one side of the door. Laura did so with her hand in her pocket, presumably grasping the handle of her revolver.

Mason held up his hand, telling Laura to wait. He opened the door but remained in place, listening for movement. Silence. He slipped in and put his back against the wall. Laura came in a second later and emulated Mason's stance on the opposite side of the door.

While keeping his gaze toward the interior, Mason slowly closed the door.

Laura whispered, "Anyone else besides Wentworth live here?"

"His wife and two teenage boys."

The drawn curtains blocked most of the daylight from reaching the interior, causing everything to be shrouded in gray. The foyer led to several rooms, left and right. Mason knew about the dining room, the front room, and the kitchen, which were on his right. He assumed the living room was on the left.

Mason nodded to Laura, and they moved forward. Mason slid sideways and peeked into the dining room. He had a clear view from the entrance to the kitchen. No one was there. He came back and motioned for Laura to keep an eye on the stairs and upper balcony, while he moved to his left and checked the living room and library.

Finding those rooms empty, he joined Laura, and they moved up the stairs. At the top, Mason signaled for Laura to go left and check the boys' bedrooms. Laura shook her head. She touched her eyes and pointed at him.

Mason shrugged and went up the right-side staircase, the way he'd gone before. Laura followed directly behind him. They stopped at the door that Mason knew was Wentworth's study. Each took a side against the doorframe. Mason whispered for her to get ready, and she pulled out her pistol and flicked off the safety. She'd been a reporter in battle zones during the war and had obviously learned how to use a pistol.

Mason put his hand on the doorknob and turned it. He put one foot inside and took a shooting stance. The room was empty, though a fire still smoldered in the fireplace. Mason stepped in with his gun still up and checked the corners. Laura came in right behind him. With some of the tension gone,

Mason could admire the way Laura handled herself. She'd taken cues from him and immediately learned how to enter a room.

They turned and faced the closed door on the opposite side of the hallway. They repeated the pattern of approaching the room, and upon opening the door, they discovered a large bedroom with a canopy bed. The bed had been hastily made, but there were no other signs of life. Mason relaxed his gun arm. They had at least two more rooms on the other side of the house, but it was doubtful the boys were home or that guards would be waiting for them there.

They left the room, moved toward the end of the hallway, and repeated the steps again. This door had been left partially open, and they could see white and black tiling of a bathroom. Laura pointed to her ear and then at the bathroom. Mason listened but heard nothing; his hearing was not what it used to be after two years of war and several gunfights after leaving the army.

Mason pushed open the door and finally heard what seemed to be trickling water. They charged in, guns ready, then stopped. Wentworth lay in the bathtub. It was full of water, red from Wentworth's blood. The man was slumped down on his back with the water covering his nose and mouth. Only his eyes poked above the surface, the lids open, eyes blank and still.

Mason stepped up to the tub and put his hand into the water. It was tepid despite the slow trickle of hot water coming from the faucet. He lifted the man's cold arm. The gashes across both wrists were so deep he could see tendon and bone. After lowering the arm back into the water, he turned on his heels and walked past Laura.

Laura joined him in the hallway. “This is going to create a firestorm,” she said in a hushed tone. “A high-ranking military government officer committing suicide.”

“He didn’t commit suicide.”

“You know that just by looking at him?”

“We can talk about this later. We still need to clear the rooms on the other side and then get out of here.”

“We’re just going to leave? You’re not going to call the CID?”

“We’re both operating under aliases and committed breaking and entering with guns we don’t have permits for. We’re the only links to Wentworth’s death, which will make us suspects number one and two.”

“Well, when you put it that way.”

“I’ll clear the rooms. See what you can find in his papers. His desk and briefcase and file cabinets.”

They split up. Mason cleared the other rooms. They were all unoccupied. The clothes were gone from the closets, and the dresser drawers were empty. He then did a full search of the master bedroom, going through the armoire and dressers. While Wentworth’s clothes seemed to be all there, his wife’s clothes and toiletries were missing. Nothing else looked out of place. He joined Laura in the study and found her kneeling in front of the wastebasket.

“File cabinets are completely empty,” she said as she removed items from the wastebasket and glanced at them.

“That’s why I know it wasn’t suicide,” Mason said and picked up the leather briefcase sitting on the chair.

“That’s empty, too,” Laura said as she threw the trash back into the trash can.

Mason stopped and looked for something else to search. "I'm sure they were thorough."

Laura sat on the floor with her hands behind her propping her up. Mason used the poker to sift through the ashes in the fireplace. The thick bed of ashes showed signs of someone already having done the same thing, but Mason moved them around anyway.

He looked at Laura, who remained in her reclined position. "Taking a break?"

She scrunched her brow while looking at Wentworth's desk. "Those two candelabras on the desk. Kind of odd to put them there. He already has a desk lamp and a hanging lamp just above his desk. Seems redundant."

"Maybe a lousy interior decorator?" Mason said and stood up from his squatting position. He shifted over to the desk and looked at the silver candelabras. Each held three candles, and they were placed on either end of the desk, with one right next to the desk lamp. He lifted each of them and checked the bottoms. Using his knife, he removed the felt padding, but the bases were solid.

"Check one of the candles," Laura said.

He removed one and snapped it in half. He held up the lower half, the other half dangling by the wick. "Yep, a candle."

"Brute," Laura said and got to her feet.

She walked up to the farthest candle on the left, plucked it from its sconce. She examined it, hefted it to test the weight, then chose another one. She repeated this process for two others, then on her fourth try, she seemed to notice something when she tested the weight. She held it up to the light, then grabbed each end of the candle with her hands and twisted. It separated in the middle. She examined the separated ends and smiled. She showed Mason. There was a hollow tube inserted through the length of the candle.

Mason hurried over and looked over her shoulder as she removed a single rolled sheet of paper from the tube. She unrolled it, revealing a series of random numbers—a long list, in fact—half of them separated by commas and the other half by dashes.

"Obviously a code of some sort," Laura said and handed it over to Mason.

"I'm coming to you next time I have to hide a secret document," Mason said.

"Reporters have to be detectives, too, you know. Stick with me, kid, and you might learn something."

"We'll look at this later," Mason said and pocketed the sheet of paper. "We should get out of here before someone from his office wonders why he hasn't shown up, and they decide to call the police."

Mason wiped down any surfaces where they might have left fingerprints while Laura put everything back exactly the way she had found them.

As they descended the stairs, Mason said, "Too bad we couldn't search this place from top to bottom, maybe even lift fingerprints in the bathroom."

"Missing your time at the CID?"

"Yes ma'am, I am."

They stopped at the front door.

"What if we're seen leaving?" Laura asked. "There's not a better way out of here?"

"The only other way out of here is out the back and over a garden wall."

"So, no."

Mason shook his head and used the handkerchief to wipe prints off the front doorknob. When all was ready, Laura took a deep breath, plastered a pleasant smile on her face, and they walked out the front door.

They smiled and chatted as they headed for the car. Mason held open the passenger's door for Laura, then got behind the wheel as if out on a Sunday drive. Once the car doors were closed, Laura let out a long breath and slumped in her seat.

"Don't get too relaxed," Mason said. "We're just getting started."

27

Mason looked at his watch again while taking a puff of his cigarette.

"There's a clock on the wall, you know," Laura said.

"Just checking to see if it's correct."

"It is. And it has been every time you look at your watch and light up another cigarette."

Mason and Laura were in the townhouse that Sebastian had taken Mason to after his meeting with Konstantin. Mason's constant pacing was threatening to wear a hole in the ratty carpet. Laura sat at a round table playing solitaire with a deck of cards she'd found in a kitchen drawer.

"Forester's the one who called this meeting," Mason said.

"I know it might be a shock to you, but not everyone runs on Mason Collins time."

"It's not like him to be late. And he didn't sound too happy over the phone, which makes me think it's not good news." Frustration drove Mason to jam his cigarette into the ashtray, crushing the life out of it. The front door opened at the same instant. Bauer stepped in and shook out his umbrella.

"Where's Forester?"

"He's coming with Kraus," Bauer said as he entered the living room. He greeted Laura and asked, "What have you got?"

"Shouldn't we wait for Mike?" Laura asked.

Bauer made his impatience clear with a stone-cold stare. "Why don't we get started? Then I can get Forester up to speed."

"Wentworth's dead," Mason said.

"We haven't heard anything. How'd you find out?"

Laura cleared her throat. "We broke into his house."

Bauer whirled around to give Mason another angry stare. "That was stupid."

"I think you mean careless, reckless, but not stupid. He was murdered, and all his papers are gone."

"He was in the bathtub with hot water," Laura said. "His wrists were slashed to the bone."

Bauer muttered something under his breath, then said, "He was ripe for the picking. We could have turned him."

"I guess that's what Carver thought, too," Mason said.

"An American," Bauer said. "A colonel, no less. That's going to stir up a hornet's nest."

"You guys should call CID so they can get there first. See if they can lift any fingerprints or dig up any other evidence."

Bauer shook his head. "We let it be. It'll be better for us if the conclusion is suicide. A tragedy, but at least that won't produce a full-blown crisis."

"A good CID investigator could figure it out."

"Then let's hope he's not that good."

"You're forgetting his wife," Laura said. "She had to know

something was going on. He must have sent them away when he knew he was in danger."

"We let it play out however it does. We stay out of it."

The front door opened again, and this time Forester came in with Kraus and someone Mason didn't know. The man looked like he was fresh off an Ivy League campus—cut features, slicked-back hair, the football quarterback fit for a poster. He smiled as he entered the living room.

Right away, Mason pegged him as an ambitious bureaucrat with a Montana-sized ego born from wealth and privilege. He found himself standing a little taller when they shook hands. Forester introduced him has Adam Kovack.

"Another CIC officer?" Mason asked.

Kovack remained silent, letting Forester speak, who looked reluctant to do so. "Adam is the deputy chief of operations for the Office of Special Operations in the occupied zones."

Mason returned a blank stare.

Forester cleared his throat, seemingly reluctant to go further.

"We're part of the new Central Intelligence Group," Kovack said. "We took over the foreign clandestine operations from the OSS and SSU."

"Just what everyone needs. Another intelligence agency."

"We're not military. The head of the CIG answers directly to the president."

"Meaning they supersede us," Forester said as if reporting the death of a loved one.

"I don't want to get into a turf war," Kovack said. "We can work together."

Mason looked between Forester and Kovack while he tried

to work out what this implied. He said to Forester, "They're not trying to take this case away from us, are they?"

"If your case involves Carver," Kovack said, "then we're not so much taking it over as shutting you down."

"You're what? This man is responsible for countless murders. You can't—"

"Do you have any proof? Hard evidence?"

Mason looked at Laura and Forester.

"I take it by your silence that you don't," Kovack said.

"Mike, you can't let him do this," Mason said.

"I've got my orders," Forester said, "and now you do too. You and Kraus still have that conference scheduled for tomorrow. I want you both to keep up appearances and go. You might be able to get your hands on more information. But you lay off Carver. Do you understand?"

"I'm a civilian. I don't have to follow orders."

Kovack stepped in front of Forester. "Mr. Collins, you can go after his lieutenants—"

"You know he's running a crime organization and even works with the Russians."

"Yes, but you've got to look at the bigger picture. The serious threat from the East. If we fail to contain the Soviets, Western Europe could fall. So far, they're winning the intelligence game, and Carver's one of the only assets we've got in Vienna who's providing us with information about the Soviets."

"In the meantime, he's exploiting and murdering innocent people," Laura said. "Including my husband. Including MPs and CID investigators."

"You guys have to understand," Forester said, "every time

we manage to embed an asset or turn a Soviet, their intelligence shuts it down."

"Carver's the only one managing to get his hands on Soviet documents and staying alive in the process," Kovack said. "As long as he's allowed to operate, he'll be able to pass on Soviet secrets to us. He has to stay where he is."

"Mike, how can you go along with this?" Mason asked.

"It's out of my hands."

"When it comes to Carver," Kovack said, "I'm calling the shots. I've gotten approval from the director of the Central Intelligence Group, who has the ear of the president. Is that clear enough for you? Is that a high enough rank for you?"

Kovack delivered the last of his speech with such an imperious tone that Mason wanted to give him a solid right cross.

Laura must have seen it, because she said, "Mason," in a warning tone.

Mason pushed past Kovack and Forester and headed for the door. Forester called after him, but he ignored the man and charged out of the townhouse.

He marched for the Buick. Laura called out his name as she came running up to him. He ignored her, too, and got into the car. Laura got into the passenger seat just as he started the car and hit the accelerator.

"Mason, calm down."

"I am calm," he said as he raced down the street.

"When you get this angry, you don't think clearly. If you go off half-cocked, you could get into more trouble than you can handle."

"I know exactly what I have to do. It's the only way to end this."

"You kill Carver, and we'll both wind up in prison or dead."

"I didn't ask you to come along."

"I want bring him down as much or more than you do, but this isn't the way to do it. You've got to be as cunning as he is."

Mason turned left so fast that the tires squealed.

Laura put her hand on his arm. "We do this smart, and we do it together. We bring him down hard, but not like this. I want you to stick around. In one piece. Stop and think. Do it for me."

Mason could feel her eyes on him and feel the warmth of her hand. He let the pressure off the accelerator, and the car slowed. He steered to the curb and switched off the engine. Laura kept her hand on his and remained silent as he took deep breaths to calm his rage.

From out of nowhere, two black sedans raced up to their car. One of them ground to a halt just in front of Mason's car. The other stopped alongside to block Mason from opening his door. It took a split second for Mason to figure out what was going on, and that moment of confusion delayed him from putting the car in reverse. Just as he did so, four men in black overcoats jumped out of the lead car with their guns drawn. Two of them went toward Laura's side, and the other two aimed their pistols at Mason's head.

Mason went for his gun, but then he heard a sharp tapping on his window. He looked to his left and saw a man aiming a pistol at his head. The two men with their guns on Laura came to her door, opened it, and pulled her out, dragging her toward the front sedan. The other two waved their pistols for Mason to get out.

Mason got the message clearly enough. He holstered his pistol and slid across the front seat. The two Russians jerked him to his feet and pushed him toward the sedan blocking his car. The street-side back passenger's door opened, and Mason was pushed inside. Konstantin was waiting for him.

"Mademoiselle Vallier has nothing to do with this," Mason said. "Let her go."

Konstantin ignored him and nodded. The lead sedan pulled out onto the street. Konstantin's driver followed. Mason peered through the sedan's windshield to see if Laura was being mistreated.

"She will be unharmed," Konstantin said. "She is temporary collateral. You satisfy my queries, and you both walk free."

"What do you expect from me in three days? I'm working on it."

The two sedans came up quickly to a Soviet zone checkpoint. A sign mounted at the sidewalk announced that they were leaving the American zone and entering the Soviet one. Once the cars passed the checkpoint, Laura and he were at the mercy of Konstantin.

Mason had to weigh his options in a split second: what to tell, what to hold back, life and death decisions. Konstantin looked at him expectantly.

"I've been following Carver," Mason said, "but he's been very careful. I haven't seen anything out of the ordinary. He keeps busy all day, meets with lots of people, and goes around with a big entourage. Meaning documents or information could be passed at any time, to anyone, anywhere."

"I made the effort to recruit you because of your resourcefulness. I expected something by now. I have the feeling you're delaying. Use that resourcefulness of yours and get some results."

"Taking my associate won't make me get faster results."

"I'm not so sure."

"I'm telling you, if you hold Mademoiselle Vallier, I'll be more worried about her safety than keeping tabs on Carver. You want me to do your bidding, then let her go."

Konstantin stared at Mason. Mason panicked on the inside but kept his expression firm, returning a cold stare of his own.

Finally, the Russian said, "You have three more days. That's it."

Mason was about to say something, but Konstantin held up his hand to quiet him. "I know you and the mademoiselle are lovers. I have a weakness for romance. I won't hold her. Not this time. But I do expect results." He said something in Russian to the driver. The driver flashed the headlights twice, obviously his signal, as the lead sedan made a U-turn at the next intersection and headed back for the American zone.

MASON AND LAURA GOT INTO THEIR CAR AND REMAINED silent until the two Russian sedans pulled away.

"Are you all right?" Mason asked Laura.

"Considering two goons who stank of vodka held me at gunpoint, yeah."

Mason shifted the car into first gear and hit the accelerator.

"I assume that was Konstantin," Laura said.

Mason nodded. "He wanted a progress report."

"And to scare you. Picking us up within the American zone

was all about showing you he can grab you anywhere. That he has the power to do anything, anywhere he wants."

"That's why I want you to get out of town."

"I'm not going anywhere."

"He's given me three days, Laura. I'm not going to have the results in that short of time. And it would mean I'd have to betray my country by compromising the only intelligence source the U.S. has got in Vienna."

Mason stopped at a checkpoint controlling the entrance to the city center. The American MP checked the papers before waving them through the barricade.

"We try to find a way to satisfy both problems," Laura said.

"The only way to do that is to give Konstantin the Russian source and kill Carver at the same time. Make it look like the Russians did it."

"If it comes to that, if we're really left with no other choice, then that's what we do. But let's come up with a better solution in the meantime."

"There is no *us*. I want you to get out of here now, while you still can."

"No. And stop treating me like a helpless female, or I'll cut your balls off before you can say Rumpelstiltskin."

Despite his anger, Mason chuckled. "Rumpelstiltskin? Is that what your mother used to say?"

A smile broke through Laura's tough demeanor. "It's the first thing that came into my head," she said, then furrowed her brow. "I still mean it, buster."

Mason parked the car down the block from their hotel. "I believe you, even if you called me buster." He switched off the motor. "Shall we adjourn to the bar? I could use a stiff drink."

"Don't we have that conference to go to tomorrow?"

"That's not until four thirty."

"Have you prepared for it?"

"Kraus is doing the speech. My job is to play the privileged asshole, remember?"

"Take away the privileged part, and you're a shoo-in," Laura said and got out of the car.

Mason joined her on the sidewalk, and they headed for the hotel.

She was steamed about something he did, but Mason had yet to figure it out.

"I don't know what's going to happen tomorrow at the conference," Mason said, "so I don't want you to go."

Laura said nothing, but her shoes pounded the sidewalk as she increased her pace.

"Did you hear me?" Mason asked.

"I heard, all right."

"Then you'll stay away?"

Laura gritted her teeth, and her eyes flared with anger.

"How about that drink?" Mason asked.

"I've had enough excitement—and you—for one day. I'm going to my room. You should do the same and try to stay out of trouble until tomorrow afternoon."

Laura surged forward, leaving Mason alone on the sidewalk. He smiled. At least she'd unwittingly given him permission to get into trouble tomorrow afternoon. He planned to take her up on that offer.

28

Mason found it hard to concentrate on what the Vienna city councilman was saying. The man, Karl Wimmer, sported an enormous mustache that squirmed as he talked, making the thing appear like a small furry animal had taken up residence on the man's upper lip. To make things more distracting, the buxom tomato on his arm, who Wimmer introduced unconvincingly as his niece, eyed him with such a steamy come-hither look that it had Mason fidgeting with the change in his pocket.

The gist of Wimmer's diatribe concerned the Soviet's expropriation of over four hundred Austrian businesses and putting a stranglehold on the steel, oil, and transportation industries. That the Soviets were stifling Austrian independence through corporate proxy.

Mason nodded and interjected "hms" and "I sees" to give the man the impression that he was listening. But most of the time, he scanned the large gathering to pick out any of Carver's cronies, to see who interacted with whom, who might be making deals or plotting their next murder.

Someone at the CIC who Mason didn't know had picked the opulent grand gallery at the Schönbrunn Palace for the conference. The palace had been requisitioned by the British for their army headquarters and their delegates to the Allied Commission for Austria. But Mason figured the CIC had chosen the baroque gallery, with its undulating stucco walls trimmed with gilding and king-sized ceiling paintings of skies filled with people floating on clouds, to entice corporate moguls to pledge money and support for a worthy cause, but Mason found it cynical considering the conference was to encourage help in fighting the starvation plaguing the city's general population, particularly orphaned children.

Kraus was standing on a dais and was halfway through a speech imploring the men of industry and finance and politics to embrace democratic values for the improvement of life for all Austrians. He talked like a Swiss banker, but Mason knew Kraus's words came from the heart.

However, most of the guests circulated with their drinks in one hand and their wives or mistresses on the other. They talked and chuckled in small groups, ignoring Kraus.

A French vice-consul general, a British attaché, and the mayor of Vienna had already spoken. The attendees were a veritable who's who of Austrian and Allied military government officials, not to mention members of Carver's criminal enterprise: Emile Gruber; Schumacher, the Austrian deputy commissioner of police; and a handful of Russian brass that Mason had spotted with Carver at the fundraiser party.

True to his cover's reputation as a drinker and ladies' man, he circulated among the crowd, making as little small talk as possible while consuming ample amounts of watered-down alcohol. Apparently, his reputation had circulated among the wives and mistresses, because he'd already fended off the advances of several of the female attendees, including a jewel-laden Frau in her sixties.

Kraus completed his speech, and a scattering of applause followed. Mason used that as an opportunity to excuse himself from the Austrian councilman, and he headed for the dais to intercept Kraus. He stopped short when Flannigan crossed his path and mounted the dais.

Kraus came up to him, and they watched as Flannigan adjusted the microphone.

"I see he took your invitation seriously," Kraus said.

"He shows up just when I was beginning to think this was going to be a waste of time."

"I was watching how the ladies have flocked to you. If your current career choice doesn't work out for you, you might consider becoming a gigolo to the wealthy."

"There's always me becoming an assassin of wisecracking Austrians."

Flannigan began his speech about how corporate sponsorship is all well and good, but sources need to be vetted to prevent exploitation.

"That's amusing coming from him," Mason said.

Flannigan continued by urging foreign investors to go slow, saying that while he and others welcome democracy for Austria, he wondered if the Austrians, who followed Hitler and the Nazis to war and genocide, should be allowed self-determination before it's proven they're able to eschew their past.

"In other words," Kraus said, "go slow so they can continue to exploit my country."

Mason no longer heard what Kraus was saying, because he

spotted Laura entering the room. She wore a glittering dress of silver and sapphire that clung to her curves and picked up the color of her eyes. Heads turned as she crossed the room, and Mason never got tired of watching her and the spectacle she caused. Normally, he'd be thrilled to see her despite telling her to say away, but this time his stomach clenched with alarm.

Carver had entered just behind Laura and began making his rounds of the well-heeled guests. Two of his bodyguards came in behind him. One stood by the door while the other shadowed his boss.

Laura smiled as she approached, though it seemed strained. "Monsieur Bossart," she said. "So lovely to see you."

"The pleasure is all mine, Mademoiselle Vallier," Kraus said.

"Mr. Anderson," Laura said and stood between him and Kraus. She turned to the room and stiffened when she spotted Carver. She grabbed Mason's hand, and her nails dug into his palm.

"Easy now," Mason said to Laura in a low voice.

"Were you expecting him?" she asked.

"No, but I didn't expect half of these highfalutin, hypocritical bastards to show up."

Carver glanced at Mason several times as he shook hands and stopped to chat with a half dozen Soviet officers. The officers all beamed. It seemed incongruous that one of the Soviet officers sported a Hitler-style mustache, while another had Adolph's hair style. Obviously, they hadn't been paying attention to current events.

Like a predatory bird, Carver would alight from one group to the next, all the while keeping one eye on Mason. And with each successive guest, he closed in on Mason, Laura, and Kraus.

"It looks like he came here to see you," Kraus said out of the side of his mouth.

Carver made eye contact with Mason once again and headed their way.

"Remember," Mason said to Laura, "you're Mademoiselle Vallier."

Laura squeezed Mason's hand harder. He put up with the pain; he knew Laura was stressed to the limit and liable to strike if she wasn't able to clamp onto something.

Carver plastered on a fake smile and approached them with his hand out. "Ah, Mr. Anderson," he said. "Just the person I wanted to see."

Mason emulated Carver's smile. He freed his hand from Laura and shook Carver's. "I'm glad you decided to join us," Mason said.

Carver looked admiringly at Laura. "I wouldn't miss it. Not with so many lovely ladies in attendance." He held out his hand to her, but she didn't take it. He seemed to enjoy the tension passing between them, and he bowed instead. "And Monsieur Bossart," he said to Kraus and shook his hand. "I understand you three are like peas in a pod."

"We've all become friends," Kraus said.

He smiled indulgently at Kraus, then turned back to Mason. "And rumor has it you've been quite curious about my affairs."

Mason's ears burned, but he maintained a congenial composure. "We've been anxious to learn about the all the VIPs in Vienna, and as you are one of the most influential figures in the city, we've been hoping to speak with you about our work here."

"I, too, had my people look into your backgrounds. Astonishingly spotless records, I must say." Carver paused to peer at each one of them. "As to your work here, while the revival of Austria is a concern to all of us, I would advise you not to be too hasty. I don't believe that Austria is ready for full democracy. I propose that the U.S. and its allies maintain a strong, governing influence to counter any Soviet aggression."

"Wouldn't countering the Soviets be better achieved if Austria is allowed to form a strong democracy?" Kraus said in a combative tone.

That came off as too aggressive for Mason just when they had an opportunity to lure him in. He leaned forward to give Kraus a look of warning.

"Let us agree to disagree," Carver said to Kraus. "But what I really wanted to talk to you two about was further investment opportunities in Austria that could benefit both the Austrians and your investors." He said to Mason, "With your contacts in the U.S."—then he turned to Kraus—"and your banking friends in Switzerland, there are many attractive opportunities available in Vienna and Austria."

"Make hay while the Austrians are still on their knees?" Laura asked.

Carver gave Laura a condescending smile, but Mason noticed something carnivorous about it. Carver returned his attention to Mason. "Perhaps we could discuss this further? I'm having a dinner party next week, and I'd be pleased if you all would come."

"Yes, of course," Mason said with as much congeniality as he could muster. "We'd be delighted."

"Then it's set," Carver said. "I'll have one of my secretaries send you the details." He bowed to them and moved to the next group of dignitaries—or coconspirators.

Laura spun around to put her back to Carver, and she let out a muted growl. Mason's spine still tingled from the encounter—not from fear but from having his quarry so close and being unable to do anything about it. He was aware that Kraus moved around in front of Laura and took her hands to help calm her, but Mason focused all his attention on Carver.

A few of the attendees applauded, and Flannigan stepped off the dais and joined Carver. A pianist started playing a Gershwin melody, causing the murmurings of the guests to grow louder.

Mason came around to Laura and Kraus. "That was pretty tough," he said to Laura. "Are you okay?"

"I feel dirty," Laura said, more to herself than to Mason.

"Mason," Kraus said softly. He tilted his head in the direction of the door. Both Mason and Laura turned around to see Carver heading for the door. He shook hands as he went, like the president exiting Congress after a State of the Union address. Then, just as he was about to walk out, one of the Russian generals intercepted him and pulled him aside. They leaned in to talk in hushed tones, and Carver's expression went from genial to serious. He nodded, glanced around the room, then left with his bodyguards.

Mason took Laura's arm. "Let's see where he's going."

Laura nodded, and they started for the door.

"Wait," Kraus said. "What about me?"

"Everyone will assume that the playboy is taking his squeeze for a ride. You've got to stay and keep up appearances," Mason said.

"Next time, I get to be the playboy."

Mason and Laura walked as quickly as they could without attracting too much attention. Carver had already exited with his bodyguards in tow.

29

Mason and Laura retrieved their coats from the British private acting as the hat-check girl, exited Schönbrunn Palace, and descended the stairs to the sprawling front courtyard. Carver's sedan, followed by another containing his bodyguards, were already on their way past the British RMPs guarding the gates. Mason and Laura rushed over to their car, jumped in, and took off after them.

It took a few nerve-racking seconds to get past the palace guards, and by the time they were out on the streets, there was no sign of Carver.

"Now what?" Laura asked.

"My guess is, he's either headed for the inner city or the American zone," Mason said. He turned right and hit the accelerator. They ran parallel to the tracks leading to the Westbahnhof train station. The tracks and the station were important targets during the Allied bombing raids, so many of the buildings in the area were nothing but shells or piles of rubble. They had to change course a couple of times due to construction roadblocks, and despite pushing the car hard and staying on the main roads, they never caught sight of Carver's or the bodyguards' cars.

To get to the inner city they would have to leave the British zone and go through either the Russian zone or the French. The French was the obvious choice, and they got through the checkpoint without much bother. Mason had hoped to catch up to Carver there, since there was a bottleneck of traffic funneling through that particular checkpoint. But there was still no sign of the two sedans.

"Face it," Laura said. "We lost him. I say we go back to the hotel. I'd like to change out of this dress anyway. The thing's cutting into my ribs and irritating my burns."

As they approached a checkpoint at the ring road and the inner city, an American MP waved for them to stop. The MP scanned their IDs and the CIC passes Forester had given them. Next to them, another sedan barely hesitated, and it took only a brief glance from one of the MPs to wave the car through without checking their papers.

Mason figured it must be a VIP of some sort, and he looked over to see who it was. Hamilton Carver sat in the back. The sedan just behind his contained the two grim-looking bodyguards. That sedan was waved through as well, and both drove away at a good clip.

The MP handed Mason back his and Laura's papers and waved him through.

"Did you see that?" Laura asked.

"With both eyes, baby," Mason said and turned right onto the ring road to follow Carver's sedans.

Mason kept his distance from the sedan with Carver's guards. After several blocks, the two sedans stopped at the checkpoint to enter the American zone. Mason held back a bit to avoid stopping too close, but the same thing happened: the MPs waved the two sedans through without checking their papers.

"I get letting Carver through, but his bodyguards?" Mason said as he pulled up and showed the MP their documents.

While the MP examined their papers, Mason and Laura kept their eyes on the sedans. Both turned right after passing several smaller streets. When the MP handed back their IDs, Mason hit the accelerator, trying to catch up before they lost Carver again.

He made the same turn and caught sight of the sedans. Carver's driver seemed to be driving at a leisurely pace, though he did make a number of successive turns. Obviously, the drivers were checking for tails, and it required all of Mason's skills to not be spotted.

Finally, Carver's and the guards' sedans pulled up to a coffeehouse very near the Vienna school of medicine and the border between the American and Russian zones.

Mason cruised past them and pulled over three doors down from the coffeehouse. He and Laura used the rear- and side-view mirrors to watch Carver. The guards got out first, scanned the area, then stood on either side of their boss's sedan. Carver got out and went into the coffeehouse.

"Kind of uncharacteristic, don't you think?" Laura said. "Him patronizing an ordinary establishment, mixing with the common masses."

"I could use a coffee right now, Mademoiselle Vallier."

"Along with a Sachertorte, Mr. Anderson."

They got out of their car and strolled arm in arm, just a happy couple.

"What do you think?" Mason asked as he eyed Carver's

bodyguards, who now flanked either side of the café. "State Department guards or hired guns?"

"Hired guns. They don't look American."

"How can you tell? Just because one looks like Bluto from the Popeye cartoons?"

The comment wasn't particularly funny, but Laura tittered anyway as they walked up to the entrance and the wary guards.

Laura, smiling and giggling, pointed to the coffeehouse as if she'd just noticed it. "Let's go in here for some pastries. It looks so charming."

"Of course, darling."

A couple speaking American-accented English was certainly not out of place in the American zone, but the guards looked them up and down all the same. The happy couple paid them no mind as they entered.

The interior was larger than the typical Viennese coffeehouse in the inner city, and it bustled with customers and waiters weighed down with trays. Carver sat in a booth at the far end of the café. He was alone and talking to the waiter. Mason picked a booth closest to the entrance with a good view of Carver through the plethora of tables in the middle of the floor. As soon as they settled in, a waitress came to them. They ordered two coffees, and Laura ordered her sachertorte.

While waiting for their coffee, they took turns watching Carver. The man was looking at an Austrian newspaper while waiting for his order. Mason scanned the faces of the other customers, trying to discern the reason Carver had picked this particular café. He heard mostly English, along with a smattering of French, the majority Americans and Brits, soldiers and civilians, which meant little except that there weren't any

Russian or Austrian contacts. He looked away when Carver glanced around the room.

"We're risking him spotting us," Laura said.

"We just say that this, by coincidence, is our new favorite place."

"Even sitting this far away from him makes my skin crawl," Laura said, and she self-consciously brushed her hair with her fingers to make sure it would cover up her burn scars. She stared at the surface of their table and frowned as if her thoughts had gone elsewhere. The coffees and sachertorte arrived, which seemed to brighten her mood a bit.

Mason watched Laura attack the chocolate cake like she hadn't eaten in weeks. He then turned his attention to the crowd, the waiters circulating around, the man dressed in a cheap black suit standing at the cash register, and then the customers, who were all talking in groups or concentrating on their coffee and pastries, seemingly oblivious to the man in the distant booth.

"Now why would Carver bother to come to such a working-class establishment?" Mason asked.

"Is that a rhetorical question?" Laura asked with a mouthful of cake. "Because the answer seems obvious. He's here to make contact with someone."

"You learn quick."

"I'm a reporter, remember?" she said without looking up from her disappearing torte.

"I know you guys are all sneaky."

Laura uttered a grunt as she snagged the last bite of her torte and held up the morsel with her fork. The sight of it dangling in front of him reminded Mason he hadn't eaten in some time, and his mouth salivated.

But instead of offering it to him, Laura popped it in her mouth and feigned shock. "Sorry, did you want a bite?"

"Sneaky."

The waiter crossing on the other side of the room caught Mason's eye. The man was different from the one who had taken Carver's order. This new waiter made a beeline to Carver's table and set a coffee and a tray of cookies down in front of him. It was very quick and subtle, and Carver tried to use a couple crossing in front as cover, but Mason spied him snatching the linen napkin and slipping it into the inside pocket of his suit coat.

Mason's gaze swept to the waiters' station and the bar, but the waiter had disappeared through the swinging door. "I'll be right back."

He got up and headed for what he assumed was the door for the kitchen. He kept his face away from Carver as he crossed the room. He pushed open the door and took one step inside.

Someone from behind asked, "Can I help you, sir? That's for employees only."

Mason ignored the man and scanned the kitchen. There were two cooks and Carver's first waiter, but not the one who had brought the tray of cookies.

The man tapped on his shoulder. "Please, sir—"

Mason pushed through the door and strode up to one of the two cooks. The man looked frightened at Mason's aggressive approach.

"There was another waiter who came in here a moment ago. Where'd he go?"

Puzzled by the question and by his manager's continued tapping on Mason's shoulder, he said, "You mean Felix?"

"If he's the one who came in here and disappeared, then yeah."

"Sir," the manager barked. He came around to face Mason. "You are not allowed in here or to question my cooks." He pointed his index finger at the cook. "Andre, you will say nothing."

Mason kept his glare on the cook, prompting the man to blurt out, "It was the end of his shift, and he just left." The cook pointed to the back door.

Mason shifted his intimidating glare to the manager, who took a step back in fear. Mason growled, "Sorry, looking for the bathroom."

The manager jabbed his finger at the swinging door. "That way. The narrow hall in the back corner."

Mason did an about-face and exited the kitchen. At that same moment, Carver was walking out of the café. The two bodyguards peeled off from the doorway and escorted Carver to his car. Mason hooked around to the other side of the room and passed Carver's table. The man hadn't touched the coffee or cookies. The napkin was gone, as was the newspaper.

He returned to Laura and laid some money on the table. "Come on, we're getting out of here."

Laura finished a sip of her coffee and rose from the table. "Where are we off to in such a hurry?" she asked as she put on her overcoat.

"I think I just saw a way Carver is being passed documents."

Laura instinctively looked at Carver's empty booth. "The waiter?"

Mason nodded and led Laura straight for the swinging door. They pushed through, ignoring the shouts from the manager. The cooks stopped what they were doing and stepped back to let them pass and exit the back door.

They were in an alleyway, and Mason just caught sight of the waiter turning right at the end of the alley. They hurried to the corner and turned in the same direction. The waiter wore a brown overcoat over his five-foot-eleven frame. He was lean, in his midforties, and walked at a fast pace. The man crossed the street, giving Mason a decent look at his face, which was round and chinless, with thick eyebrows and a seemingly permanent five-o'clock shadow.

"What do you plan to do when we catch up to him?" Laura asked.

"I just want to see where he's going," Mason said and quickened his pace.

The waiter crossed the street again and got into a Mercedes that was idling at the corner. Mason tried to see the driver or anyone else in the car, but daylight reflected off the glass and obscured his view. It looked like the driver wore a military cap, but he couldn't tell from which country.

He stopped, prompting Laura to do the same. "Did you get a look at who was waiting in the car?"

"Just the driver, and a man waiting in the back. Both were in uniform."

"It's time to have a talk with the manager."

Mason and Laura turned to see a man standing right behind them. Laura let out a yelp of surprise, and Mason shoved his hand in his pocket to go for his gun. A split second later, his face registered. It was Bauer.

"What the hell are you doing here?" Mason asked.

"I should ask you the same thing," Bauer said. "You have orders not to follow Carver."

"We stopped by for a coffee, then Carver just happened to come in," Laura said. "We followed a man we thought might be one of his contacts, but it turned out we were wrong."

Mason kept his stern expression, but he smiled on the inside at Laura's adept lying.

"And what's your story?" Mason asked Bauer.

"It was my job to keep an eye on Carver. One of my agents called me to tell me he was in the coffeehouse, but I only got here just as Carver was leaving. Then I heard the manager yelling about an intruder in the kitchen, and I came out to see what was going on."

Bauer's reason sounded plausible, but Mason had the impression he was lying just as adeptly as Laura.

Bauer must have seen something in Mason's probing gaze, because his expression flashed through several changes, from smug to sheepishness before turning hostile. "You two get out of here before I call Forester and tell him you violated his strict orders."

Mason continued to stare at Bauer until he felt Laura tug on his arm. Reluctantly, he let Laura guide him around Bauer and back in the direction of their car. After they'd gone a few yards, Mason pulled away from Laura's grasp and retraced their steps back to the end of the alleyway. He looked around the corner and saw Bauer going through the back door to the coffeehouse's kitchen.

When Laura came up to his side, Mason said, "Remind me to keep him at arm's length from now on."

30

Mason parked the car on Kärntnerstrasse a block down from the hotel. He got out, as did Laura. They remained silent while entering the hotel, crossing the lobby, and taking the elevator. Mason asked for the fifth floor. Laura said nothing.

They exited the elevator, and Mason said, "Your room is on this floor?"

"We're not done talking."

"Okay. My room, then."

They went to Mason's room and entered. Mason went straight for the desk, which held several bottles of alcohol.

"I'm going to have a drink," he said. "Can I pour you something?"

Laura stopped in the middle of the room and crossed her arms. "I thought we were going to talk."

"We are," he said as he poured two fingers of scotch in a glass. "No reason we can't do both."

Laura huffed in exasperation but said, "I'll take the same."

Mason poured scotch into a second glass and walked over

to her. When she took the glass, Mason noticed her hand shook slightly.

He held up his glass. “Just what the doctor ordered.”

They clinked glasses and took a sip. Laura was putting on a brave face. She’d been through a lot, and Mason could tell she was still wound tight from being so close to her husband’s murderer.

“It’s almost seven,” Mason said. “What do you say I call room service and order up some dinner?”

“We talk, then eat,” Laura said.

“I order, we talk, and by the time we’re done, our dinners will be here.”

“Plying me with alcohol and a candlelit dinner?”

“Mademoiselle Vallier, I wouldn’t presume.”

“As long as we’ve got that straight, go ahead.”

Mason called room service and ordered two steak dinners and a bottle of wine. He sat on the bed and pulled out the piece of paper they’d found at Wentworth’s. Instead of sitting on the bed next to him, Laura pulled up a chair and turned Mason’s hand so they could both examine the coded message.

“I noticed you didn’t tell Bauer or Forester about what we found,” Laura said.

“Didn’t I?” Mason said, feigning innocence. “I must have been distracted.”

Laura gave him a skeptical look. “Neither one of us is a code breaker, but I’m glad you held it back.”

“I’ve had some experience in ciphers from my time in army intelligence. And I cracked the code in Garmisch that got us into this trouble to begin with.”

“Okay, genius, what’s it about?”

“First, I’m sure they passed coded messages back and forth

all the time. So, what was in the message that made Wentworth feel he had to hide it away from everything else?"

"He was the head of the military government's political arm. That involved politicians from Austria and the Allied powers. Maybe a secret meeting. A time and place?"

"He could easily memorize something like that." Mason studied the symbols on the paper. "It doesn't seem to be a very sophisticated code. My guess is, you match up the numbers and Roman numerals with a text that spells out a message. So, all we have to do is figure out what text was used to encode the message."

"The text could be from a book," Laura said. "The Bible being the most obvious." She got up from her chair and opened the bedside table drawer. She shut it again. "That'd be too easy."

"Even if there were a Bible in there, it'd be in German. In fact, the text—if my theory about this code is correct—could be in German. Even in Russian."

They both fell silent. Mason assumed Laura was doing the same as he: contemplating the seemingly impossible task of determining which language and text might solve the code.

"It has to be a text all the players have in common."

"We have to start somewhere." Mason got up and called room service again and asked that they send up a Bible with the dinner order. When he hung up, he said, "That'll get them guessing what we plan to do with a Bible over a steak dinner." He turned and noticed Laura pouring another two fingers into Mason's glass, and then she did the same for herself. Her hand still had a slight tremor, and he was beginning to think the day's events were not the only cause.

He walked up close to her. They stared at each other for a

long moment. Mason gently took the glass out of her hand and put it on the bedside table. His hands didn't shake, but his heart pounded in his chest. Slowly he leaned in and kissed her on the lips. Though she breathed rapidly, she kept her hands at her sides. But then she kissed back, and they wrapped their arms tight around each other. Mason's head spun with a flurry of emotions, while the rest of him turned hot with passion. Laura choked back a tear and held him even tighter.

Someone knocked on the door and said, "Room service."

They broke their embrace. Laura turned away, embarrassed and seemingly confused. She said nothing as Mason went to the door, checked the hallway through the peephole, then opened it. A man in a black-and-white uniform entered with a rolling tray and began to set up the dinner on the table by the window.

Mason looked at Laura, but she only stared at the door. The man finished, and Mason tipped him. The man left, gently closing the door behind him. They were alone again.

"I shouldn't have let you do that," Laura said.

Mason searched for the right thing to say but failed to find it.

Laura avoided looking at him. "Let's just eat." She sat at the table.

Mason joined her. "I guess we'll save the bottle of wine for another time."

Laura muttered a yes and begin to cut at the steak.

They ate for a while, then Laura said, "What's next?"

"Laura, I know you lost your husband—"

"Hold it right there. I meant what should we do next in our search for Valerius? I say we go after the waiter at the coffee-house and see what he has to tell us."

Mason nodded. "He and that note are our only leads."

A quiet moment passed between them, then Laura said, "I still have feelings for you, but I need time. I haven't been able to bury my husband or mourn his death properly."

"I understand."

"Good," she said, putting her napkin on the table and rising from the chair. "I'm not hungry anymore."

Mason got up and walked her to the door. He opened it for her. "I'll see you in the morning?"

Laura nodded and left. Mason watched her move down the hallway before closing the door. He strode over to the table and took one more bite of his steak. He then put his pistol in the shoulder holster, donned his overcoat, and walked out the door.

Mason locked the hotel room door and turned toward the elevator, when he saw Kraus staring at him. Kraus stood in the hall by his door and wore his overcoat. He had his hands on his hips and a frown on his face as if he'd just caught a child trying to sneak out of the house.

"Where are you going?" Kraus asked.

"Out," Mason said and headed for the elevators.

Kraus caught up to him. "I heard Laura leave your room and just knew you couldn't sit still without wreaking havoc somewhere."

They stopped at the elevator door, and Mason pushed the button.

"Why do you insist on doing these things alone? I'm here to help."

"Haven't you been busy with the police commissioner and Gruber?"

"Bauer came by looking for you, and he told me of your

and Laura's encounter with Carver. I knew that would make you do something you'd regret later."

"I get enough of that talk from Laura. You can't come with me."

The elevator bell sounded, and the door opened. Mason stepped in, and Kraus entered right behind him. Mason stared at the door as the operator pulled the lever for the ground floor, and Kraus stared at Mason.

Moments later the operator announced the lobby floor, and both got out. Kraus kept on Mason's heels through the lobby and out the door. Mason paused outside and checked the street for anyone watching, then he headed for the car. Kraus kept silent while remaining at Mason's side. Mason unlocked the driver's side door and got in. Kraus stood at the passenger's door and tried to open it, but it was locked. "Open the door."

Mason ignored him as he started the car's engine and put it in gear.

"I'm not letting go," Kraus said loud enough for Mason to hear.

With a groan of frustration, Mason leaned over and unlocked the passenger door. Kraus got in and gave Mason a satisfied grin.

"You're going to come along without knowing what I plan to do?" Mason said, more as an accusation than a question.

"I've got your back. That's all you need to know."

"Okay, but you better hold on tight, 'cause you're not going to like what you see."

Mason hit the accelerator.

31

The last three customers left the coffeehouse, all Americans, one man and two women. The man cracked jokes, and the women chuckled halfheartedly. Mason dismissed them, noncombatants in this personal war of his. He stood in a dark doorway across the street. Kraus stood next to him. Traffic passed on the main street at the intersection to his left and was busy for ten p.m.

The coffeehouse, being the only establishment on the small street, made for a quiet place to wait. He could see his target through the window—Felix, the waiter who passed something to Carter. Felix wiped down the tables and put the chairs on top, while the manager counted the money in the register, and another waiter started mopping the floor.

"I wonder if you could move over a little," Kraus whispered to Mason. "This doorway is pretty small."

Mason slid over. "I didn't ask for you to come."

"Don't start that again."

Mason saw the wisdom in not going around in circles with

their argument and decided to change the subject. "Where are you with the police commissioner and Gruber?"

"Gruber is always trying to cook up one banking scheme or another. I'm not biting, so he's not saying much. The commissioner, on the other hand, told me in confidence that they know someone is getting too close to the top of the organization, and it's making them nervous—"

Kraus stopped when Mason put a hand on his shoulder to quiet him. Footsteps approached them. The person tread lightly, the pace quick, and walked on the balls of their feet. He knew that walk anywhere.

Mason stepped out in front of Laura. Her expression remained neutral, though instinctively she did take a half step back.

"Jesus, what are you doing here?" Mason growled.

"I knew you'd do something like this, so I grabbed a taxi and followed you."

There was some movement near the coffeehouse window, and Mason pulled her back into the doorway in the shadows.

Kraus made himself as small as he could and tipped his hat. "Mrs. Talbot."

"Herr Kraus," Laura said.

"Well, ain't this cozy," Mason said with resentment in his tone.

"Stop whining," Laura said.

"This isn't a stakeout, it's a jamboree."

"I knew you'd try to slip out on me."

"I was going to make sure he stayed out of trouble," Kraus said.

"I appreciate that, Peter, but he's more likely to get you into trouble than you keeping him out of it."

Mason shushed them both when he saw Felix slip on his overcoat. The waiter said something to his coworkers and stepped out, locking the door behind him. Before departing, he scanned the street.

Mason, Laura, and Kraus pulled back further into the shadows. Mason noted Felix's vigilance, the first hint he was more than a mere waiter. Felix paused at the doorway. He put on his homburg hat and gloves while tilting his head as if sensing his surroundings. He then proceeded to his left and walked with a sure gait.

Mason waited until the waiter had a fifty-foot lead, then said, "Laura, you stick with me, and Peter, you stay on this side of the street and keep a parallel course."

The three of them crossed the street and matched Felix's pace. Mason had parked his car at the bottom of the street. If he timed it right, they could get the waiter in the car without much difficulty.

So far, the waiter seemed confident enough to not look behind him. If the guy got spooked and bolted, there wouldn't be much use in running after him. Mason had one chance. He closed the gap, keeping his right hand in his overcoat pocket and on the pistol while he found the blackjack with his left. He motioned for Laura to get behind him.

A car turned onto the street and passed them. Mason used the noise to increase his speed. The waiter turned the corner, and Mason was right behind. He pulled out his pistol and turned the corner.

A zip of fabric, a blur of motion, and Mason's jaw exploded with pain. Quick hands grabbed at Mason's gun. Then several blows with a nightstick disarmed him. With a whoosh, the nightstick struck the side of his head. Stunned, he stumbled back.

Kraus was on Felix and tried to pin his arms, but Felix had a thirty-pound advantage. The man jerked out of the hold and brought the nightstick down on Kraus's arm. Kraus cried out in pain. The waiter kicked Kraus in the chest, and he flew backward, slamming into a car, then dropping to his knees.

Laura cried out from a blow, enraging Mason, and despite the shock from the blows of the nightstick, he attacked. The waiter swung his nightstick, but Mason dodged it.

Both men threw blows and blocked fists, until Felix froze.

Laura had her revolver jammed in Felix's neck. "Drop the stick and get on your knees."

Felix dropped the stick, but instead of dropping to his knees, he yelled, "Help!"

Mason swiped the blackjack across the back of Felix's skull. The waiter went down to the pavement and barely moved.

"Are you okay?" Mason asked Laura.

She nodded. "He got me with that stick across my stomach. It just knocked the wind out of me."

Mason looked over at Kraus, who held his arm and looked to be in pain.

"I think he broke my arm."

With moves practiced countless times, Mason quickly handcuffed the man and pulled a hood over his head. With Laura's help, they hoisted the waiter and rushed over to Mason's car. Fortunately, the Buick's trunk was large enough to accommodate a small village, so with a little folding, the waiter fit easily.

Mason glanced around to see if there were any witnesses,

while Laura helped Kraus get into the front passenger's seat. She got in back, and Mason got behind the wheel and took off.

"We should get Peter to the hospital," Laura said.

"No," Kraus said. "I'll be fine. We do what we came here to do, then I'll go."

"It's your decision," Laura said. "But if it gets worse, we drop everything and get you to a doctor." She looked at Mason in the rearview mirror. "Where are we taking him?"

"I've got a nice cozy spot already picked out."

32

"I know this looks bad," Mason said to Laura and Kraus, "but I'm not going to hurt him too much, okay? I might rough him up, but that's it. So, I don't want either of you to call out or scream. If it gets too much for you, then walk away to another part of the basement."

Laura stood some distance from Mason and his captive. She had a hard time looking in his direction, but she nodded. Kraus sat on a chunk of concrete that had fallen from the upper floor. He looked pale but otherwise fine. He, too, nodded his assent.

Mason walked over to Felix. He patted the waiter's cheek, and the man stirred. Felix was blindfolded and strung up by his wrists with the rope tied around an exposed cement beam in the basement of a bomb-damaged building. The waiter flinched and immediately struggled with his bonds. He growled through the gag across his mouth. His rapid breathing created clouds of vapor in the cold air.

"I was worried you wouldn't wake up," Mason said. He strolled over to a large chunk of falling concrete and sat.

Beside him was a small fire, and within was a broken piece of steel rebar heated to crimson red.

Mason held up the ID card he'd found in the man's wallet. "Felix Egger. But that's not your real name, is it?" he said in English. "And I know you're not just a waiter. You couldn't have learned those fighting moves in the war. Not as an ordinary foot soldier anyway. Perhaps an Abwehr Brandenburger?"

Egger tried to maintain a stoic expression, though Mason detected a tick of recognition when he mentioned the Nazis' special forces unit.

"Now, Felix, I'm going to ask you a series of questions, and I'd appreciate honest and direct answers. Since you're blindfolded, I'll describe the scene a little. We're in the basement of a bombed-out hotel. I'm sitting next to a fire, and there's a steel rod in there that's heating up nicely. I hope I don't have to use it, but I'm determined to get some answers out of you. Are you with me so far?"

Egger said nothing. The only sounds where the crackling fire and Egger's labored breathing. Mason uses a wad of cloth to pick up the metal rod. He walked over to Egger and held it close to the man's face. Egger recoiled once he felt the heat. He renewed his struggles against the ropes as he sucked in air.

"I asked if you're with me so far."

Egger nodded once.

"The war is over, Felix," Mason said as he returned the rod to the fire. "Any information you give me won't betray your country. It won't tarnish your honor. I want you to think about that." He stepped up to Egger and got in close to his face. "You're a waiter, and I'm sure they pay you pennies. What have you got to gain by holding back information? Whoever is paying you won't give a damn whether you live or die. You're expendable, a waste product." Mason paused to let that sink in. "Now I'm going to pull off the gag. If you scream or yell out, no one's going to hear it. But most importantly, doing either will get me very upset. Do you understand?"

Egger nodded again. Mason untied the gag and pulled out the cloth jammed in his mouth.

Between gulps of air, Egger asked, "What do you want?"

"No, no, no, I'm asking the questions. All I want to hear from you are answers. For example, I saw you passing information to Hamilton Carver. Who gave it to you?"

"I don't know what you are talking about."

Mason hit Egger in the stomach hard enough to cause pain but not enough to rupture his organs. Egger writhed and sputtered as he fought to recover.

Mason looked over to Laura and Kraus, and both looked squeamish. He put his index finger to his lips to remind them not to make a sound.

"I'm sure you've been trained to withstand torture, as I have, but everyone breaks. Sure, you might resist the pain for a while, but to what end? Why don't we bypass all that nonsense? You tell me what I want to know, and I'll let you go. Eventually."

"Do you think I'm stupid? Once you have what you want, you'll kill me."

"No, I won't. I promise. But if you don't give me what I want, I'll leave you hanging here until you freeze to death. This building's condemned. No one will find you. At least not before it's too late. Now, who passed the intelligence to you to give to Carver?"

Egger hesitated. Mason got out his knife, moved around to Egger's back and sliced open the man's shirt. After a few more cuts, he ripped off the tattered shirt, leaving Egger naked from the waist up. Laura flinched. Egger shuddered, and Mason felt sure it was from fear and not from the cold.

In a short, sharp jab, Mason used the knuckle of his middle finger to punch the nest of nerves just below the waiter's sternum.

Egger's mouth popped open as he tried to breathe. To no avail. Punching that grouping of nerves paralyzed his chest muscles and diaphragm. He shook against the bonds. A moment later the paralysis subsided, and he sucked in air.

"I'll ask you again—"

"I don't know!" Egger yelled. "I've never heard his name. You think the man is going to tell me who he is just before handing me stolen documents?"

At least one thing was confirmed—he did pass stolen documents to Carver.

"Describe him," Mason said. "Russian? Did he wear a uniform? Any distinctive traits?"

Egger hesitated.

"Come on, Felix, if you're telling the truth, and you don't know him, then describing him won't give me much. Are you refusing because *you're* the Russian spy?"

"I hate the Russians. They raped my mother, my sister, when Vienna fell."

Now we're getting somewhere, Mason thought.

"But despite your hatred of Russians, you still accepted something from one of them to pass on to Carver. That means you work for Carver."

Egger said nothing, but his silence told Mason he guessed correctly.

"Describe the man," Mason said.

"I can't."

"You can't or you won't?"

Again, Egger said nothing.

Mason marched over to the heated rod and brought it back to his captive. He hovered the rod near the man's face. It was only for an instant, but it was hot enough to drive the man to recoil as far as the bindings would allow.

"Burning your face or torso is a waste of time," Mason said. "If you don't give me what I want, this thing goes up your ass. You hear me?"

Egger burst out, "I don't know his name. Tall, clean-cut. Maybe midthirties. Black hair. No uniform, just regular clothes. I have no idea if he's Russian because he never says anything. I swear."

Mason had led enough interrogations to sense that Egger was telling the truth. "Is he the only one passing on intelligence or messages?"

Egger stopped breathing. His muscles tensed, as he prepared himself for pain.

Mason leaned close to the waiter's ear. "One thing you have to realize, Felix. I lose everything if I don't get results fast. I will die. That's why I won't stop. I'm a desperate man, and desperate men will do anything. Do you understand? You will either live through the night reasonably intact, or you'll end up a broken man, but I will extract everything I need from you."

Mason paused to let that sink in. "Is this courier the only one passing on information or messages?"

Egger shuddered again. The skin on his torso fluttered like that of a horse in reaction to a fly. Mason knew well that the anticipation of pain could be worse than the pain itself. He was tortured relentlessly by a sadistic Nazi SS officer. He could still remember the agony, the fear, the helplessness. Those memories brought up acidic bile to his throat. And despite his playacting as the torturer, his abdomen squirmed.

He looked over at Laura, and she stared at him with a look of horror in her eyes. She turned and walked away.

Egger said, “Yes, there are others.”

Mason said nothing; silence was sometimes the best way to get them to talk.

“Mr. Carver owns the coffeehouse,” Egger said. “He, his lieutenants, any business contacts, suppliers and buyers, exchange information and messages.” He turned his head to try to face Mason, though he missed the mark, instead looking at Mason’s shoulder. “But I don’t know what’s in them. I pass stuff around, do some small jobs for him. That’s all.”

“General Flannigan or Emile Gruber?”

“Both, I think. A couple of times. Occasionally a British or French officer. That’s all I know. If you wanted more, you picked the wrong man.”

“What are the small jobs you do for Carver?”

The waiter’s face twitched just slightly but enough to tell Mason the man was about to lie.

“What kind of jobs, Felix?”

“Nothing important. Get his wife flowers. Pick up his clothes at the tailor’s.”

“You’re lying.”

Egger started panting again and licked his lips. He might be a good soldier, but he was a lousy liar.

“Packages, messages, money? Drugs?”

“I’m just a waiter,” Egger said, his voice turning to begging. “I do what they tell me.”

"You're allowed to pass on the messages in the coffeehouse. Carver trusts you. Trusts you enough to handle important—not to mention incriminating—information. Your small jobs are as a courier—"

"He must have dozens of couriers."

"No, Felix. A man in his position can't afford to risk too many hands on his secrets. He chose you to handle his Soviet packages. When's your next job? What are you carrying?"

He clamped his mouth closed and shook his head violently. He braced again for more pain.

"I'm running out of patience," Mason said. "Why don't we just cut to the real stuff?" He stuffed the cloth in Egger's mouth, then put the gag back in place. "I don't want to listen to you scream."

He used his knife to cut Felix's belt, then yanked his pants and underpants off and tossed them aside. With another length of rope, he tied a knot around Egger's ankle, wrapped the other end around a vertical beam, and pulled. Egger's left leg stretched sideways, leaving him to prop himself on the toes of his right foot. Mason repeated the process, attaching and pulling on another rope, causing Egger's right leg to stretch in the opposite direction. Now he dangled by his wrists.

Egger screamed through the gag. He shook almost to the point of convulsing.

Mason walked up to him and said in his ear, "This is going to really hurt." He moved around behind Egger, grabbed one butt cheek and pushed it to the side. "You'll survive this, but you'll be shitting in a bag the rest of your life."

Egger tried to yell out something through the gag. It seemed he was trying to say something, which was good enough for Mason; he had no intention of following through with such a brutal act.

Mason let go of Egger's butt cheek, then yanked down on the gag and pulled out the wad of cloth.

Egger kept repeating, "Please, don't. Please, don't."

"Then talk!"

"Tomorrow night, 2200. I'm taking something from Mr. Carver to a Russian courier."

"Where's the meeting?"

Egger growled through his humiliation.

"Where is the meeting, Felix?" Mason yelled.

"Stadtpark, by the east side of the lake."

"Where's the package?"

"I don't have it. Someone is to pass it to me in the plaza in front of Karlskirche."

"Who?"

"I don't know." Tears leaked beneath Egger's blindfold. "Please." He shivered uncontrollably.

Mason had enough. Nausea bubbled up from his guts. A primitive part of his psyche urged him to kill and bury Egger just to get rid of the source of his shame and guilt. Instead, he blew past Kraus and walked away into a far, dark corner of the wrecked basement and sat on a pile of rubble where he, too, shook.

33

By Mason's reckoning, it was close to five a.m. when he parked the Buick a block away from the Bristol Hotel. He switched off the engine and sat for a moment, rubbing the exhaustion from his eyes. Or maybe to rub away the visions from the evening.

Laura and Kraus had remained silent the entire way back, and neither of them moved. Mason felt their eyes on him, and he felt ashamed, then angry, wanting to yell at them that he'd warned them.

Finally, Laura and Kraus made moves to exit the car. Mason forced his hands to release the steering wheel and reached for the door handle. Just then, a black sedan came from the opposite direction and made a hard stop beside his door. Mason instinctively went for his pistol. He stopped when he saw Forester was behind the wheel.

Mason rolled down the window. "What the hell—" He stopped when he saw Forester's grim expression.

"Follow me," Forester said. "All of you." With that, he took off.

Laura and Kraus got back into the car, and Mason started the engine and made a U-turn to follow. Forester drove fast, but not so much that they would attract attention. They left the inner city and crossed into the American zone. Forester made so many turns and double-backs that Mason wasn't sure exactly where they were, except that they kept going deeper into the American zone and the outlying reaches of Vienna's suburbs.

Forester finally pulled into a short driveway leading to an isolated house near a bomb-damaged rail line and the Hernals cemetery. They both parked in the gravel courtyard in front of the house. Mason, Laura, and Kraus got out, but Forester said nothing as he made a beeline for the front door.

Once there, Forester did a visual sweep before opening the door and entering. Laura, Mason, and Kraus followed. Forester turned on a floor lamp, revealing a shabbily furnished living room.

Forester noticed Kraus supporting his arm and asked, "What happened to you?"

"I fell. I think I broke it."

Forester gave Kraus a skeptical look, then glowered at all of them. "Where have all of you been?"

"Out," Laura said.

Forester was about to say something but then appeared to change his mind. "Forget I asked," he said. "I don't want to know. Whatever the reason, it was better that you all weren't at the hotel. They might have picked you up otherwise."

"What are you talking about?" Mason asked. "Who was going to take us?"

"CID and Kovack from the Central Intelligence Group," Forester said.

"If this is about Carver—"

"It's not. The last batch of Soviet documents Carver received had a communiqué saying that you, Mason, are passing on intelligence to the Russians. They want Kraus and Laura for questioning. They're floating a possible conspiracy charge against them."

"That's crazy. I told you about being contacted by Konstantin. But I sure as hell didn't give him any information."

"According to the internal Soviet chatter, you have."

"It's a setup. Carver planted that to get rid of me. He must know I'm after him."

"That'd be a pretty elaborate ruse. Why not just have you killed like he has all his other enemies?"

"The only explanation is that he knows I'm working for you. Killing me would create too much of a headache. This is cleaner."

"How would he know that?"

"It's obvious, isn't it? Someone on your team must be feeding him information."

"Now you're sounding desperate."

Mason wanted to hit something. "That bastard dies. This is all a load of crap." He looked at Forester. "Did you bring us here so your boys can pick us up?"

"Mason," Laura said. "Mike is risking his career getting us away from the hotel and to somewhere safe."

"For some stupid reason, buddy, I believe you," Forester said. "The problem is CID brass, my superiors, and CIG think otherwise. You've already admitted to being in contact with Konstantin, and that he offered information on Valerius in exchange for spying for him. You were seen getting into his car several days ago, and the communiqué mentions you being turned while you were in prison."

"I didn't cooperate, even when he threatened to have me killed or sent to a gulag. I only escaped that fate because I escaped the prison."

"If your theory is true, how would Carver know you've been talking to Konstantin?"

"Because someone on our side leaked that information."

"Sir," Kraus said, "I have been with Mason since his time in that prison, and I can vouch for his character. I'm sure all of us here can."

Forester thought for a moment, then said, "It's a shaky theory, but a possibility. I'll look into it."

"You do that," Mason said.

"In the meantime, I'll take Kraus to get his arm looked at. You and Laura stay put. Only I know about this place, so you'll be safe here for now, until I can convince them it's a ploy to put you out of action."

"*If* you can convince them."

Forester fell silent for a moment, then looked at his watch. "It's after six. I better get out of here. But first, I need a drink."

"You've got booze in here?" Mason asked.

As Forester walked over to a corner cabinet, he said, "I use this place sometimes to get away."

"You mean to entertain young ladies."

"I take the fifth."

Mason and Kraus joined him at the cabinet, and Forester poured them both large portions of whiskey.

"You know when Mike said it's after six, he meant morning," Laura said to Mason.

"It's a bracer for the shit day I'm about to have."

"And I need something to ease the pain," Kraus said. "Not to mention last night."

"In that case," Laura said, "I'll join you."

Forester poured a whiskey for Laura. They all clinked glasses and drank. Mason didn't stop until he consumed the whole thing.

"You didn't answer my question earlier," Forester said as he looked at the three of them. "Where were you?"

Mason looked at Laura and Kraus while he considered his response. Neither of them looked ready to stop him, so he said to Forester, "We picked up a waiter from a coffeehouse and took him someplace where he and I could have a conversation."

"What waiter?" Forester asked. "Do I need another drink before I hear this?"

"Laura and I followed Carver yesterday—" He held up his hand to quiet Forester. "He showed up unexpectedly at the conference and made a point to let me know he was looking into us. Then he left after speaking surreptitiously to a Russian general. I got curious, so we decided to follow him. We tracked him to that coffeehouse on Hahngasse and witnessed a waiter passing him something in a napkin. Something Carver took pains to hide. We were pretty sure of it then, and I know for sure now, that's how the Soviet operative is passing on secrets to Carver. Right under everyone's noses."

Forester's face twisted in anger. "And you two just forgot to tell me?"

"Sorry, Mike, we should have. But the point is, we know one place Carver gets his intelligence."

"And that helps us how?"

"It turns out, Carver owns the coffeehouse," Mason said.

"And according to the waiter, he and his cronies use the place to pass information back and forth, make deals, and relay instructions for his operations."

"That'd be great intel if we didn't have hands-off orders for him from the higher-ups. As long as he's giving our side useful intelligence, then that coffeehouse is a no-go zone."

Laura cleared her throat. "Uh, well, one of those waiters is who Mason persuaded to talk."

Forester glared at Mason. "God dammit, Mason. You disobeyed direct orders."

"Before you burst an artery, I got something else. This waiter, a Felix Egger, runs errands and does pickups for Carver."

"That's not enough to get you off my shit list."

"When did that happen?"

"About thirty seconds ago."

"Then get your eraser ready: the waiter is to rendezvous with a Soviet contact and pass on something from Carver."

Forester stared at Mason as he pondered. "Could be drugs. Could be money."

"Whatever it is, we need to find out what."

"When? Where?"

"I'm not going to tell you."

"You what?"

"I'm going to do it, and I don't want you sending your boys over there, or for you to feel a sense of duty and pass it on to Kovack. *You're* under the hands-off order, and as an army officer, you have to obey them. I don't."

"Don't give me that pile of crap," Forester said.

"Plus, there's someone in your group giving Carver the heads-up."

"We don't know that."

"You want to risk it?"

Forester didn't have an answer.

"Laura and I will go," Mason said and looked at Laura for confirmation.

Laura stood and stepped up next to Mason in a defiant gesture.

Mason looked at a deflated Kraus. "Peter, you're not going to be much use with your arm in a sling."

"You can't keep me out of this. I can help."

"He could act as another lookout," Laura said.

"I'm certainly not the only man in Vienna with his arm in a sling," Kraus said. "Karlsplatz is a big space. You'll need me as a third to cover that amount of area."

"You'll need at least four to pull this off," Forester said.

Mason smiled. "You're on." He turned to Kraus. "You, too, if you don't have any complications with your arm."

Forester finished his drink. "That means I should get him to a doctor. Then I'd better show up at headquarters before anyone wonders where I've been."

Forester and Kraus started to leave, when Mason said to Forester, "Oh, I left the waiter, Felix, tied up in the basement of the bombed-out hotel on Saltztorgasse. The one near the river."

Forester nodded. "I'll pick him up and keep him under wraps."

Forester started to go again, but Mason said, "Mike." Forester turned, and Mason added, "Thanks."

Forester said to Laura, "Try to keep him out of trouble until tonight, will you?"

Mason watched Forester and Kraus leave, then he turned to pour another drink. Laura put her hand on his glass.

"You've already had the equivalent of three drinks. I need you to be at least semiconscious."

Without looking at her, Mason pulled the glass out from under her hand and poured another two fingers. He walked over to the sofa and sat, then leaned his head back onto the cushions.

Laura sat on the other side of the sofa. "What's gotten into you? Ever since I got here you've been more sullen than I've ever seen you."

Mason said nothing and took another sip.

"You tormented that man to get what you wanted."

"I saw your face last night while I was doing it. I'm afraid I lost you."

"That display upset me, yes, but I was more worried you've stepped over the line so many times that you won't find your way back again."

Mason raised his glass to her. "Here's to you becoming a fine shrinker of heads." He took another sip of whiskey.

"I know you, Mason. It doesn't take much imagination to figure out what you're thinking." She slid a little closer and turned to face him. "You did it for me, for us. For all the people in your life that Valerius has taken away from you."

"The day you arrived I'd just stabbed a man to death," Mason said. He couldn't look at Laura and stared straight ahead. "I did it face to face. It felt like murder for the first time in my life."

Laura looked away, and they sat in silence for a moment. Finally, she said, "What would've happened if you did let him live?"

"He would have reported me to his Soviet superiors. He would have blown my cover, forcing me to run or get thrown back in the prison. Or worse."

"You did what you needed to survive. I for one am glad you're here with me. That you'd do anything to stop this evil man from killing more innocent people. Given the chance, I'd kill him with my bare hands."

"No, you wouldn't. It would haunt you. I still see the faces of the people I killed."

"How about the faces of the people you saved?" Laura asked. "The ones you protected from harm?" She got up and knelt on the sofa and leaned in close. "This is the face of someone you saved and loved."

Laura took the glass from Mason's hand and placed it on the coffee table, then kissed him. He pulled her in and kissed her firmly. Warmth flooded over him, and he forgot everything but the touch of her soft lips and her body pressing into his. She guided him down to the sofa cushions with her, and they embraced, kissing and touching. In the heat of passion, Mason tugged at her clothes. His need for a connection, his need for release, overwhelmed him.

She stopped him and gently pulled his hands away. Then she undressed him slowly, and he did the same for her. They made love, never leaving the sofa. Mason never felt so alive as he did then. Danger was all around them, but he didn't care. For a while, he could forget.

34

Sunday evening's mass had just finished, and the worshipers emerged from Karlskirche and filed out onto the broad, circular plaza of Karlsplatz. Mason leaned against a tree at the southwestern edge of the park that bordered the western side of the plaza. The throngs of people made it difficult to spot anyone who might be there with the intention of passing on stolen documents.

The plaza and the park were the premier places for black marketeers, and where Mason had first come to pick up Valerius's scent by following the drug dealer. Adding to the chaos of the plaza, a covey of black marketeers and a handful of prostitutes emerged from the shadows of the park and mingled with the churchgoers in an attempt to sell their wares. A few Russian soldiers and police wandered the area in twos and threes, but they seemed more interested in the bargains than policing. The courier had chosen the perfect time and place for a clandestine exchange.

Mason carried a briefcase, which according to Felix, he was to set on the ground, shake hands with the courier—

whoever that was. Then, after a brief conversation, he was to pick up the opposite case. The courier would know Felix by sight, which put Mason at a disadvantage. He had donned Egger's brown overcoat and homburg hat, and they did have a similar build, but the similarities ended there. Mason hoped to get a good look at the courier before the man got close enough to spot the ruse.

Mason was counting on Forester or Laura to have a better view from their position at the park's northern edge near the wide boulevard. Or Kraus, who watched from the southern corner of the church. He tried to peer over the heads of the crowd to see if he could spot his companions, but the crowd was too dense.

After Forester had picked up Egger and taken him to their hideout, they had gotten a little more information from him, including that he was to wait for the courier at the southern edge of the reflection pool in front of the church. Instead of waiting at the designated spot, Mason remained thirty feet back in the tree line.

The crowd began to thin slightly. The time of the rendezvous had passed by ten minutes. Mason began to worry the courier had seen him, suspected the ruse, and fled. And the longer he stayed out in the open, the greater the chances one of the CIC boys or CIG agents would spot him.

Mason debated whether to abort the mission when he saw a tall male figure cutting through the crowds. The man neither stopped to chat nor checked out the black marketers or prostitutes. By his rigid, quick stride, he was a man on a mission.

Mason lowered his head, letting the brim of his hat cast a shadow across his face. He could still see the man from the waist down, and he watched his target's footsteps as the courier moved toward the reflecting pool. Then the man stopped.

Mason expected that, because he, as Egger, was not at the rendezvous point. That was Mason's cue. He moved toward the pool, the briefcase in his hand and his head tilted forward. Instead of aiming directly for the courier, he strode toward the rendezvous point as if running late. A group of five teenagers passed him. They must have been selling something, because they stopped right where the courier had hesitated and surrounded him. Mason took a chance and lifted his head to see what was happening.

The courier looked straight at him, and though he maintained a neutral expression, a flash of alarm registered in his eyes. He said something Mason couldn't hear to the five teenagers and passed them something. Then he spun on his heels and dashed for the park.

Mason took off after him, but the five teenagers rushed him and blocked his path. They yelled at him and grabbed onto his coat. Mason fought them off, but he'd lost precious seconds.

The courier drove a wedge through the crowds. Mason dodged the same people. Some scolded him, while others scurried away. It was not unusual to see an undercover cop chasing black markers, but the last thing he wanted was attention from Russian soldiers. He caught a glimpse of the courier entering the park. Mason hit the tree line twenty-five yards behind him.

The courier had long legs, but Mason was faster, and he poured on the speed. Then, just as he closed the gap, the courier whipped around, took a knee, and aimed his pistol.

Mason planted his feet and dived behind a tree. An instant later he heard a collision of bodies and grunts of a struggle. He looked out from behind the tree and saw that Forester had tackled the courier. They fought for control of the gun. The courier flipped Forester over and lowered the gun to shoot Forester in the head.

Mason raced up, taking out his blackjack, and struck the courier at the base of his skull. With a yelp, the man fell forward onto Forester and ceased to move. Forester shoved the courier off his body, pulled the gun from the man's hand, and put it in his pocket.

While Forester caught his breath, Mason picked up the briefcase and opened it. He quickly checked the documents. "Looks like diplomatic communiqués and classified intelligence papers."

Laura rushed up. "The black marketers are starting to come back. We've got to do something with him before we're seen."

The courier groaned. His eyes opened, and he started to get up. Forester pushed the man back down and clamped his hands onto his mouth. The courier thrashed as he tried to call for help.

Breathless, Kraus came racing up to them. "The Russians and Austrian police are becoming curious."

In a flash, Forester opened his switchblade and jabbed it against the courier's neck. "Who gave you those documents?"

The courier shook his head. He was defiant, but his eyes betrayed his terror.

Forester placed the tip of the blade next to the man's left eye. "Which piece do you want me to take first? Because I'll take them all until I get some answers."

"Mike, we've got to go," Laura hissed.

Forester ignored her and pressed the tip harder against the courier's left eye. The man's muffled screams seemed loud in the near-empty park.

Mason had enough of men screaming in pain. "Mike, we can get it out of him later."

"I know this guy," Forester said. "He's a clerk with the CIC, and a traitor." He looked at the man with fury in his eyes. "I'm going to enjoy cutting pieces off of you. Who gave you these documents?"

The courier tried to say something and stopped struggling to show he was ready to talk. Forester eased off the pressure on the man's mouth.

"Help!" the courier yelled and managed to squeeze out from under Forester's body. As the courier tried to stand, Mason swung the blackjack again, striking the side of the man's skull. Stunned, the courier fell silent.

"We've got to get out of here," Mason said. "Now."

"There." Laura pointed to a narrow alley between two buildings beyond the southern edge of the park. "We act like he's too drunk to walk."

Mason and Forester hoisted the courier, putt their shoulders under each armpit, and hurriedly dragged him toward the alley. Laura grabbed Mason's briefcase while Kraus gathered the other briefcase and the courier's hat. Kraus rushed ahead to make sure there was no one in the alley. Behind them, the beams of two flashlights and the sound of Russian voices came from the area they had just vacated.

Agonizing seconds later, they managed to get the tall man into the alley. Kraus pointed to a short stairway leading to a basement door. Mason and Forester struggled to get the unconscious courier down the stairs, then laid his limp body on the cement.

"You two stay with him," Forester said to Mason and Laura. "Kraus and I will get the car and bring it around to the back of this building." He and Kraus climbed the ten steps and disappeared.

Blood streamed from the side of the courier's head.

Mason examined the wound and checked the man's breathing and pulse.

"He's got a pretty bad concussion," Mason said.

"I just hope he recuperates," Laura said as she breathed heavily from fear and adrenaline. "We need him alive to answer more questions."

Headlights lit up the access road behind the building. A moment later came the sound of a car engine. Mason sneaked up the steps and saw Forester's car come to a stop at the end of the perpendicular alley. He went back down the stairs and picked up the courier by the shoulders. Laura took his legs, and they heaved the body up the steps. Forester and Kraus arrived and gave Laura a hand. They rushed over to the car and dropped the courier into the trunk. The four of them got in, with Forester getting behind the wheel. Laura joined him in front, and Mason got in the back with Kraus.

Forester said to Mason, "That waiter said he was to rendezvous with someone in Stadtpark, right?"

"Yeah, on the east side of the pond."

"All right, I'll drop you near the Stadtpark, then we've got to get our guy somewhere before he starts banging on the trunk lid."

Forester backed out of the alley and traveled the brief distance to the ring road. In less than five minutes, he pulled the car over just shy of the southwest corner of the park.

Forester handed Mason a small Leica camera. "You're not going to go in there to do anything else except get the best photos you can of the contact. You're maybe two hundred yards from the rendezvous point. Don't engage the contact unless you have no other choice. Just get a good look at him or her, try to get some good photos, and get out of there." He asked Laura to retrieve a pair of binoculars in the glove compartment.

Laura did as he asked, but instead of handing the binoculars to Mason, she kept them. "I'm going with him."

Mason wanted to object, but she flashed him a nasty look that convinced him it was better for his health to keep his mouth shut.

"Are you sure?" Forester asked. "This is a favorite spot for spies and assassins, and we're technically in the Russian zone."

"Someone has to watch Mason's back," Laura said.

"He can take care of himself."

"I'm right here, you know," Mason said.

Forester ignored Mason and said to Laura, "Once you get a good look at the contact, head for the Annakirche on Annagasse. It's not more than six blocks from the park." He turned to Kraus. "I need you with me, okay? We'll get the courier to a safe place, then I need for you to sit on him while I go back for Mason and Laura."

Kraus nodded and seemed slightly relieved he wouldn't have to risk getting arrested by the Soviets.

"Once we've got the courier secure, I'll come back for you there," Forester said to Mason and Laura. "Good luck."

Mason and Laura got out of the car and entered the rectangular Stadtpark.

35

The Vienna river sliced lengthwise through Stadtpark with several bridges linking the two sections. Mason and Laura were in the larger portion, which had an open lawn broken by stands of trees and crisscrossed by walkways and formal gardens. The teardrop-shaped pond was in the center. A smattering of dead leaves still clung stubbornly to the trees, and a few couples strolled the walkways. A group of kids—homeless by the look of their clothes and forlorn faces—huddled around a bonfire, and they reminded Mason of the orphans he'd befriended in Munich.

Laura took his arm. "Remember, we're just another couple out for a moonlit stroll."

"The sky's overcast."

"Killjoy."

They took a walkway that paralleled the ring road and afforded glimpses of the pond. A thicket of trees lined the eastern side, where the recipient of the documents was supposed to be waiting. Next to the trees was a small, boarded-up building, which could provide cover for whoever waited on the other side.

When Mason and Laura passed the Franz Schubert monument and the halfway point of the pond, they turned off the path. Being careful to use the trees as cover, they approached the pond's shoreline. While Mason kept a lookout, Laura used the binoculars to scan the other side. Two soldiers walked the path Mason and Laura had just left. If they just happened to look to their right, Mason and Laura were in plain view.

Mason gently lowered the binoculars from Laura's eyes and kissed her. The two soldiers chatted as they passed, and when the sounds of their conversation faded, Mason broke the embrace. They both made sure the two soldiers continued on their walk before returning to the task at hand.

"Too bad we're not someplace a little more cozy," Mason said.

"You mean you've never made love to a girl in a public park on a blanket of wet leaves?" Laura asked as she scanned the area opposite the pond through the binoculars. She stopped. "Ten o'clock." She handed Mason the binoculars. "By an oak about five yards up from the shoreline."

Mason looked where Laura had indicated. He spotted the silhouette of a man leaning against a tree. "It's too dark to make out his face, but he just checked his watch and seems impatient."

"Not surprising. The handoff was supposed to have happened five minutes ago."

"We'll have to get closer if we want to make an ID and get a photo," Mason said as he continued to watch the man. "He's in uniform, but I can't make out which army."

He lowered the binoculars and made a signal for them to head for the north end of the park. Staying within the tree line and the shadows, they made their way along the shore of the pond. A pathway at the northern tip took them around to the other side. The smaller of the two boarded-up buildings came up on their left, and Mason judged they were close enough to observe.

He and Laura huddled under a weeping willow. Mason took out the camera, while Laura looked through the binoculars. The man still stood near the same tree, looking both ways, then at his watch.

Mason focused the lens on the man's darkened face. A moment later, the man ignited his lighter, then brought the flame up to his face to light a cigarette.

"Hello," Mason said as he snapped several photos. "Colonel Sergi Bogdonovich. GRU, Soviet military intelligence."

"Do you think he's the one passing on Soviet secrets to Carver?"

"Assuming the courier is doing Carver's bidding, then it stands to reason that Bogdonovich is the Russian mole." He lowered the camera. "But what this really means is Carver is a double agent. We've got him."

Mason took several more photographs, then a split second before the colonel extinguished the flame, he saw a second man appear out of nowhere. He was standing in front of the colonel. The colonel's expression was frozen in surprise and fear. Mason's heart jumped into high gear. He swore he knew the man.

Just as darkness returned to his subject, two bright flashes lit up the colonel's face again. And this time, the flash also lit up the other man.

It was Bauer.

A heartbeat later came the sharp snaps of a suppressed pistol. Laura sucked in her breath, and asked in a harsh whisper, "What just happened?"

Mason's mind was still processing what he saw as the colonel dropped to the ground. The shock and surprise of watching Bauer kill the man had made him doubt his eyes.

"Bauer just shot the colonel," Mason said.

"Bauer?" Laura hissed with surprise.

Shouting erupted in Russian. Then two soldiers ran in hot pursuit of the fleeing Bauer. Two more soldiers cut off Bauer's escape and grabbed him. Bauer started yelling in Russian while fighting them off. Being an intelligence officer, that in itself was not surprising, but it was the tone that left Mason puzzled; it was almost as if Bauer was shouting commands.

More shouting in Russian and heavy bootsteps. Only this time they were much closer. Mason and Laura turned to see the two Soviet soldiers running for them a hundred yards away, pistols out.

They took off running through the trees toward the southern end of the park. The pursuing soldiers had attracted another team of soldiers. That pair broke into a run from the outer edges of the park on an interception course.

"This way," Mason said and led Laura back around the northern end of the pond.

The intercepting soldiers had to push through a thicket of tree branches and shrubs, slowing them down. Mason and Laura went around the pond and continued toward the southern end. Mason knew their best bet was to cross the ring road, exiting the Russian zone into the inner city.

They reached the intersection of two pathways at the

southern end of the pond and dashed across the open lawn. Not too far behind them, Mason could hear footsteps in the fallen leaves, bodies crashing through the bushes. At another intersection of pathways, Mason took Laura's hand and steered her diagonally through a wooded area and toward the ring road. There would be checkpoints and patrols controlling the border of the two zones. They'd surely pick up more pursuers, or worse, run directly into a contingent of Soviet soldiers guarding the main routes into the inner city.

Mason turned perpendicular to the broad boulevard. "As fast as you can," he said to Laura, and they crossed the road just in front of a passing tram that paralleled the ring road. He then headed straight for a small clothing shop occupying the ground floor of a partially fire-damaged office building.

"Where are we going?" Laura asked, breathless.

Her question was answered when Mason, still moving at full speed, kicked open the closed shop's front door. He was betting everything on a rear entrance; otherwise, he'd just led them into a dead end.

36

Mason and Laura pushed past racks of clothes in the darkness, past the cashier's counter and into the back hallway. Mason felt a flood of relief when he saw a rear exit. He jerked back the two deadbolts and flung open the door.

Outside they found themselves in a courtyard. Piles of debris from the damaged buildings had been discarded in the square space and distributed in random piles. Bicycles and trash cans lined the four walls, but there were no alleys. No means of escape.

"There," Laura said and pointed to the opposite wall at two rear entrances.

They raced across the courtyard. When they cleared a tall pile of debris, they saw a man in a white apron standing at one of the doors, smoking a cigarette. Startled by their quick approach, the smoker stepped aside, allowing Mason and Laura to charge through the door.

They were in a restaurant's kitchen, and the two cooks and the dishwasher stood in shock as Mason and Laura sprinted through the kitchen and pushed through the swinging door. Only two tables still had diners, and a waiter was about to lock the door.

Mason yelled in German, “Coming through!”

The waiter jumped aside. Mason and Laura exited the restaurant onto a small side street. Both had to stop for a moment to catch their breath.

“Do you have any idea where the Annakirche is?” Mason asked.

She shook her head. “Just that it’s on Annagasse.”

Mason looked right, then left. They had to make a choice, and fast. On instinct, Mason led them left. They came upon an intersection with a wider street. Though the curfew was in effect for the locals, a scattering of uniformed men with their dates or groups of soldiers were still out, leaving restaurants or going to bars.

Running would attract too much attention, so they slowed to a quick walk and turned right onto the wider street. At the next intersection, they turned right again. They continued that way, making a zigzag pattern, turning at each intersection while still heading toward the center of the city.

Laura checked behind them. “Maybe we lost them.”

“Could be they’ve been held up at the border.”

“Don’t count on it. The Russians aren’t about to respect policing protocol.”

“And even if they did, I’m sure they’ll call the international police to pick us up.”

They quickened their pace despite the risk of attracting attention. The problem was, they still had no idea how to find Annakirche or Annagasse. Finally, Laura stopped a couple of

British soldiers and asked sweetly for directions. The two soldiers eyed her with lust in their eyes until she asked for the church. One of them gave her directions.

Laura thanked him and rejoined Mason. "We've gone too far into the center. We have to double back."

Laura led the way. They turned and retraced their steps for two streets before turning left. A four-men-in-a-jeep passed by at one point, forcing them to duck into the shadows, but they finally reached the corner of Annagasse and Kärntnerstrasse and saw why they missed the street: it extended only one block with that name. Restaurants and a few bars were lined along the ground floors of the mostly four- and five-story buildings. The restaurants were closed, but the bars were still open.

Laura started to turn onto Annagasse, but Mason pulled her back behind the corner building.

"We check out the location before we go any farther."

They both peeked around the corner. The church was halfway down the street. The walls of the other buildings touched those of the church, making it one long string of establishments. The only thing that set the church apart was the gilded domed tower that rose above the rooftops.

There was a man standing just outside the church's entrance. He smoked a cigarette as he looked both ways, presumably waiting for them. It was Forester.

"There's Mike," Laura said and started to go.

Mason had to pull her back again, and she looked at him quizzically. He pointed to a parked car with its engine still running a few doors down from the church. The light from a bar's neon sign cast the driver in silhouette.

Mason whispered, "Two doors down, on the other side of

the church, there's a guy standing in the shadows of the doorway."

As Laura looked, the man leaned out from the shadow to peer at both ends of the street.

"It's Kovack," Mason said. He and Laura ducked back behind the corner building. "They picked up Mike, and they're using him to lure us in."

"They must have figured out that Mike was hiding us."

One block down, on another major street, an MP jeep passed by.

Mason looked at Laura. "We could turn ourselves over to Kovack. That'd be better than getting picked up by the MPs or the Russians."

"Then it's all over," Laura said. "Spotting a GRU colonel smoking a cigarette in a park, not to mention Bauer shooting him, won't be enough to get Carver arrested." She nodded at the camera still hanging around Mason's neck. "Do you think you got the colonel or Bauer on camera?"

"I don't know. It was dark. I just kept hitting the trigger. I did hear Bauer speak in Russian."

"I did, too. And he didn't sound like he was pleading his innocence."

"The documents in the courier's briefcase come from Carver. Bauer shoots Bogdonovich, a GRU officer …" Mason shook his head. "There's something I'm missing."

"We'd better lay low until we can figure this all out. Not only is Kovack after us, but now the Russians suspect we're involved in Bogdonovich's murder."

Mason smiled at her. He was proud of her courage, smarts, and determination.

Laura slugged his arm. “Don’t give me that patronizing look.”

“Okay, okay. You don’t have to slug me to get your point across. I was going to say that I’ve got an idea where we can go.”

“Then stop with the goofy eyes and get going.”

Mason took her hand and led her deeper into the city.

37

Mason and Laura sneaked up to the gate of Wentworth's house. Mason picked the lock while Laura kept a lookout. In seconds, they were through the gate. Mason knew how to tackle the three front door locks, but picking them by cigarette lighter slowed him down. It took several agonizing moments, but he finally got the better of them, and they entered the dark, cold house. Since the city's electrical grid was still under repair, the streetlights were out, making the interior almost black. The faint outlines of the windows provided the only orientation.

"We leave the lights off in front," Mason said. "I don't want anyone to notice we're here. At least this is one of the last places they'd come looking for us."

"But they will eventually. Then what?"

"I haven't figured that part out yet."

"While we're doing that, why don't we try to find whatever he was using to decipher that message."

"Better than a swift kick in the ribs."

"I forgot about your fondness for hayseed commentary."

Mason shrugged and flicked on his cigarette lighter. Following the faint light, they mounted the stairs.

The door to Wentworth's study was wide open. They stepped inside, and Mason went over to the desk and turned on the lamp. The light revealed furniture that had been pushed aside. Papers were scattered on Wentworth's desk and the desk drawers left open. The paintings on the wall hung askew. Fingerprint dusting clung to any hard surface that might have latent prints.

Obviously, the U.S. Army's criminal investigation division had searched for clues to the cause of Wentworth's untimely demise. Since the books on the shelves were relatively untouched, Mason gathered that, surprisingly, no one from Carver's crew had come in after the police to search the place for themselves. Or at least they hadn't tackled the bookshelves. Or they found what they were looking for after killing Wentworth, and this would be a waste of time.

Mason backed up and stood next to Laura to stare at the shelves.

"There must be five hundred books," Laura said.

"We start with the obvious ones," Mason said. "The ones with wider circulation, and ones with Roman numerals."

"That's assuming your theory about the message is correct."

"Better than playing tiddledywinks."

Laura gave him a mock glare. "Why am I beginning to think playing that game will be a better use of our time?"

MASON CLOSED ANOTHER BOOK AND DROPPED IT ON A PILE. He stretched and stepped back to look at all the shelves at once. The clock indicated it was after one a.m., and they had only eliminated half the books. On the floor in front of him were three piles, the one on the left being the most promising. The middle one represented "probably not," and finally on the right was the "no way in hell" group.

Both he and Laura had been concentrating on the promising pile, but out of boredom he decided to take a gander at the ridiculous. He plucked the one on top. It seemed particularly absurd: A U.S. Army officer's field manual. He went over to the desk and sat. With pencil in hand and a blank sheet of paper before him, he rubbed the tiredness from his eyes and opened the manual.

He had memorized the first string of numbers and Roman numerals after hours of doing the same with a multitude of other books, and he started with the table of contents. The table of contents indicated that the book was broken down into chapter numbers and sections of chapters by Roman numerals. Mason began with the simplest method, which was a matter of pairing a number with a Roman numeral, then going to the page indicated.

On the first try, the first sentence, in fact, none of the text on the page, made any sense in the context of a decoded message. He was about to rip out the page in frustration, when he noticed, in very small, very neat handwriting, a name entered at the bottom of the page: Maj. Morozov. With the name in mind, he looked at the text again and deciphered "Five units," then a date.

"I think I found the right book," Mason said.

Laura stood up from the floor and stepped up to the desk to look over Mason's shoulder. "An army field manual?"

"Seems ironic, doesn't it?"

Mason continued to match the figures with the names while Laura looked on. As there were only close to one hundred numbers and figures to decipher and transcribe, it came together quickly.

"It looks like a laundry list of names, dates, and payments," Laura said as she read what Mason had written down on the piece of paper. "General Baranova, ten units. Here's Gruber, five units, and Flannigan, twenty-three units, all in the last two weeks."

"Six Russians, three Americans, four Austrians, then one British major, and a French colonel."

"Wentworth must have funneled bribes or profits to some of Carver's powerful cronies," Laura said. "I'm guessing a unit is a substantial amount of money. Since the dates of those payments are all recent, this list must be just the latest figures—"

"To enter in a master file," Mason said, completing the idea.

They both looked around the room.

"Do you think that master file is still here?" Laura asked.

"Whoever killed him had plenty of time to find it. They either already have the master file, or they thought they'd gotten it when they took everything from his file cabinets."

"If they didn't find anything in the files, they would have come back here and taken an axe to the place."

"Or they will very soon," Mason said.

Laura straightened and turned to the door. "Maybe this wasn't the best place to hide out, after all."

"Tonight might be our only shot at finding that master file before they do," Mason said as he scanned the room for possible hiding places.

The sound of the front door opening reached their ears. Then came the hushed murmur of men's voices.

Mason turned off the desk lamp, then they sneaked across the room to the opposite side. Mason pulled out his pistol and, as quietly as he could, pulled back the slider to load a bullet into the chamber. He looked at Laura, who held up her hands in frustration.

"I must have left mine in Forester's car," she whispered.

Three pairs of footsteps ascended the stairs. Two pairs approached the door, meaning one man had stopped at the landing.

Mason and Laura instinctively pressed their backs against the wall. The door opened. The hinge side was to them, so the door blocked them from view. A flashlight beam pierced the darkness, then a man stepped into the room. It was too dark to see the man's face, and fortunately for Mason and Laura, he didn't bother to sweep the entire study with his flashlight. And surprisingly, neither did he hit the wall switch for the hanging lamp over the desk.

Instead, he aimed his flashlight on the desk and headed for it. Apparently knowing exactly where he was going. He only paused for a moment to take in the chaos of the bookshelves before going over to the desk. He switched on the desk lamp, causing Mason and Laura to draw back further into the shadows.

Mason felt Laura become rigid with alarm. It was Flannigan.

Flannigan took hold of the desk chair and adjusted its position. He stood on the chair and reached over the edge of the hanging lamp's glass shade. Mason heard a metallic click, then Flannigan put both hands on the edges of the lamp shade and turned. Though the hanging lamp appeared to be suspended from a chain, the lamp and chain were rigid. And as Flannigan turned the shade, a muffled pop sounded, and a square section of the ceiling separated from the rest. With each turn, the lamp and section of the ceiling dropped lower.

Finally, when Flannigan was satisfied, he stretched high and reached into the opening in the ceiling. After a moment of feeling around, he pulled out a rectangular book. He got off the chair and laid the book on the table. After adjusting the position of the desk lamp, he opened it and leafed through the pages.

Mason took advantage of Flannigan's fixed attention on the book to creep forward. He had the blackjack ready in his left hand in case the man heard him approaching. He stepped carefully to avoid any creaking floorboards.

Mason put the barrel of his gun against the back of Flannigan's head. "Don't move, or I'll blow it off."

Flannigan gasped in surprise and raised his hands. He chanced a glimpse back. "Anderson? What the hell?"

"I'm here for another client," Mason said, lying. "He wants that ledger."

"Maybe we can make a deal." He wiggled a finger in the direction of the book. "That ledger contains enough information to get rid of Carver and use it our mutual advantage. Outside of Wentworth, I'm the only one who knew where to find it."

"Sorry, no deal," Mason said. "Now, I want you to turn slowly and kneel on the floor."

Flannigan spun and took a swing at Mason. He called out, “Nick!”

Mason blocked the swing and hit him with the handle of his pistol.

Flannigan stumbled backward into the desk lamp and fell to the floor. The lamp went with him, crashing to pieces next to him and plunging the room into darkness.

At that same instant, the man outside the office kicked the door open and fired at Mason. Fortunately for Mason, it was too dark for accuracy, though with each shot, the shooter got closer to the mark.

Mason dived behind the desk and aimed, but Laura charged and threw all her weight against the door. It slammed into the shooter’s head and pushed him into the doorframe.

The shooter got off another round before the door trapped his gun arm against the doorframe. Flannigan cried out.

The shooter shoved the door open, flinging Laura backward.

Mason was ready and fired his pistol three times. The man crumpled to the floor.

Laura tried to slam the door shut, but the shooter’s feet prevented her from shutting it completely.

Mason heard rushing footsteps in the hallway. “Laura! Get in the corner!”

Just then, a submachine gun opened up. Bullets ripped through the plaster wall and pelted the room.

Laura let out a scream.

38

Mason tried desperately to see if Laura had gotten out of the line of fire in time. Bullets pinned him down, forcing him to stay behind the desk.

Despite the danger, he tensed his muscles, ready to dash across the killing field, when he saw her crawling toward the corner of the room. "Laura, you okay?" he yelled over the sounds of the machine gun.

"Yes," she said.

The shooting stopped. The only sound was Flannigan gasping for air. Then the floorboards creaked. Mason could only guess at the man's position outside the door, but he opened fire anyway, putting five bullets into the wall. A heavy thud followed.

Mason jumped from his spot, grabbed the ledger, and ran to Laura. He helped her to her feet, and they rushed to the door. He stopped Laura just inside the doorframe and peeked out into the hallway.

Two flashlight beams rose up from the ground floor, and they swept the landing. A man downstairs called for Nick and

Frieder. Mason assumed those were the names of the two shooters motionless at his feet.

Mason removed the empty magazine from his pistol and popped in his spare. He started to creep down the hallway. Halfway there, someone began running up the stairs. Mason aimed his pistol at the landing, estimating a point chest-high. A fast-moving shadow appeared at the landing, and Mason fired twice.

He'd aimed a little too high, and the man bounded back down the stairs. At least two submachine guns responded in short bursts. Wood and plaster exploded.

Mason retreated to the study and to Laura. "Trapped," he whispered. "See what you can do for Flannigan."

Laura went over to Flannigan, who groaned in the darkness near the fireplace. Mason remained at the door and watched the stairs. He had six bullets left in his remaining magazine. Against two or three shooters with submachine guns, and possibly others with pistols. Definitely outgunned.

As quietly as he could, he checked the first shooter's Luger pistol. Four rounds. He picked up the Thompson submachine gun. The thirty-round box magazine was empty, but while searching the shooter's body, he found a twenty-round spare. He belted the Luger and put the loaded magazine into the Thompson.

Laura came back to him and whispered, "Hit in the shoulder. He's in shock, and he's going to bleed to death if he doesn't get to a hospital."

Mason yelled down the hallway, "Your boss is—"

The front door banged open, and gunfire erupted. Mason pulled Laura inside and pushed the door closed. No telling who was shooting at whom. Another gang? The Russians?

When the gunfire began to abate, he could hear men speaking in Russian. They must have been hunting for Mason and Laura, and they simply followed the sound of the gunfire.

Mason led Laura away from the door and gave her the dead shooter's Luger. "I can't let them take either of us. They'll either shoot us down where we stand or send us to die in a gulag. Use this only as a last resort."

Despite her fear, Laura accepted the pistol and readied herself for a last, desperate gunfight. "Where are you going?"

Mason didn't respond and marched over to the door. He opened it just enough to point the submachine gun down the hallway. He fired off a short burst. The men below returned fire, though it stopped an instant later.

Mason was about to shoot off another burst, when he saw the beam of a flashlight travel across the wall. It was coming from the back of the house. They were going to try to come at them from the rear. He rushed to the window and saw the light beam came from the top of the wall behind the garden.

The person pointing the beam at them turned the light on himself.

It was Kraus. He waved his arms and motioned for them to come to him.

Mason looked down. The sloped roof of the back porch reached up to within four feet of the study's windowsill. "Are you up for jumping?" Mason asked Laura.

Without responding, Laura rushed over to the window and threw it open. She climbed out, and Mason helped her reach the porch roof. He strode over to the door, poked the submachine gun out into the hallway, and fired another burst until the magazine was empty. The Russians blindly returned fire. Mason threw the now useless gun on the floor and rushed over to retrieve the ledger where he'd dropped it. With one long stride, he leapt out of the window.

As Mason slid down the roof, he heard multiple footsteps running up the stairs. Flashlight beams lit up the bullet holes in the walls.

Laura had already climbed down and waited for him in the middle of the backyard. Mason threw the ledger down to Laura, held onto the edge of the roof, and dropped down. Just behind him, gunfire erupted. Bullets shattered the three windows. The Russians weren't taking any chances before risking entry.

Mason caught up with Laura and tucked the ledger under his arm like a football player running for the end zone. They raced for the wall. Kraus lowered his hand to help them climb. Laura got there first. She jumped and latched onto Kraus's hand. He pulled her up as Mason boosted her from behind.

Mason tossed the ledger over the wall and leapt for Kraus's hand. Kraus nearly tumbled off the wall but grabbed onto the barbed wire. He groaned as he pulled Mason up.

Voices shouting in Russian erupted from the upper floor. Boots hit the porch roof. Then several shooters opened up with their submachine guns.

Bullets slammed into the brick wall just as Mason and Kraus jumped down and landed on the other side. They joined Laura, and all three ran through the rear door of the apartment building, down the short corridor, and out onto the street.

"This way," Kraus said and hooked left.

Half a block later, Kraus jumped behind the wheel of a Horch Phaeton convertible. Mason got in back, while Laura got in the front passenger's seat. The engine roared to life, and Kraus hit the accelerator. The car lurched forward and gained speed. They passed the apartment building just as three men in Russian uniforms burst through the front door.

The Russians opened fire. Bullets zipped past them or impacted the trunk or pierced the windshield.

Kraus turned left at the intersection and put on the speed.

"How did you get your hands on this car?" Mason asked.

"I stole it," Kraus said and looked back at Mason with exhilaration in his eyes.

Laura slapped Kraus on the shoulder, getting his attention. She was too breathless to do anything but point forward, reminding him to keep his eyes on the road.

"I'll make a gangster out of you yet," Mason said to him.

Two sedans came out of nowhere, pulled into the intersection and stopped, blocking their escape. Kraus slammed on the brakes and brought the car to a stop just yards from the two vehicles.

Kraus jammed the car into reverse, but four men got out of the blocking sedans and pointed pistols and shotguns at them.

Mason tapped on Kraus's shoulder and shook his head; there was no way they could make an escape. Then he recognized one of the men standing with the others. Kovack.

Mason felt a mixture of relief and dread; they wouldn't die from Russian bullets, but their futures didn't look very promising, all the same.

Kovack and another man sauntered up to the Horch. He looked straight at Mason. "You're under arrest."

39

Mason sat alone in an interrogation room at the U.S. Army's CID headquarters. Having been a criminal investigator for the CID in Munich and Garmisch-Partenkirchen in Germany, he found it disconcerting yet interesting to be on the other side of the table. Like any interrogation room, there was a shaded lamp hanging from the center of the ceiling, a battered table, and chairs that were bolted to the cement floor. Three of the walls had strike marks and indentions from heads being thrust against them at full force, breaking up the monotony of the dingy, white walls. There was, of course, the two-way mirror dominating one wall perpendicular to the hallway.

A CID investigator, who couldn't have cared less that Mason used to be one of them, had grilled him for an hour—at least Mason figured it had been an hour, since there were no clocks in the room and they'd taken his watch. Then the young investigator was suddenly called from the room. That was twenty minutes ago.

Between being picked up near Wentworth's townhouse and

now, he hadn't seen Forester, and he wondered if he was sweating it out in another interrogation room like he was. He also wondered if they were giving Laura and Kraus the same treatment. He hoped they were okay. At least both of them were now relatively safe.

Mason was about to light up another cigarette, when the door opened, and Kovack walked into the room. He wore a sneer and flared his nostrils like he was trying to mimic some tough-guy G-man he'd seen in the movies. He slapped a thick file folder on the table and sat opposite Mason. What he neglected to remember was that Mason had plenty of experience as an interrogator, and the thick-file routine was a rookie technique to make the perp think they had the damning weight of evidence against him.

"You really fouled things up," Kovack said.

"For you, maybe."

"You had orders to steer clear of Carver, and now you've blown his cover and exposed him to the wrong people."

"I exposed him as the killer and traitor that he is. You only wanted to protect that asshole so you'd look good to your superiors by serving up flimsy morsels of intel on the Russians. He's a cold-blooded killer."

"Are you really that damned naïve? We're not the first agency to use killers for the sake of U.S. counterespionage. The CIC has looked the other way when they've hired ex-Gestapo and SS mass murderers."

"Carver's been working as a double agent."

"You haven't got any proof."

"What about us witnessing Agent Bauer shooting a Soviet colonel?"

"Agent Bauer is still in Soviet hands. He's reportedly

admitted to the shooting but claims he acted on his own. He says Carver had nothing to do with it."

"That's bullshit, and you know it. What about the courier we caught with classified documents originating from Carver's office?"

"Mr. Collins, you seem to think that you can talk your way out of this. But I have to inform you that this interview is just a formality. You're already destined for trial and prison. If there's something you want to come clean about, now's the time."

"For what? Trying to stop a killer? Bring down a criminal gang? Exposing a traitor? It sure as hell can't be for disobeying orders. I'm a private citizen."

"I can make sure that the Austrian police arrest you for murder, kidnapping, and breaking and entering."

"Whose side are you on?"

Kovack seethed at the question—what Mason was aiming for—and said, "I can also charge Mrs. Talbot and Peter Kraus on an aiding-and-abetting rap, accessories to murder. I can arrange that if you don't cooperate and come clean." He leaned forward, giving Mason a sinister smile. "You forget that we don't operate like a police department. If we want someone to disappear, we can make that happen."

There was a sharp rapping on the two-way mirror, causing Kovack to launch back in his chair and clamp his mouth shut. A moment later, the door opened, and Mike Forester put a foot in the door. He said nothing as he stared at Kovack. Behind him, standing in the hallway, was a middle-aged man in a tailored suit. He looked grim. The man tilted his head to signal that Kovack should join him in the hallway.

Kovack's facial muscles fell, and he turned pale. He glared

at Mason, then stood and left the room. When Kovack and the middle-aged man disappeared out of sight, Forester stepped in.

"Mike," Mason said, happy to see the man. He instinctively tried to stand, but the handcuffs chained to the table prevented him from doing more than lifting his butt off the chair.

Forester called in an MP, who came over to Mason and removed the cuffs. He said nothing while the policeman finished his task.

When the MP stepped out and closed the door, Mason said, "I see you're off the hook. That's good."

Forester sat across from him with a tired groan. "Hanging around you has put five years on me."

"Don't say I never did anything for you."

A crack of a smile broke through Forester's serious expression.

"Is Kovack in trouble?" Mason asked.

"I'd say he's ripe for reassignment. That guy in the hallway was Kovack's boss, the deputy director of CIG. He came into town to see what's what, so I thought he might like to listen in on the interview."

"That was a sly move. Remind me to stay on your good side."

"News to me that I have a good side," Forester said.

"Kovack told me the Russians have Bauer, and he's refused to implicate Carver in anything."

"That's right. Our people and the Soviet counterparts are trying to hash out a deal as to who gets to go at him first. My bet is he'll sing whatever tune gives him the best chance to escape Soviet-style justice. He'll talk."

"What about Flannigan?"

"The Russians finally turned him over. They patched up his wound, then proceeded to beat him to a pulp. He's so happy to be back with us that he's talking. But he's also refusing to implicate Carver."

"What about Carver?"

Instead of answering, Forester lit a cigarette. He offered one to Mason, but Mason declined. "They're bringing him in for questioning," Forester said.

Mason raised an eyebrow as he peered at his friend. "I don't like the sound of that."

"It's complicated."

Mason leaned forward in anger. "Come on, Mike. Even if Bauer and Flannigan aren't talking yet, you've still got the ledger. And that courier must have said something. You've got to have an open and shut case."

"We'll see if we can get Carver talking, but I have my doubts. And, unfortunately, the ledger doesn't point back to Carver, either. Everything we have is hearsay or circumstantial. He's also a high-ranking diplomat and a friend to a bunch of power brokers in Washington."

"Did you search his premises?"

"CID is doing that now, but Carver was very careful. I doubt they'll find much. We're trying to build a case, but this could be a major embarrassment to the State Department. To the president. Carver will be stripped of his commissions. They'll make up some excuse as to why he suddenly resigned, but unless we find more proof, he'll probably avoid any jail time."

"He was passing on classified documents to the Russians. He's a traitor."

"We caught a courier with classified documents from Carver's office, but we didn't catch Carver in the act. The courier said he got the briefcase from someone who got it from someone else. We're tracking it back to the originator, but it's going to take a little time. For all we know, someone in Carver's office or one of his lieutenants is responsible. Plus, the U.S. got some good intel on the Soviets because of him. Their thinking is, he did more for us than for them. I think Kovack and his superiors at the CIG are more pissed at you than they are at Carver."

In utter frustration, Mason coiled his muscles tightly and shot up from the table. He turned to the two-way mirror, tempted to put his fist through the glass.

"Mason, you got enough to shut him down. He's being forced to go back to the States with his tail between his legs and a tarnished record. And you did it without landing a murder rap. He's done. He won't be able to go after you or Laura, ever again."

"Good luck keeping Laura quiet. A hardheaded reporter with a front-row seat to a State Department and army coverup."

"You want to see her?" Forester asked.

Mason turned to look at Forester. "You mean I can walk out of here?"

Forester wordlessly stubbed out his cigarette and went to the door.

"You kept me in chains after I was free to go?" Mason asked.

Forester ignored the remark and exited the room. Mason caught up to him a moment later, and they walked down the corridor toward the main offices and the exit.

"You're not completely in the clear," Forester said. "At

least as far as the CID or the Austrian authorities are concerned. There's still the abduction of an Austrian citizen and killing Flannigan's bodyguards."

"Mike—"

"I know, self-defense," Forester said. "I'll try to make it go away, but I doubt you'll ever be welcome back in Vienna."

Farther down the hallway, two MPs came around a corner from the opposite direction, and they were leading a handcuffed man by his arms. The man's head was turned, but then he looked straight ahead. A burst of electricity surged up Mason's spine, and his muscles went rigid. It was Carver. It took all of Mason's control not to jump on the man and beat him to a pulp.

Carver's face twisted in anger when he saw Mason. "You're a corpse, asshole."

The MPs had to yank him in close to control him. As they passed, Carver yelled, "You hear me? Dead. And your girlfriend, too."

Mason spun around to attack, but Forester pushed him against the wall.

"Don't do it, Mason. It's not worth it."

Mason took a deep breath and nodded. Forester released him, and they continued their walk. A moment later, Forester stopped at a door and opened it. He moved aside. Mason stepped past him and entered a small lounge area.

Laura was sitting with Kraus on a small sofa. When she saw him, she jumped up and hugged him. Mason didn't want to let go and hugged her tighter. Kraus, with his arm in a cast, stood next to the sofa, looking on. Mason smiled and nodded at him, and Kraus nodded back. Mason and Laura broke their embrace and turned to look at Forester.

"I'll have to find you a safe place until this is all calms down," Forester said to all three of them. "You managed to piss off a bunch of people … again. I'll make some arrangements."

Forester seemed to be finished speaking but remained where he was. Suddenly, he had a hard time looking at them; if he'd had a hat, he would have been turning it in his hands.

"If you have more bad news, you might as well spill it," Laura said.

"Do you promise not to do anything rash once you hear what I have to say?"

"I might do something rash if you don't get on with it," Mason said.

Forester's gaze went elsewhere as if he was having an argument in his head. Finally, he cleared his throat and said, "Bauer and Flannigan have both said they'd never heard of Valerius. They even laughed when we suggested that Valerius was Carver's moniker. And so far, Carver has denied it. It's beginning to look like whatever Carver is guilty of, chances are he's not your guy."

Mason's insides turned upside down. "That's not possible. They're all lying."

"We haven't found anyone or anything to corroborate that he's Valerius. You pegged Carver as a criminal boss at that fundraiser, but you made the wrong assumption or someone steered you wrong. Or the Valerius moniker is some kind of gangland myth."

Mason was stunned into silence, and he didn't notice Forester leaving. He knew Laura was saying something, but he didn't listen. He was too busy running through everything he'd learned up to that point, trying to weave the events in another direction. If Carver wasn't Valerius, then who …

Mason turned to Laura and Kraus. Despite his urge to bolt out of the room, he gave Laura and Kraus a look of resignation. "You two stay here. I'm going to find the bathroom."

He could tell Laura didn't quite buy it, but she simply nodded. Still resisting his impulse to charge out of the room, he calmly stepped out into the hallway.

40

Mason had to move fast. Laura wouldn't stand still for very long, and Forester might return to the room at any moment. The problem was, he had no idea where to look first. He strode down the hallway as if he belonged, heading deeper into CID's labyrinth of hallways and offices.

CID headquarters was in the Stiftskaserne, a complex of buildings that formed a rectangle with a large courtyard in the center. It was also home to the 796th Military Battalion, as well as the provost marshal's offices. The CID offices were on the second floor, amidst a beehive of law enforcement personnel—not the ideal place for Mason to contemplate the theft of valuable evidence.

He figured what he was looking for would be in the evidence room or someplace where analysts pored over it and catalogued the information contained within.

He stopped at an unmarked door, rapped quickly, and opened it. A CID investigator was on the phone. He stopped talking and glared at Mason.

"Sorry, wrong room," Mason said and shut the door before

the investigator had time to question what he was doing wandering around headquarters.

At the next door, Mason did the same thing. An empty office. The next one was an interview room, with a perp handcuffed to the table. Mason shut the door and continued. There were several rooms with the doors wide open, affording Mason enough of a view into each room to determine he could move on, all the while hoping he wouldn't open one and come face to face with Forester making arrangements or Kovack getting his ass chewed.

Around the next corner and in another corridor, he came up to a door labeled Evidence Room. He entered a large space where several clerks circulated through rows of shelves of collected evidence. An MP sat at a small desk just inside the door. He looked up expectantly at Mason.

"I'm with CIG," Mason said. "Deputy Chief Kovack sent me to pick up the evidence from this morning."

"ID, please," the MP said and held out his open hand.

Mason patted his suit jacket, then shrugged. "I left it at my desk. Kovack will chew me out if I come back empty-handed."

"You should have thought of that before you came in here. I can't let you in without ID."

Mason glanced around the room, at the desks for the two clerks, the counter to sign in evidence, and the clerks shelving items. Fighting his way through the guard and clerks was not an option.

"Produce an ID or leave," the MP said.

Mason turned on his heels, walked out of the room, and continued. Two doors down, he entered a room that had a two-way mirror. It was an observation room and was empty. When he entered, he saw why: Kovack's boss was grilling him inside the interrogation room. The microphone had been muted, but it was obvious by the man's gestures that Kovack was in deep trouble for threatening violence during an interrogation. But more importantly for Mason, the room was otherwise empty. Neither Kovack nor his boss was in possession of the evidence.

Two final rooms. Two more chances to find the ledger before Mason would have to walk away without it.

The next door was the access to the interrogation room. Then, at the end of the corridor, a sign declared the room was Captain Avril Patterson's office, the CID detachment's commanding officer.

His last chance.

Mason plucked some files off of a table near the door, clutched them to his chest, and walked with purpose into the room. It was the anteroom, where the captain's male secretary was on the phone talking heatedly to someone on the other end. The secretary looked up. Mason signaled that he would go directly to the captain's office.

With that, Mason headed in with haste.

The secretary dropped the phone receiver to his shoulder. "Where are you going, sir?"

Mason continued and said, "The CIG director ordered me to leave these files personally on the captain's desk."

He stepped in and immediately saw the ledger sitting on the captain's desk. He put the files down, grabbed the ledger, and strode for the exit.

By that time the secretary was on his feet. "You can't go in there."

As Mason crossed the anteroom, the secretary came around his desk to cut off Mason's escape. "Where are you going with that?"

"Orders," Mason said without stopping.

The secretary seized Mason's shoulder and pulled to turn him. Mason used the motion to spin and throw a solid right to the secretary's jawline. The man fell back, hitting the desk on his way to the floor.

Mason didn't bother to watch whether the man stayed down. With long strides, he retraced his steps, passing others in the succession of hallways and listening at his rear for any kind of pursuit. He turned his head away when he passed the room where Laura and Kraus still waited for him. Then it was a matter of traversing one more corridor, which he did. But as soon as he reached the main lobby, a flurry of noise broke out behind him. From somewhere in the corridor, several men yelled for him to be stopped.

Most people in the lobby seemed confused over the fuss, prompting Mason to pour on the speed, and he exploded out the front door. As he bounded down the steps and onto the sidewalk, he knew his next mission would be to find a phone and make a series of risky calls—well, next was to get far away from CID headquarters before a squad of MPs tackled him and threw him in the stockade.

Just as he made it to the paving stones, and beige sedan screecched to halt in front of him. Mason prepared himself for fight and flight, but then he saw Kraus hanging out the front passenger's window with Laura behind the wheel.

"Get in!" Kraus yelled.

Considering the circumstances, Mason had no other choice. He jumped in the back seat, and Laura punched the accelerator.

Laura sped down the Viennese streets like a professional racecar driver, forcing Mason had to hold on to the backs of the front seats to stay upright. "Damnit, you guys," Mason said, "now that you were safe, I wanted you to stay that way."

"Neither one of us was going to let you do this alone," Laura said and took another sharp turn.

"How did you know I was going to do anything?"

"The look in your eyes," Kraus said. "I've seen it a dozen times, and craziness always follows."

He didn't have a retort for that one. He looked around and realized they were in a completely different car. "Okay, now where did you get *this* car?"

"The kaserne's courtyard parking lot," Kraus said. "The keys were in it, fortunately."

"We've got to get off the streets as fast as we can. The MPs will be on our tail any minute."

Laura turned down a street no wider than an alley, forcing people to hug the buildings to avoid getting run over. "What's the plan?" she asked Mason.

"The plan is for you to let me out, and you guys find a safe place to hide."

"Not a chance," she said. "We didn't risk our hides just to be your taxi service. You stole that ledger from the CID for a reason."

"We want to help," Kraus said. "No, we insist."

"What I plan to do is certainly stupid, not to mention dangerous. I can't let you guys go along."

"If this has anything to do with exposing Valerius, then I'm coming along whether you like it or not!"

Mason glanced at the rearview mirror and saw the determination in Laura's eyes. He knew that look as well as she knew his, and she was deadly serious. Kraus glared at him, too. There was no time to argue.

"For this to work, you two have to do exactly as I say," Mason said.

"What's first?" Kraus asked.

Mason opened the ledger and turned to a page, where a list of deciphered names had been inserted between the pages. "Get me to a phone."

41

Mason emerged from the rubble of a building and crossed Kärntnertrasse. He passed by the Bristol Hotel and came up on the roofless opera house on his right side. Along the base of the once grand opera building lay a long line of rubble excavated from the bombed-out ruins, and wooden scaffolding now covered large portions of the exterior walls. The many arches on the ground floor were boarded up, and now, in the early dawn hours, the building seemed abandoned and left for dead.

But as Mason approached the front that faced the ring road, he could pick out the silhouettes of men in the faint morning light. They were strategically placed at various points near the entrance. As he got closer, he could see they were in civilian clothes, though their demeanors were those of toughened soldiers ready to pull out their concealed weapons at the slightest provocation.

They had arrived earlier than Mason had hoped. One of the phone calls Mason had made after escaping CID headquarters was to set up a meeting here at the opera house. It was to be at seven a.m., and he'd planned to get there an hour early to scope out the best way to escape if things went south. Now he had no choice but to walk into a trap of his own making.

The men kept one eye on Mason while still watching the surrounding area for any threat. Mason navigated the gauntlet of men and turned right onto a path that cut through the piles of crushed brick and stone. Two men flanking the single entrance pivoted as Mason passed through the opening and entered the lobby.

By some miracle, the bombings and the resulting devastating fire had spared the grand entrance, foyer, marble staircases, and frescoes. The elegant statuary and gilded torchères remained, but all the glitter and color had taken on a dark patina from the smoke and dust.

A bull in human form stopped in front of Mason at the short set of stairs going up to the foyer. He said nothing, only waved his hands for Mason to raise his. Another guy half his companion's size came up and held out his hand and motioned for Mason to give him the ledger from Wentworth's study. Mason handed over the ledger, then opened his overcoat, and the bigger man patted him down for weapons. Finding none, the he stepped aside to let Mason pass.

Mason followed the smaller man up the eight steps and onto the grand staircase, which split halfway up into left and right staircases. The rear edge of the landing marked the beginning of the damaged portion of the building. Where there had once been a set of doors was now sheets of plywood with a doorway cut in the center. The faint odor of smoke still lingered in the air, along with a metallic tinge that stuck in Mason's nostrils.

Beyond the improvised door, they entered a scene of

devastation. The massive iron girders that once supported the roof were now strewn around the auditorium. The stage no longer existed, and neither did the orchestra pit or the backstage facilities. Blackened wood and piles of brick, concrete, and plaster had replaced them. The seats had been gutted by fire and buried under rubble, and more iron beams twisted as if they'd writhed in agony from the inferno. Above him, the sky was an indigo blue from the prolonged autumn dawn. The tiers of balconies and boxes stared back like empty eye sockets, blinded by the inferno, witnesses to the destruction of war.

Mason's guide into the petrified inferno continued down a path cut through the remains of the seating area. The path had been cleared for the workers who were beginning to clear away the rubble. Four more men stood where the stage had once been. Tucked under their arms, they had PPSh-41 Russian submachine guns, easily identifiable by the round drum magazines. Two more men revealed themselves by moving into place on opposite sides of the grand tier, one level up.

Mason approached the remnants of the stage, then heard the crunch of footsteps crossing the charred wood and coming from the backstage area. Out of the shadows, Konstantin emerged. He was dressed in civilian clothes topped by a tailored gray wool overcoat.

"Eight men with submachine guns," Mason said to Konstantin. "You weren't taking any chances."

"You said you had something that would provide the proof I need to find the traitor."

"I figure, once I give you what you want, these guys have orders to shoot me down."

"I don't need these men to do that. I'd be happy to pull the trigger myself."

A guard held up his hand to stop Mason from going any farther than the lead edge of what was once the orchestra pit. Mason's escort rushed up to Konstantin and handed over the ledger.

"Rather dramatic of you to pick this spot," Konstantin said. "How many operas have had their hero undone by their own hubris, I wonder."

Konstantin stepped over to a small table that had been set up to one side of the proscenium and set the ledger down. He lit a small lamp, put on his reading glasses, and leaned over the table. Without looking up, he said, "I hope this contains irrefutable proof of the traitor who passed on secrets to the Americans."

"We both know that's not what you really want."

Konstantin straightened and took off his reading glasses. He was calm and deliberate in his movements, including placing his glasses in their case and pulling out his pistol. He turned to face Mason and loaded a bullet into the chamber. "You are familiar with how little patience I possess. But I'll indulge you. What is it I really want?"

"To take down Carver, so you can take over his organization's territory."

Konstantin aimed his pistol at Mason. Adrenaline pumped through Mason's body, turning his guts cold.

The Russian peered at Mason with a furrowed brow. It was as if he sensed some oddity in Mason's behavior. "I'm an intelligence officer and a patriot to the motherland," he said with a raised head as if delivering the lines to an audience. "I want to know the traitor's name. Who gave Carver secret Soviet documents?"

"You see, I realized Carver hasn't been in Germany or Austria long enough to have such a wide reach of lieutenants and assassins. But you, as a member of the Soviet forces, have been in the West for almost two years. Being with the almighty NKVD, then MGB, you could set up your network with a reign of terror. When I busted up—"

Konstantin fired. The bullet screamed past Mason's ear.

The effects of the adrenaline doubled, but Mason ignored them. "When I busted up that crime ring in Germany, it took down the American and British networks. But no Russians. And of the Americans, only Carver remained, mostly because he'd just gotten started taking over Vienna and western Austria. That cut into your growing territory. He stopped your expansion, and you needed him out of the way. The problem for you was that he's an American diplomat. Going after him yourself could expose you to too much risk. That, and incur the wrath of any Soviet military brass profiting off Carver. What better way to get to him than by using another American bent on revenge? Use me to go after the man I vowed to kill. Valerius."

Konstantin fired his pistol again. It felt like a sledgehammer struck Mason's left arm. The pain was so intense that it brought him to his knees.

"I will keep shooting until you tell me why you brought me this ledger, and what you hoped to accomplish by accusing me."

Mason controlled the spinning in his head and returned a defiant stare at Konstantin. "You sent assassins to kill me, and when that failed, you sent assassins to kill anyone related to the case. Including Laura McKinnon, three CID officers in Garmisch, a convicted witness, two friends in Tangier. Why not just kill me when you realized I was here in Vienna?"

"Yes. I used you. To great effect, I might add. I'd studied your file. I knew you to be tenacious, and you would stop at nothing to have your vengeance on Valerius. It's just that you had the wrong man. I let you believe it was Carver. You're right: that investigation in Germany crippled my enterprise there. It took some time to recover, and by that time, Carver had gained control over Vienna. That made you more valuable alive than dead. The only reason you were able to slip out of the Soviet zone that night and make it to the center of the city is because I ordered it. If there are names in that ledger that point to Carver's Soviet coconspirators, then your debt is paid in full, though I can't let you live."

Mason heard the creaks of footsteps on wooden floorboards, and Konstantin's gaze and the aim of his gun shifted to the source.

Mason looked behind, then up. Laura stood at the back of the grand tier. "Laura, I told you to stay away from here. Get back."

Laura had a pained expression as she looked at Mason, but then her face became twisted in fury. "You killed my husband," she said to Konstantin.

"Unfortunate, but true."

Konstantin shouted an order in Russian, and the two guards on the same level as Laura moved for her. At that moment, the sounds of a multitude of footsteps and guns being readied echoed in the vast space as if coming from everywhere. Men in civilian clothes and Russian soldiers began streaming into the auditorium and across the tiered balconies, while others moved forward from backstage. Then Forester and Kraus joined Laura.

Konstantin turned in alarm when thirty-plus men pointed their guns at him and his men. Three men in Russian officers' uniforms stepped through the plywood doorway of the foyer and entered the auditorium.

Mason struggled to his feet and glared at Konstantin. "The Soviet names in the ledger? They're the ones who had an interest in keeping Carver in business. I called them and invited them here. You, of course, know General Baranova, Major Morozov, and Colonel Vasiliev."

The ranking officer, Baranova, yelled something in Russian. Konstantin's men dropped their weapons. He yelled something else directed at Konstantin, which Mason assumed was the general saying he was under arrest. But the man known as Valerius kept possession of his pistol.

Mason heard rushing footsteps behind him, then Laura and Forester came up to him. Forester checked his wound while Laura helped him remain on his feet. She scolded him for his recklessness, but Mason kept his attention on Konstantin and the general. He'd gambled with his life and wanted to see if the risk had been worth it.

Konstantin and the general exchanged words.

Forester translated for Mason and Laura. "The usual crap," Forester said. "He's innocent, that they have no evidence. Then the general saying they don't need evidence."

"Meaning they'll dump him into a gulag for the rest of his life or execute him," Mason said.

Konstantin looked at Mason with a smile of resignation. In a lightning move, he brought his pistol up. Mason shielded Laura and clenched in anticipation of a bullet boring into him.

Instead, the man jammed the pistol's barrel under his chin and fired.

Some of the general's soldiers reacted to Konstantin's movements, and they put more bullets into him as he collapsed.

Valerius was no more.

The incredible relief, the pain, and the loss of blood were too much for Mason. His knees buckled, and he fell to the floor. He felt hands on him and heard Laura's voice as his consciousness faded. As his vision constricted, the only thing he was truly aware of was the image of Konstantin's eyes, wide and lifeless, as if staring into the depths of hell.

42

Mason squinted against the sunlight as he exited the Stiftskaserne. He held up his right hand to shield his eyes, since his left lay useless in a sling. The sun hung low and grazed the top of the kaserne buildings, and it was surprisingly warm for a November day. Or maybe the summer-like sensations were magnified because he'd just spent two weeks in a darkened cell awaiting his hearing.

He scanned the expansive courtyard and spotted Forester leaning against a black sedan. Kraus was there too, and he waved. While Mason was happy to see that his old friend, and his new one, were there to greet him, his heart still sank when he saw no sign of Laura.

He walked across the courtyard toward the two men and entered the area in shadow. He suddenly felt cold and pulled his overcoat around his crippled arm. It wasn't just the drop in temperature that made him shiver; he was now adrift, his enemy vanquished, leaving him without a purpose.

Kraus was the first to meet him. He smiled and shook

Mason's hand like jacking the handle of a dry well. "You look healthy for a wounded man."

Mason ignored the pain from Kraus's jostling. "Unfortunately, my body seems to be getting used to the abuse."

Forester threw his cigarette to the pavement and met Mason a few steps from the vehicle. "I don't see any handcuffs or guards."

Mason nodded and shook Forester's hand. "The CID chief and MP battalion commander wanted to send me to Leavenworth, but the provost marshal and the army brass thought it better to just get rid of me. I'm to report to the Tulin air base. They're putting me on a plane for the States this evening."

Kraus's face dropped with disappointment, but Forester nodded knowingly. "I volunteered to take you to the air base, if they decided to cut you loose."

Forester walked around the sedan and opened the passenger's door. Mason hesitated, not wanting to stay but not wanting to be forced into heading home after so many years either.

Kraus remained next to Mason. "I have to stay here. I'm on assignment."

"You're not going home?" Mason asked.

"There's nothing for me back in Linz. I lost all my family, and the CIC has taken me on as an agent," Kraus said and beamed with pride.

"Congratulations, Peter," Mason said and shook his hand.

"He's a natural," Forester said. "Plus, he learned from the best."

Mason wished him good luck, then looked at Forester.

"I'm sure you have a bunch of questions," Forester said. "We'll talk on the way."

Mason said good-bye to Kraus, stepped around the car, and got in the front passenger's seat. Forester closed the door and climbed in behind the wheel. He started up the engine and headed for the courtyard exit.

Mason looked back at Kraus, waved, then faced the front. "I was hoping against hope that Laura had decided to stay. At least until I got my freedom."

"None of us were sure if you'd get out, or when. And you know she had to go to England to see her husband's parents and visit the grave."

A surge of emotion left Mason speechless.

"Give her time," Forester said as he stopped at the gate. He showed his paperwork to the sentry. When the sentry waved him through, Forester pulled out onto the street. "She loves you. I can see that. But you can't expect her to forget everything and just blithely move on before she deals with her loss."

"She told me to look her up in Boston, but I'd lay odds that after a couple of days at home, she'll get antsy and take on another risky assignment."

They rode in silence a moment, then Forester said, "I do have some good news for you. That ex-partner of yours from Garmisch, Abrams? He's going to pull through. He should be at Walter Reed by the time you get back."

"Good news. Thanks for telling me." Some of the lead weights lifted off his shoulders. "What about Carver? They wouldn't tell me anything while I was locked up."

Forester said nothing as he took a turn.

"Let me guess," Mason said, "he got off scot-free."

"Not exactly. He was forced to resign, but he's already taken a lucrative private job in the U.S. At least Flannigan is going to prison, and the Austrians are finally going to put the screws to Gruber. A couple more of Carver's lieutenants will take the fall, but Carver, with his rich family and powerful friends, will come out okay."

"Did you think things were going to change?"

That dreary assessment brought on the silence again. Mason watched the beauty and ruins of Vienna pass by his side window.

Finally, Forester said, "I lobbied to get you in CIC and come work for me, but no one wants you in Vienna. Ever."

"Thanks for the offer, but I wouldn't want it anyway."

"Mason, you haven't got a dime to your name. What are you going to do once you get back to the States? Live off your grandmother?"

"I've got another idea. I need you to take a little detour before we get to the air base."

Forester looked at his watch. "It'd better not be too long. Your flight leaves in a few hours."

"We'll get there in time. It's a place in the Russian zone on the outskirts of the city."

"The Russian zone? Are you crazy? Konstantin's gone, but some of his buddies could have survived the purge. And I don't have authorization to drive anywhere I want in their zone."

Mason fished a folded piece of paper out of the inner pocket of his overcoat and held it up for Forester to see. "A one-time-only entry pass from one of the Russian generals who are profiting rather nicely from Konstantin's downfall."

"How did you get ahold of that?"

"One of a certain general's proxies came to see me in jail. The general is so grateful I helped take down Konstantin that he offered to do me a favor."

"And that one-time pass is it?"

"I wouldn't accept anything else."

"Why is entering the Russian zone so important to you?"

"Take me there, and you'll see."

Forester let out a groan of frustration, but he steered the car south toward the Russian zone.

They passed through the checkpoints without a hitch. The paper in Mason's possession had the guards scrambling to accommodate them. It worked equally well with the couple of patrols that stopped them on their way. Mason had memorized the streets and led Forester deep into the tenth Bezirk, or district. His time in Vienna had been arduous and pivotal, but Mason remembered every step he'd taken on that first night upon entering the city.

People were out on foot or pulling wooden wheelbarrows containing their possessions, their children, or wood for their fires. The Trümmerfrauen were at work, and so were several steam-powered excavators that pulled at the ruins.

Mason spotted the street he'd been looking for and directed Forester to make a right turn. Since the street had suffered a great deal of damage, the burned-out skeletons of the buildings all looked the same. But Mason had memorized the number of buildings between his destination and the corner they had just rounded.

He started counting as Forester drove slowly, but when he got to the tenth, he felt as though a rug had been pulled out from under him.

"Stop," Mason said.

Forester did, and Mason got out. He mentally went through the path they'd taken and verified the number of buildings from the corner. He was in the right place.

The building before him, the one where he'd penetrated the basement and hidden the diamonds and jewelry, was no longer there. The only thing remaining of that bomb-damaged building was a heap of rubble.

Workers had torn down the structure, by controlled explosion or machinery, and they had left the remains of the six-story building where it had fallen. The heap was at least fifteen feet high, and it was so dense that there was no way he would ever find a way to enter the basement and reclaim his valuables.

Mason was unaware that Forester had come up next to him until the man spoke. "I take it this building isn't the way you left it."

Mason shook his head. "There's probably five-grand worth of valuables buried under that rubble."

"A tough break."

"Maybe God is trying to tell me something. I took that loot off of two of Valerius's lieutenants. Men I killed or left for dead."

"I thought you didn't believe in God."

"I don't. Not really. But that doesn't mean God got the message."

Forester put a hand on Mason's shoulder. "Come on, buddy. Let's get you to the air base."

"You know I'm not going to get on that plane."

Forester removed his hand. "Yeah, I figured that."

"Are you going to try to stop me?" Mason asked as he continued to stare at the rubble.

Forester pulled something out of his coat pocket and held out an envelope for Mason.

"What's this?"

"Your new passport and traveling papers," Forester said. "I was supposed to give them to you just before you boarded the plane. But under the circumstances..."

"Thanks, Mike," Mason said as he pocketed the envelope.

Forester reached into his pants pocket and pulled out a small wad of cash. “And here’s forty bucks. It’s all I have on me, but it’ll hold you for a little while.”

Mason took the money. “I’ll pay you back.”

“You’ll be paying me back by letting me know that you’re settled in somewhere. And out of trouble.”

“Like I said, I’ll make sure you get the cash.”

They shook hands, and Forester said, “Good luck.”

“Good luck with explaining how I slipped through your fingers.”

“I’ll figure out something. I’ll see you Stateside some time.”

All Mason would offer was, “Yeah.”

Without another word, Forester went back to the car and started the engine. Mason turned south, with his back to Forester’s car, and started walking.

And he never looked back to watch his friend drive away. That would have made things harder. He was still a long way from somewhere, and it was going to take a long time to get there.

Did you enjoy this book? You can make a big difference in my career!

Reviews are the most powerful tools in my arsenal when it comes to getting attention for my books. Like most readers, I'm sure you weigh reviews heavily once you've seen the book's cover and read the description. And without reviews, a reader might move on without giving a new author a try.

That's where you can come in: An honest review of this novel —or any of my other novels—just might be the thing that convinces them to read and discover new stories and authors. Like me!

If you enjoyed this book, I would be very grateful if you could take five minutes to leave an honest review on the book's Amazon page.

Leaving a review is easy:

1) Go to the book's page on Amazon
2) Scroll down to the reviews section and click on the "Write a customer review" button just below the stars rating bars
3) Select a star rating
4) Write a few short words (or as long as you like)
5) Click the submit button

Thank you very much!

ALSO BY JOHN A. CONNELL

THE MASON COLLINS SERIES

Madness in the Ruins

It is the winter of 1945, seven months after the Nazi defeat, and Munich is in ruins. A killer is stalking the devastated city—one who has knowledge of human anatomy, enacts mysterious rituals with his prey, and seems to pick victims at random. It falls upon U.S. Army investigator Mason Collins to hunt down the brutal killer. In a city where chaos reigns, Mason must rely on his wits and instincts, and he's driven to places he never could have imagined: from interrogation rooms with unrepentant Nazi war criminals to the bowels of the crumbling city.

Madness in the Ruins is the first in a series that will follow Mason Collins to some of the most dangerous and outrageous spots around the globe. **"…this is going to be a must-read series for me."** ~ ***Lee Child, #1 New York Times bestselling author of the Jack Reacher novels***

Haven of Vipers

Mason Collins risks everything to hunt down a gang of ruthless murderers in a case that will take him from a Hollywood-style nightclub and a speeding train, to the icy slopes of the Bavarian Alps. As both witnesses and evidence begin disappearing, it becomes obvious that someone on high is pulling strings to stifle the investigation—and that Mason must feel his way in the darkness if he is going to find out who in town has the most to gain—and the most to lose…

Haven of Vipers is the second in the Mason Collins crime-thriller series that Steve Berry, bestselling author of *The Patriot Threat* and *The Templar Legacy*, said: "Excitement melds with adventure as the tangled threads gradually unwind, revealing treachery coming from all directions. The whole thing is reminiscent of early-Robert Ludlum, and makes you clamor for more."

Bones of the Innocent

Mason Collins grapples with a web of lies, secrets, and murder as he races against time to save the lives of abducted teenagers in a case as twisted as the streets of Tangier's medina. And as he digs deeper, he realizes everyone has a hidden agenda, including those who harbor a terrible secret. And just as Mason begins to unravel the mystery, the assassins have picked up his trail. Now, Mason must put his life on the line to find the girls and discover who's behind the heinous crimes before it's too late. If he lives that long…

Bones of the Innocent is the third in the Mason Collins series of historical crime thrillers that bestselling author Lee Child said, *"This is going to be a must-read series for me."*

STANDALONE HISTORICAL CRIME THRILLER

Good Night, Sweet Daddy-O

1958 San Francisco

Struggling jazz musician, Frank Valentine, suffers a midnight beating, leaving his left hand paralyzed. Jobless, penniless, and desperate, Frank agrees to join his best friend, George, and three other buddies to distribute a gangster's heroin for quick money.

What he doesn't know is that George has more dangerous plans. Inexperienced in the ways of crime, Frank quickly slips deeper and deeper into the dark vortex of San Francisco gangsters, junkies, and murderers for hire. To make things worse, Frank's newfound love, a mysterious, dark-haired beauty, is somehow connected to it all.

And when it becomes clear that a crime syndicate is bent on his destruction, Frank realizes that the easy road out of purgatory often leads to hell.

GET A FREE MASON COLLINS NOVELLA

The relationship between writer and reader is a special one for me. If you are interested in going beyond what you read here and wish to receive occasional newsletters from me with details on my writing life, new releases, special offers, and other news, you can sign up to my mailing list, and I'll send you a free Mason Collins series prequel novella not available anywhere else.

You can get the novella by going to: https://johnaconnell.com/subscribe

Thank you!

ACKNOWLEDGEMENTS AND AUTHOR'S NOTES FOR TO KILL A DEVIL

The destruction by bombs and battle, the deprivations, and the intrigue of Vienna is often overlooked compared to Berlin. While Berlin's destruction was far more extensive, Vienna and the Viennese suffered on a larger scale than I had expected. And like Berlin, Vienna was divided into four separate zones, each under one of the Allied powers, the Americans, British, French, and Soviets.

What was unique is that Vienna's old city center was administered collectively, by the four powers, making it a hot bed of intrigue and espionage. Anyone who has watched the movie *The Third Man* has gotten some idea of the post-WW2 conditions and atmosphere of the city. I found the history of Vienna during that post-war period fascinating.

I tried to portray Vienna as it was in late 1946 using non-fiction sources, photographs, and maps, and many of the places depicted in the story are factual, though some of the minor locations are figments of my imagination.

A word about the American intelligence of that time. During the period of To Kill A Devil, the CIA had yet to be created. When the Office of Strategic Services, or OSS, the principal clandestine organization during World War Two, was disbanded in the fall of 1945, the covert assets were handed over, temporarily, to the Strategic Services Unit, then to the Central Intelligence Group, which formed the Office of Strategic Operations. All very confusing, but these permutations of the U.S. central intelligence gathering organizations evolved into the CIA in 1947.

If you're interested in further reading on post-WW2 Vienna, the following is a list of the main sources that I leaned on heavily for facts and inspiration:

- After the Reich: From the Liberation of Vienna to the Berlin Airlift, Giles MacDonald
- In the Ruins of the Reich, Douglas Botting
- Endgame 1945: Victory, Retribution, Liberation, David Stafford
- America's Secret Army: The Untold Story of the Counter Intelligence Corps, Ian Sayer & Douglas Botting

Also, an invaluable tool was the website www.usarmygermany.com – a great site providing unit histories, maps, photos, personal accounts, even telephone directories, all pertaining to the U.S. Army's presence in Europe from the beginning of the post-WW2 period to the end of the Cold War.

ABOUT THE AUTHOR

John A. Connell writes spellbinding crime thrillers with a historical twist. In addition to his standalone, Good Night, Sweet Daddy-O, he writes the post-WW2 Mason Collins series, which follows Mason to some of the most dangerous and turbulent places in the post-World War Two world. The first, Madness in the Ruins, was a 2016 Barry Award finalist, and the series has garnered praise from such bestselling authors as Lee Child and Steve Berry. In a previous life, John worked as a cameraman on films such as *Jurassic* Park and *Thelma and Louise* and on TV shows including *NYPD Blue* and *The Practice*. Atlanta-born, John spends his time between the U.S. and France.

You can visit John online at: https://johnaconnell.com

And feel free to contact me at john@johnaconnell.com

I'm also on Facebook, Twitter, Bookbub, and Goodreads

Printed in Great Britain
by Amazon